HALLIE B

AUTTIE GRACE

EMPIRE

TO EARTH AND BACK

This is a work of fiction. Unless otherwise indicated, all the names, characters, businesses, places, events, and incidents in this book are either the product of the authors' imaginations or used in a fictitious manner. Any resemblance to actual persons, living or dead, or actual events is purely coincidental. All situations and descriptions are for your entertainment only and should not be relied on for accuracy and should not be replicated.

If someone tells you that the blue sky in this book symbolizes the ache of sadness in the characters' hearts or that Fitz's red hair symbolizes built-up anger, that person is wrong. The truth is, you can interpret this story however you want (within reason of course, if you think this book is a call from a supernatural being to murder half the population, get help... immediately :) All we're trying to say is that everything depends on your point of view, and everyone interprets things differently, especially in books.

Cover and spine illustration by germancreative

This book has been typeset in Merriweather

ISBN 978-0-578-29390-5

https://hastoriesofficial.com

TABLE OF CONTENTS

PROLOGUE

All I wanted to do was scream. The darkness was suffocating. Between the overwhelming feeling of fear and the adrenaline coursing through me, I felt like I had just run a marathon.

I couldn't remember anything. Not my name, where I was, or who I was with, nothing. A million questions swirled through my head. This place was so unfamiliar. Nothing felt right. Nothing felt *real*. The surrounding air was bitter and cold, spreading a numbness through my veins. I felt like a prisoner, probably because I *was* one. What did I do to deserve this?

A dark figure towered over me. I could see the outlines of other people, their faces hidden in shadows. I felt a sense of familiarity. I just couldn't pinpoint it.

I jolted. Someone had grabbed my hand.

From the smothering darkness, I heard a whisper, "Focus on my hand. It'll be okay. We will be okay."

My throat was dry and scratchy. I couldn't reply. The mysterious voice had somewhat calmed my nerves. Ironic, considering I had no clue who they were. I tried to do as they said and focus on the hand clasping mine.

Think, think, think.

I tried to survey my surroundings. It was dark, except for a bit of light leaking in from under the door. I was sitting down. My wrists weren't bound. I'd take that as a good sign, but there were at least three burly figures flanking the walls of the room. Not good.

I felt someone wince and realized I had tensed up again. I loosened my vice-like grip on the hand intertwined with mine.

Sorry. I thought, figuring it was no use to attempt to speak again. *Alright, somehow you got yourself into this mess; now you just have to get out. Easy.*

At least I was thinking clearly again. Well, clearly for someone with a major case of amnesia.

I did a second survey of the room and silently cursed. No windows. The only way out was the door. I looked up to see if I could find any grates in the ceiling, but it was too dark to tell. No big loss. Watching people climb through the ventilation system in movies was probably way easier than doing it myself. Plus, I had no actual plan for getting high enough to even reach the ceiling.

The door.

If I wanted to get out, I'd have to use the normal person way. Not like they were just going to let me waltz out, anyway. Judging by what appeared to be a gun in each looming figure's hand, they weren't going to have second thoughts about using force to keep me in here. What were these people waiting for? If they wanted me dead, they would have killed me already. No, they were definitely waiting for something or someone.

A noise interrupted my inner monologue.

I heard a scuffle of feet and a clicking sound, like typing on a keyboard. A single beep sounded outside the door, and the handle turned.

Then, as quickly as it had started, the world went black, and my surroundings were dragged into the shadows.

CHAPTER 1

THE START OF THE EMPIRE

Long, long ago, our world was nothing but a meteoroid drifting through the universe. Known as the Prima Stella, *the meteoroid was made of molecules that allowed it to attract small bits of hydrogen and oxygen from the folds of the galaxy. The elements collided, creating water. Once the water was collected, a sprout began to grow, its roots intertwining with the falling star. With every passing day, it grew taller, and the roots grew thicker.*

For years and years, it grew, blossoming into a massive, beautiful tree known as the Lignum Vitae. *As more years passed, the tree and meteoroid attracted countless drops of water. The* Tertia Aquae, *the water around the* Lignum Vitae, *was formed as a protective barrier.*

Centuries later, a second shell had formed around the orb of water: the Quartus de Terra, *the layer of land on which we live. Life flourished on this new planet, and so did we.*

We called our world Esprit and created our Empire to unite us all under one rule. Laws were formed, and leaders were elected to construct and protect the peace. Battles were fought, and wars were won throughout history, but the Empire held fast. Among the leaders who protect and govern our world is the Director. A vital and elite position, the job of the Director is one not taken lightly. *The Director is in charge of overseeing the Empire and adjusting issues that arise.*

Ingenuity and creativity led to new technologies, and these innovations led to others. Many minds worked tirelessly on one invention that stood out among the rest. The protective rings around our planet have continued to keep floating debris from entering our atmosphere, keeping us safely hidden inside for centuries.

And still today, at the center of it all, grows the Lignum Vitae. *Without it, our planet would cease to exist; crops would die, and land would crumble. As long as we protect the* Lignum Vitae, *Esprit will continue to thrive.*

"Now, class," said Mrs. Nour, "Who can summarize—"

A loud snoring sound coming from the front row interrupted her. She turned towards the class and walked towards the desk of the culprit.

"Maybe Mr. Eve can summarize the start of Esprit for me?" she said calmly, for she had dealt with this kind of behavior from Asher Eve since the first day of school.

"Wha—huh—umm—wha?" Asher awoke with a start.

Asher was sixteen and not the best student. His wavy brown hair stuck to one side of his face as he lifted his head from its resting position on the desk. His blue eyes looked around in confusion as if he had forgotten where he was.

"Please summarize our lesson on the start of Esprit," Mrs. Nour repeated.

"Umm, well, here's the thing, Mrs. Nour," Asher started, unsticking the hair from the side of his face.

"I'm sure the entire class would love to hear your newest

excuse, but, frankly, we don't have enough time to go through one today. Why don't you save it for next year's teacher?" she retaliated.

It was the last day of school, and Mrs. Nour was obviously not in the mood to deal with Asher's antics.

"Delphi, why don't you summarize our final lesson?" Mrs. Nour asked, turning to Asher's twin sister.

Delphi looked up from her elaborate doodling and blew her wavy brown hair out of her eyes.

"Well," she started, "we began as a rock, and..." she described what Mrs. Nour had just taught.

When she got to the new technologies; a tall, pretty girl with dark green eyes; a deep warm tan; and short, curly dark brown hair cut her off.

"Technology, such as the protective rings around Esprit..." the girl finished the summary for Delphi.

Delphi turned around and mouthed "Thank you," to her best friend, Meeka McBella.

Meeka tended to play tag team with Delphi in class. They were inseparable since the age of five when Meeka moved to the The Metropolis, the capital of Esprit. The high-tech capital city played an essential role in the society of Esprit. Built on clean energy and advanced sciences, the city allowed the rest of the world to run smoothly and safely.

"Well done, girls," Mrs. Nour said, ignoring that Meeka had interrupted.

After all, Meeka and Delphi were Mrs. Nour's favorite students. At least, according to Asher.

Meeka smiled, and Delphi gave Asher a look that basically

said, 'You're an idiot.'

Asher rolled his eyes and looked down at his desk.

"Show offs," he muttered under his breath.

The final lesson of the year was over, and chatter started to fill the classroom. Some students resorted to the screens of their *cursors* for entertainment, while others grouped up with friends.

"Nice going, Asher," Meeka teased, leaning over her desk.

"Oh, shut up. It's the last day of school. I'd rather not be learning," he replied, turning in her direction.

"Sadly, it's still a *place* of learning," Delphi chimed in, finishing her sketch.

Suddenly, the bell rang. The year was finally over. The students rushed out of the classroom and piled into the halls. Asher got up, thankful that he stayed awake in class just enough to avoid summer school. Meeka and Delphi were the last to leave the classroom.

"Have a wonderful summer!" Mrs. Nour called to her former students.

Out in the hall, Delphi and Meeka talked about plans for the summer.

"So, what are you going to do over break?" Delphi asked.

"I don't think I have any plans. My parents are going to be working a lot," Meeka said.

Delphi groaned. "Mine too. We could probably disappear all summer, and they wouldn't even notice."

Meeka nodded. "My mom has been in her lab a lot lately, working late nights and whatnot. My dad is basically doing the same. I went to his office the other day and saw stacks upon stacks of papers. The Empire has been working them hard."

"Maybe our parents are just going through some workaholic stage or something?" Delphi suggested, shaking her head. "Although, mine have always been work-addicts, especially with their positions on the Board of Governance. They probably think that the world will explode if they come home for too long."

Meeka chuckled. "They *do* have an important job. The only person with more power is the Director."

"You better not be taking their side."

"No way. I was just stating all the facts."

"You forgot the part where they hire you as a babysitter because they can't take care of my little sister themselves."

"It's not all bad. It just gives us an excuse to hang out more." Meeka nudged Delphi with her shoulder. "Speaking of your little sister..." She checked her watch. "Aw, crud! We're late to pick Opal up!"

They dashed outside and met Asher in the parking lot with his best friend and Delphi's personal nuisance, August Ray. August was a year younger than Asher, Delphi, and Meeka. His green eyes surveyed the two girls as they stopped in front of him, finally resting on Delphi.

"Hello there," he said as he ran his hands through his blonde hair.

"August is gonna walk home with us," Asher told Delphi.

"I thought Mom and Dad banned him from the house after you two set fire to the carpet last year," Delphi told him.

"Oh, come on, Elphi, that was a looong time ago. Besides,

admit it, you've missed me," August taunted, displaying his usual smirk.

Delphi ignored him and turned back to Asher. "Does he have to come?" she asked.

"Hey, you get to have Meeka over every day. It's only fair that August can come too," Asher said.

Delphi sighed. "Fine, but I really don't appreciate the nicknames."

"Come on, guys! We have to go get Opal!" Meeka yelled to them, already heading to the primary school.

Delphi ran to catch up with Meeka while the boys trailed behind. A salty ocean breeze blew past them as they ran past the train station and cut across the junior high campus. Other students were milling around, talking with friends, or on their way home. Meeka, Delphi, Asher, and August wound around them and took a shortcut through the field to reach the primary school.

When they finally got to the school, Opal was outside waiting. She had her arms crossed and was tapping her little foot.

"You guys are late," Opal said when they walked up to her.

Opal was an adorable little girl who, having two older siblings and Meeka always around, tended to try to act older than she really was. She typically wore her dirty blonde hair in double braids, and her big blue eyes looked bigger than ever.

"I'm so sorry, Opal, we lost track of time," Delphi said, hugging her little sister.

Asher came over and scooped Opal up.

"Put me down!" she yelled. "I'm too big to be picked up

anymore. I'm in second grade now!"

"Oh, okay, little girl," Asher said, setting his squirmy little sister down.

Meeka went over and took Opal's hand. "Can I still hold your hand, though?" Meeka asked.

"I think it's acceptable," Opal said.

"Jeez, that is one sassy little girl," August whispered to Asher.

Asher laughed. "Tell me about it."

They walked down the sidewalk, passing vivid green trees and many houses with bright gardens and grand designs. Flowers along the sidewalks escorted them to their driveway.

The Eves' house was huge and elegant, with large windows and a glass dome serving as the roof of the foyer. The stark white exterior contrasted with the colorful bushes and flowers in the front yard, all trimmed and neatly cut by a gardener. A series of stairs led up to the front porch and a set of double doors at the entrance. Dark green and blue ivy clung to the wall above the french doors. The house wasn't cozy and definitely didn't give off a homey vibe. It looked more like a place where you would have to be dressed up to enter and be told to *touch nothing*.

When they reached the front door, August's pocket dinged. He took out his *cursor* and checked the screen. "Aw, *dautor!*"

"What's wrong?" Asher asked.

"My mom just texted me. My cousin's coming over for the summer, and my parents want me home to greet him or something. I completely forgot," August said. "I've got to run. See you later!" And with that, August jogged away.

"Oh, thank God, he's gone." Delphi sighed.

"What do you have against August anyway, Delphi?" Asher asked.

"Um, have you met him?" she replied.

"Fair point. He's an acquired taste," Asher agreed.

"We'll just go with that," Delphi said.

She unlocked the door, and the Eve siblings and Meeka walked inside.

Chapter 2

Fitz

The doorbell rang a few hours after the Eves and Meeka got home.

"I'll get it!" Delphi called.

She got up from the couch where they were watching a spy movie. Their takeout was strewn across the countertops in the kitchen, and the clock on the wall said it was eight o'clock.

Delphi went into the foyer, where a large tree grew in the center, and opened the door. She immediately regretted answering it. August was standing in the frame with a short red-headed boy.

"Oh, it's you," Delphi said.

August opened his mouth to speak, but Delphi slammed the door closed before he could get a word out.

"Asher! It's August!" Delphi yelled.

Outside, the red-headed boy threw August a confused glance.

"She loves me," August told him.

The other boy's eyebrows shot up so far they were hidden under his mass of curls. "Uh-huh," was all he said.

Asher got up and walked over to the door. "Well? Where is he?"

"Outside," Delphi replied in a flat tone.

"God, Delphi! That's like the fifth time you've slammed the door in his face this *year*," Asher remarked.

Delphi shrugged and sat back down on the couch next to Meeka.

"Sorry about that," Asher said as he opened the door to let August and the other boy in.

"Don't worry about it. I'm used to it by now," August replied. "Oh, and this is my cousin, Fitz." He gestured to the other boy.

"Hey," Fitz waved, staring up at the glass dome ceiling of the foyer. He was the same age and had the same green eyes as August, but that was where the similarities ended. He was much quieter and had a curly mass of red hair on his head.

August eyed the living room. "Ooh, what are we watching?" He jumped over the back of the couch and plopped down. "Cool, a car chase. Those are my favorite scenes."

Fitz and Asher walked over to the living room and sat down in two of the armchairs.

"So, where are your parents tonight?" August asked, tousling his blonde hair.

"Eh, some charity ball thing. It's mostly just for show, though. Have to keep up appearances and all that rubbish," Asher said.

"At least it goes to a good cause. My parents are there too," Meeka remarked.

"While your lame old parents are at boring charity events, mine left for vacation to Litore. Fitz and I get the whole house to ourselves," August said as he relaxed his arms behind his head and chewed on a pretzel stick.

"Are you done talking yet?" Opal whined, crinkling her freckled nose. "I'm trying to watch the show."

"Sorry, Opal, but I think it's time for you to go to bed anyway," Meeka suggested.

"Can I pleeease stay up a little longer?" Opal pleaded with big eyes. "I won't tell."

"I don't think so," Meeka said. "Come on. Delphi and I will tuck you in."

"Okay." Opal pouted as Meeka and Delphi took her hands and headed to Opal's bedroom.

"Night, Opal!" Asher called to her as they walked upstairs.

Once in bed, Delphi and Meeka tucked Opal in and kissed her goodnight. They turned on the flower nightlight and turned off the overhead lights. Leaving the door ajar, the two girls headed downstairs.

Half an hour later, they heard a loud crash coming from upstairs. Meeka, Delphi, and Asher rushed up the staircase to find the source of the noise, leaving August and Fitz in the living room. The light was on in the master bedroom.

They burst through the door. "Opal, are you in here—" Meeka was cut off by the sight of a gigantic mess of objects scattered across the carpet. Opal was sitting in the center of the pile, clutching a small chest and holding her scraped knee.

"What happened in here?" Delphi asked. "Are you alright?"

Opal nodded, tears welling up in her eyes. "I couldn't sleep, so I went exploring in Mommy and Daddy's room," she

sniffed and continued, "I saw this pretty box up on the shelf."
She held the chest out for them to see.

Delphi took the surprisingly lightweight chest out of her
hands, and Meeka picked Opal out of the heap of trinkets.

"I—I climbed the shelf to get the box, and it fell over,"
Opal continued, starting to cry.

"It's okay," Meeka said, rocking Opal.

"What made you want the chest in the first place?" Asher
asked.

"It wa—wasn't here last time I—I explored, so I wanted to
che—check it out," Opal replied through her tears.

"Why don't we go get you washed up, okay?" Meeka said
to Opal. "Asher, can you please clean up this mess?"

Asher saluted Meeka, "Yes, M'lady."

Meeka carried Opal into the bathroom, and Delphi
followed. When she passed Asher, Delphi patted him on the
shoulder. "Smooth, very smooth."

"I don't know what you're talking about," Asher said with
an air of dignity.

"Sure you don't," she replied and walked into the
bathroom, still holding the chest.

While Meeka bandaged Opal's wounded knee, Delphi
inspected the chest. The cool, lightweight metal of the chest
showed no signs of damage from the fall. As her eyes
continued to scan the container, she noticed a pattern of
intricately designed white vines covering its surface. If she
looked closely enough, she could see a small keyhole in the
mass of painted ivy.

"Hey, Meeka?"

"Hmm?" Meeka replied, busy attempting to put a bandage on a squirmy Opal.

"Can I borrow one of your hairpins for a second?" Delphi asked.

"Umm, sure," Meeka said, handing a pin to Delphi. "But I'm pretty sure picking locks with hairpins only works in movies."

"Well, it's worth a shot," Delphi replied. "And how do you do that?"

"Do what?" Meeka asked.

"Read my mind," Delphi said, smiling. "You've been doing it since we were five!"

Meeka laughed, "Just open the chest."

Delphi inserted the pin into the keyhole and felt around until she heard a click. She opened the chest. Inside, there was a fragile, orb-shaped object about the size of a baseball. It was smooth and coated in frosted white glass. Upon further inspection, she noticed a symbol etched into the glass. It was a marking of a tree made of three curved lines. She racked her brain to remember where she had seen this symbol before. Delphi scooped the orb out of the cushioning surrounding it inside the chest. The minute her fingertips touched the cold material of the object, her eyes clouded over, and she saw an image of a tall building in the middle of a large city. She blinked the image away, thinking it was just her vivid imagination getting the best of her. Suddenly, another vision appeared in a flash of light. This one was of a broad man dressed head to toe in black. He was wearing sunglasses and holding... was that a gun? The weapon was pointed directly at

Delphi. Delphi screamed and tossed the orb into the air.

"Woah!" Meeka caught the orb just in time. "Are you okay?"

"No, not okay. Did you see those, those flashes?" Delphi asked.

She had sat down in the corner of the bathroom. Her knees were tucked to her chest, and her head was down. She felt sick.

Meeka finally got the bandage on Opal. "What flashes?" she asked, starting to feel very concerned for her friend.

"Flashes of light and then pictures. I don't know. Forget I said anything. I think I'm going to throw up." Delphi edged closer to the toilet.

Meeka had a worried look on her face. Delphi looked even paler than usual.

Opal, meanwhile, looked disgusted. "If you're going to throw up, I'm leaving," she said and hopped off the counter. When she opened the door, Asher and August were in the hall. Asher's hand was up, about to knock.

"We heard a scream. Is everything okay?" Asher asked. He looked up over Opal's head and saw Delphi sitting in the corner. "Is she alright?"

"Nope," Opal said. "She's starting to halluckinate."

"I think you mean 'hallucinate,'" Asher said.

"That's what I said," Opal replied and walked past the boys, unfazed.

Asher and August walked into the bathroom. Meeka was crouching next to Delphi and handing her a cool washcloth.

"What happened to you?" Asher asked Delphi. "Opal says

you're hallucinating now."

"Yeah, do you need a broad manly shoulder to cry on?" August moved closer to Delphi, only to be hit with a death stare.

"I don't see anyone with that description here," Delphi countered.

"I was talking about me!" August said.

"Dude, you're younger than me," Delphi pointed out.

August whined, "Only by a year!"

"You whine like a baby, though," Meeka mumbled.

Luckily, August didn't hear her, and if he did, he chose to ignore her comment.

"It doesn't matter," Delphi said, struggling to her feet. "I just freaked out because I had some weird visions." She recounted what she had seen.

"Halluckinating!" Opal yelled from a distance with a childish giggle.

Asher laughed. "Yeah right. What are you, a seer?"

Delphi glared at him.

"Wait, you're serious? Do you need a doctor?" Asher asked.

"Yes, I'm serious, and no, I don't need a doctor," Delphi said.

"A *doctor*, Asher, really?" Meeka asked. "What were you planning on saying? Hey, my sister here is seeing random pictures of impending doom. Can you fix her?"

"Well, when you say it like that, it doesn't sound like it would go over well," Asher said, contemplating how that discussion would go.

Meeka stifled a laugh.

Back downstairs, Meeka brought the chest with the orb in it into the kitchen and made some tea to calm Delphi down.

Fitz got up to examine the chest. "What's this?" he asked, reaching to open it.

"*STOP!*" Delphi yelled, making Fitz jump. "Do *not* open that."

Fitz backed away from the intricate box and went back into the living room.

Meeka rejoined everyone in the living room when she finished making Delphi's tea. August tried to sit next to Delphi on the couch, but she hit him with a pillow. He ended up sitting in the armchair that was previously occupied by Asher. Opal sat down in Meeka's lap, and they continued the movie.

An hour later, Meeka went back into the kitchen to clear the counters and wash the dishes. Fitz also got up and decided to nonchalantly look at the orb. He opened the chest and took the sphere out. It fumbled in his hands, and he dropped it into the sink.

Meeka quickly pulled it out and handed it back to Fitz. "I thought we told you not to touch this!"

Fitz tightly gripped the orb, afraid to drop it again. A faint humming sound started coming from the object. It grew louder and louder until it sounded more like someone was banging on pots and pans.

Everyone in the living room got up to find the source of the noise.

"What's that annoying sound?" Asher asked.

"I think it's coming from the orb thingy," Fitz said.

"You touched it?" Delphi exclaimed.

Fitz's face went red with guilt. "Oops?"

All of a sudden, the orb opened. Inside was a small silvery button. Everyone moved closer, curious. Opal jumped to get a better view of the open sphere and accidentally hit Fitz's arm. He awkwardly attempted to save the orb from slipping out of his grasp and unintentionally pushed the button.

A burst of light protruded from the object, and the banging noise stopped. The group waited for a second, breathing heavily. Then the world was turned sideways, and the kids were churned into a mass of light and color. They tried to scream, but no sound came out. Within seconds, the group had been spit out of the pastel surge and onto a cold, hard floor.

CHAPTER 3

QUINN & MACY

"Ow," Fitz groaned.

"I think I'm gonna vomit," Asher said, running to a garbage can.

"I think I broke my everything," August complained, sprawled across the floor.

Groups of tourists were giving the kids funny looks.

"What are *you* looking at?" August asked.

They quickly turned around and continued looking out of the windows.

Opal stood up. "I'm a little dizzy," she said.

"How is she standing?" August asked no one in particular.

"She's seven; her bones are basically rubber," Meeka explained, attempting to stand herself. She lost her footing and slid back down to the ground. Asher stopped barfing into the trash, took a tissue out of his pocket, wiped his face, and came over and helped Meeka up.

Delphi had managed to get herself over to a wall of windows and pull herself up. "Guys, where in the name of all things normal are we?" she asked, looking out of the window at a sprawling city.

"Umm, I want to say a city, but I think I'm seeing double

right now," August said, finally getting up and stumbling over to Delphi.

Opal staggered over to the window and pressed her face against the glass. "Wow! It's so big!"

Meeka, Asher, and Fitz went over to look at the view.

"Umm, guys?" Asher asked. "Wasn't it just dark out?"

Meeka looked at her watch. "It says it's nine thirty-seven."

"Maybe it's broken?" Fitz pointed out.

August pulled out his *cursor*. "It's dead! But I just had a 90% battery five minutes ago!"

Meeka, Delphi, Asher, and Fitz pulled theirs out, too.

"Nope, dead," Asher seconded.

"Mine too," Meeka said.

"Yeah, black screen," Fitz mumbled in agreement.

Delphi walked over to a clock hung on a wall. "This says it's two o'clock."

"We must have traveled through time!" August said.

"Traveled through time? Really, dude?" Asher replied.

"Well, how else do you explain somehow appearing in this city, out of nowhere, where it's daytime again?" August asked.

"Dreaming?" Asher hypothesized.

"All of us? At the same time? In the same freaking dream!" Delphi asked, turning toward Asher. "This is crazy! Absolutely nuts! What the heck is happening?"

"I agree with Delphi," August said. "And besides, if this were actually my dream, Delphi would have kissed me already."

Delphi scrunched up her face in disgust.

"He really isn't subtle, is he?" Meeka whispered to Delphi.

"Not. One. Bit."

"Ok, so if we're not dreaming and we definitely haven't traveled through time," Asher said, giving August a look, "then what's going on?"

"Let's all just calm down and retrace our steps," Meeka said. "What were we doing right before we ended up here?'

Fitz turned towards them, "The orb," he said. "It started making weird noises when I dropped it in the sink."

"How the *infernum* did you manage that, dude?" August asked his cousin.

Fitz shrugged and continued, "When you guys came over, the orb opened."

"Yeah, we were there. Can you get to the point?" Delphi said, still irritated with Fitz for touching the orb.

Fitz turned a violent shade of red. "Uh, yeah. The point is that I accidentally pushed the button, and we ended up here."

"Okay, so all we have to do is get the orb, push the button, and we can go back home," Meeka said.

"Yeah, easy." Delphi nodded.

"Well, where is the orb?" Fitz asked.

"You mean you don't have it?" August asked.

Fitz shook his head.

"But you were the last one to touch it," August said.

"It must have slipped out of my hands when we went through that swirly light thing," Fitz guessed.

"Butterfingers," August remarked.

They scoured the room for the sphere. A glint of light

caught Asher's eye.

"Hey, guys! I found it." He picked the orb up as the rest of the gang ran over.

"Okay, now we need to open it," Meeka said. "Fitz, do you remember how you did it last time?"

"I told you, I dropped it in the sink, and it opened. I don't know how," Fitz replied.

"So, we just have to drop it in a sink?" August asked.

"Uh, guys," Delphi said, looking around.

"Yeah?" Meeka asked.

"Where's Opal?" Delphi asked, looking around more frantically.

"There!" Asher pointed to a group of people walking toward an elevator. Opal was stuck in the wave of people and was being moved along with them.

"Opal!" Meeka yelled as the gang dashed towards the elevator.

Asher, Meeka, Delphi, August, and Fitz just reached the elevator when it closed with Opal inside.

"*Dautor haec faex!*" Meeka cursed while madly pushing the down button on the elevator.

"Woah, Meeka, I didn't know you had that kind of language in you. I'm mildly impressed," August said. Meeka ignored him and continued to violently pummel the elevator button.

Finally, the elevator door opened, and they rushed inside. Delphi pushed the ground floor button. A hidden speaker in the elevator kept repeating the same mantra, "Feel the heart of New York City."

"What floor were we on?" Fitz asked, fidgeting. "And I've never heard of New York City."

"Me neither, but I haven't memorized every single city on the planet. And I think we were on the 86th floor," Asher said, pointing to a screen that was counting down the floors. "So what are we going to do, check all the floors until we find Opal?"

"No," Delphi said, "Before the door closed on us, I caught a glimpse of someone pushing the ground floor button."

They reached the ground floor to see Opal walking outside of the building. They rushed through the doors and scanned the small crowd of people for a sign of her. Finally, Meeka spotted her entering a candy shop across the street.

"Seriously?" she cried out.

They ran across the street and onto the opposite sidewalk.

Suddenly, Delphi collapsed. Everything had gone blurry, and she had lost feeling in her legs. The blaring city noises around her were getting quieter, and the panic-stricken voices of Asher and Meeka were muted. All she could see were their mouths moving in alarm. She felt sick. She had gone deaf to the sounds around her and could only hear a constant throbbing noise inside her head. Then everything went dark.

All I wanted to do was scream. The darkness was suffocating.

Between the overwhelming feeling of fear and the adrenaline coursing through me, I felt like I had just run a marathon.

I couldn't remember anything. Not my name, where I was, or who I was with, nothing. A million questions swirled through my head. What did I do to deserve this? This place was so unfamiliar. Nothing felt right. Nothing felt *real.* The surrounding air was bitter and cold, spreading a numbness through my veins. I felt like a prisoner, probably because I *was* one.

A dark figure towered over me. I could see the outlines of other people, their faces hidden in shadows. I felt a sense of familiarity. I just couldn't pinpoint it.

I jolted. Someone had grabbed my hand.

From the smothering darkness, I heard a whisper, "Focus on my hand. It'll be okay. We will be okay."

My throat was dry and scratchy. I couldn't reply. The mysterious voice had somewhat calmed my nerves. Ironic, considering I had no clue who they were. I tried to do as they said and focus on the hand clasping mine.

Think, think, think.

I tried to survey my surroundings. It was dark, except for a bit of light leaking in from under the door. I was sitting down. My wrists weren't bound. I'd take that as a good sign, but at least three burly figures were flanking the walls of the room. Not good.

I felt someone wince and realized I had tensed up again. I loosened my vice-like grip on the hand intertwined with mine.

Sorry. I thought, figuring it was no use to attempt to speak again. *Alright, somehow you got yourself into this mess; now you just have to get out. Easy.*

At least I was thinking clearly again. Well, clearly for someone with a major case of amnesia.

I did a second survey of the room and silently cursed. No windows. The only way out was the door. I looked up to see if I could find any grates in the ceiling, but it was too dark to tell. No big loss. Watching people climb through the ventilation system in movies was probably way easier than doing it myself. Plus, I had no actual plan for getting high enough to even reach the ceiling.

The door.

If I wanted to get out, I'd have to use the normal person way. Not like they were just going to let me waltz out, anyway. Judging by what appeared to be a gun in each looming figure's hand, they weren't going to have second thoughts about using force to keep me in here. What were these people waiting for? If they wanted me dead, they would have killed me already. No, they were definitely waiting for something or someone.

A noise interrupted my inner monologue.

I heard a scuffle of feet and a clicking sound, like typing on a keyboard. A single beep sounded outside the door. The handle turned.

Then, as quickly as it had started, the world went black, and my surroundings were dragged into the shadows.

✳✳✳

"Delphi! Delphi! Wake up! Come ON!" Asher was desperately shaking Delphi awake.

"Dude, relax. She's still breathing, and it hasn't even been a minute yet," came August's voice.

Delphi opened her eyes. She was lying down on a bench a few feet away from the candy shop that Opal had entered a few minutes before. Asher was on one side of her, still holding her shoulders.

August was sitting on her other side. "Hey, beautiful," he said, smirking when he saw her eyes open.

Delphi ignored him and asked, "Where's Meeka?"

Fitz was pacing back and forth in front of the bench. Asher and August were sitting on either side of Delphi, but there was no sign of Meeka or Opal.

"Don't worry, she went into the candy shop to find Opal," Asher replied. "What you *should* be worried about is what happened to you."

"I'm fine."

Asher shot her a look.

"No, really. I'm okay." The headache and blurriness had passed, and she could hear again, but the whole thing had shaken her pretty badly. She knew she wasn't fooling anyone, but Asher and his *twintuition* would have to give up for the time being. "It was just another flash thing."

"At least tell us what you *saw*," Asher said, looking

pleadingly at her, begging her to cooperate.

"Well," she started, "I looked up at the tall building that we had just come out of, and everything went blurry and then, nothingness. I opened my eyes, and I was in a dark room—" A blaring pain behind her eyes suddenly cut her off. She felt like she was going to pass out again. She squeezed her eyes shut and managed to regain control. She took deep breaths until the pain had disappeared to a faint throbbing in the back of her mind.

Asher went wide-eyed. "Are you okay?" he asked.

"I'm fine, I'm fine." She took a few more deep breaths.

Before Asher could pester Delphi anymore, Meeka walked out of the candy shop, holding Opal's hand. A guy around the age of eighteen walked out behind her. They were arguing about something. The rest of the group jogged, or in Delphi's case, stumbled over to Meeka.

Meeka was still arguing with the guy when they came up next to her. She didn't even notice them.

The guy she was arguing with was tall and had dark, almost black, chin-length brown hair and navy blue eyes. A little girl, about Opal's age, was holding his hand. She had the same olive tone and dark brown hair, but hers was curly. Within her frame of curls, the little girl's big navy eyes shone. She and Opal were giggling with each other like they had been friends forever and didn't just meet each other in a candy shop.

"You should keep better track of her," said the guy.

"Don't lecture me. I had everything under control," Meeka replied, furious.

"Under control? There was some weirdo in there staring her and my little sister down!" the guy replied, starting to raise his voice and gesturing to the two little girls.

"Well, how come I didn't see any 'weirdo'?" Meeka asked, obviously not convinced. "For all I know, you're some weirdo."

"It was some big guy in a fancy black suit. He was wearing sunglasses inside, which was a little weird, but there's no way you could've missed him. He stuck out like a sore thumb in that candy shop!" The guy was really annoyed. You could hear it in his tone.

"Okay, sure—" Meeka trailed off mid-comeback. She had just noticed the rest of her group watching her squabble with the stranger. "Delphi, you look terrible."

"Thanks." Delphi chuckled. "Before you ask, I'm fine, really."

"What happened, though, when you fainted?" Meeka asked, not quite ready to dismiss Delphi's pale features that fast.

"Don't ask," Asher said. "When we tried, she almost passed out, again. All we know is that she got another flash."

"What if you draw it?" Meeka wondered out loud. "Would that cause the same reaction?"

"Only one way to find out," Delphi replied. "Does anyone have paper I can borrow... and maybe a pen?"

The guy who was just quarreling with Meeka took out a folded piece of paper and a pen. "Here, use this," he said. "It's got a shopping list on the back, so just turn it over." He had seemed to soften up a bit after seeing an ill-looking Delphi.

"Thanks. And you are?" She asked, taking the paper and heading to a bench outside the sweet shop.

"My name's Quinn, Quinn Russo," he said to the group. "And this is my little sister Macy." He motioned to the little girl still holding his hand. Macy and Opal were in the midst of a very stimulating conversation about the pros and cons of cupcakes.

Meeka begrudgingly introduced herself and the rest of the gang. "My name is Meeka, and that's Delphi," she pointed to Delphi, who waved without looking up from her drawing. Delphi had situated herself on a bench in front of the candy shop, with Asher looking over her shoulder to watch her sketch. "Next to her is Asher, the blonde one is August, and the kid next to him is Fitz. And of course, this one," she raised the hand that Opal was still holding. "Is Opal. "

"Woah," Asher said. Delphi had just finished her drawing. She had captured the eerie aura of the black room perfectly. There were four dark walls (including the one assumed to be out of view), three burly figures (each holding a gun), two empty folding chairs, and a partridge in a pear tree. Delphi even drew the door slightly ajar with light coming from behind it like it had been when her flash ended.

The rest of the group, including Quinn, gaped at the drawing. It was oddly unsettling, and they hadn't even been trapped in the room like Delphi had.

Just then, Quinn looked up. A man in a black suit and dark sunglasses had just walked out of a store a few doors down from where the group was standing.

"There!" he said, pointing to the man. "That's the guy I

saw in the store!"

Everyone turned around and saw who Quinn was gesturing towards. Unfortunately, with their luck, the man had spotted them too and was slowly advancing toward them. "Uh, I think we should get out of here," August said. "If I've learned anything from movies, it's that the big guy in dark sunglasses is *not* your friend."

"I hate to say it, but August's right," Delphi admitted.

"Hmm? What was that again?" August asked, with no attempt at hiding his smirk.

"There is *no* way you are getting me to say it again," Delphi replied. "Quinn, do you have a car nearby?"

"Yeah, it's just over—" he realized his mistake too late and blushed, "Umm, actually, no, I don't have a car." The lie wasn't wholly unbelievable since they *were* in a city where most people rarely owned cars, preferring to use taxis and subways. But he had fumbled, and it was apparent that no one believed him.

"You're a really bad liar," Delphi observed.

"We don't have time for this!" Fitz blurted out and then blushed. "I—I mean... Oh! Just look!" He pointed back to the guy in the tux, who had started to run towards them.

"Uh-oh. We need to go," said Asher, "Go, go, go!"

CHAPTER 4

ADRENALINE RUSH

They sprinted across the street and down the sidewalk to Quinn's car. Quinn fumbled with the keys and pushed the unlock button.

"Everybody in!" Meeka ordered.

Quinn helped Macy into the back of the silver Subaru and hopped in the driver's seat. Meeka climbed into the seat next to him. Delphi herded August, Fitz, Asher, and Opal into the backseat. Once they were piled in, with Macy in her car seat, Opal on Delphi's lap, and Fitz, August, and Asher awkwardly smushed into a single seat, Quinn took off.

Sirens sounded, and a loudspeaker turned on. "This is the FBI. If the silver Subaru does not pull over, we have the authority to shoot."

"Oh... Great," Quinn said as they sped down West 34th Street.

Asher looked out the back window and saw three black vehicles racing towards them. "If this thing goes any faster, now would be the time to floor it."

"Trust me, I am," Quinn retorted as he swerved and just missed a red Toyota. "Who are you people, anyway?"

"Maybe you should have asked that before letting us into

your car," Meeka pointed out.

"Well, I'm asking now!" Quinn was starting to lose his temper.

"First, just tell us where we are," Delphi said.

"You're kidding," Quinn said as he drove into the wrong lane and was almost flattened by a taxi. He looked in the rear-view mirror and saw everyone's serious expressions. "Okay, well, welcome to New York City." As if on cue, two car alarms went off, and a taxi driver started cursing at them. Quinn winced, "Uh, it has its, um, *charms.*"

Delphi looked out the window. "Charming."

Abruptly, Quinn slammed on the brakes.

"What the *infernum* are you thinking?" Meeka yelled.

"It's a red light!" Quinn said.

"*RUN IT!*" shouted Meeka.

Quinn floored the gas and swerved onto the sidewalk. People yelped and jumped out of the way.

The little girls giggled in the back, "Weee!"

Asher turned green. "I'm gonna throw up!"

"*Not* on the seats. There are barf bags back there," Quinn responded.

Delphi glanced at the floor and threw Asher a plastic shopping bag. "Here!"

Asher started vomiting the second the gunshots began.

"*GET DOWN!*" Meeka screamed, ducking behind her seat. Everybody bent down and covered their heads with their hands.

"*HOLY SHIT!*" Quinn shouted.

The rearview window shattered.

"We need to shake them!" Delphi yelled over the roaring in her ears.

"I know! Let's chuck things at them!" August said.

"That is... actually not a terrible idea," said Asher, pausing from puking.

"Ok, who's the best at throwing?" Delphi asked.

"Don't look at me. I can catch, but I can't throw to save our lives," replied Meeka.

"I can," Asher said. He climbed over August to get closer to the window.

"Ouch, jeez! Get off of me, dude! Come on!" August blustered.

"What should I throw?" Asher asked.

"Here, take this." Delphi handed him the bag he was just barfing into.

"Oh, that's gross!" Meeka said, ducking at another round of shots. "On second thought, just do it!"

Asher aimed at the car behind them, threw the bag, and it hit the windshield. The car swerved and crashed into an unoccupied bench on the sidewalk.

"There are still two more cars!" August yelled.

"Really? I hadn't noticed!" Delphi replied, crouching over Opal at another round of bullets.

They were now off the sidewalks and on 8th Avenue.

"I have an idea," Quinn said. "Hang on!"

"Don't need to tell me twice," Fitz mumbled.

Quinn turned left onto a side road.

"What are you doing? Turn right onto the larger road!" Meeka yelled.

"*WOULD YOU LIKE TO DRIVE?*" Quinn retorted.

"Actually, I would," Meeka said. She grabbed the wheel, and the car swerved into another lane, cutting off a line of vehicles. Other drivers wailed their horns.

"*WHAT THE HELL?* You can't just *do* that! *You're* going to get us all *KILLED!*" Quinn snapped while he tried to grab hold of the wheel.

He attempted to get the car back into control, but Meeka tried taking over once more.

"Last time I checked, *you* offered to let me drive! Now let me!" Meeka attempted to take control, but Quinn used his arm to move her out of the way.

"Why can't you just make this easier on everyone? Let me *DRIVE YOUR CAR!*"

"No. Be happy I even let you guys into my car! You people are insane. I'm here doing you a favor. Stop telling me what to do!" Quinn said impatiently while looking into his rearview mirror. Meeka didn't listen and moved over, taking the wheel. Quinn lifted his arms as if he was surrendering.

"Oh yes, so happy that I have to get into a stranger's car! Yay me! Living the life of my *dreams!*" Meeka said sarcastically. She managed to run two red lights while avoiding crashing into a herd of pedestrians. "See, easy. Maybe you should start listening to me! I know what I'm doing!"

"Remind me to *NEVER* let anyone I don't know in my car again," Quinn said as he started to slow down.

"*FLOOR IT!*" Meeka yelled as they turned into the lane of oncoming traffic. Quinn did as she said. They started to slightly lose the FBI, but not by much.

Meeka took her hands off the wheel and the car almost ran into a delivery truck. Quinn grabbed the steering wheel just in time and jerked it right.

"How about you warn me next time you are *DONE DRIVING!* You complete psychopath!" Quinn yelled, turning his head to look at Meeka.

"When will you shut up?" She rolled her eyes.

"Can we stop arguing and just work together and get the *infernum* out of here?" August interrupted.

"*SHUT UP!*" Quinn and Meeka yelled in unison.

Everyone sitting in the back exchanged looks of alarm. Meeka and Quinn continued to argue non-stop, somehow managing not to crash.

In close pursuit, the FBI dodged a street light with much better accuracy than Quinn as they raced to catch up.

"What the hell is happening?" Quinn asked as he swerved around oncoming traffic. "Who are you people? Why is the frickin' FBI chasing us?!"

"Just help us get out of this, and then we'll explain," Delphi replied.

"Yeah, you have a whole lot of explaining to do. When I woke up this morning, I wasn't planning on getting shot at."

"Well, you did run with us." Asher pointed out.

"That's because when someone's chasing you, *YOU RUN!*"

"Isn't that the first sign of being guilty?" August asked.

"Great, guilty by association. That's just perfect!"

Quinn veered suddenly to the left, and everyone toppled to the right. Asher, August, and Fitz became even more squished against the window, and Meeka's elbow hit Quinn's phone on the center console. The phone made a ding noise, and a woman's automated voice emanated from it. "What can I help you with?"

"*What?*" Meeka shrieked.

"It's just Siri. Siri, turn off!" Quinn yelled, maneuvering onto the sidewalks again.

"Ok, I stopped playing your music," Siri said.

"No, damn it! Could you just shut her off?" Quinn asked Meeka, crashing into a few sidewalk benches and returning to the road.

"I don't know how to respond to that," said Siri.

"Just shut up, you stupid box!" Meeka yelled at the phone.

"That's not nice," Siri replied.

"Why in the world would you want your electronics to talk to you?" Meeka yelled at Quinn.

"I don't know! It's supposed to be helpful. Right now, I have bigger problems to deal with!" Quinn yelled back.

"I'm not sure I understand," Siri said.

Meeka glared at the phone and then looked up. "Turn left!"

Quinn noticed the black FBI vehicles coming from the right and did as she said.

"Recalculating. Recalculating. In ten feet, turn right on—"

"Stop *TALKING*!" Meeka yelled at Quinn's phone.

"Playing 'Stop Talking' from your library," Siri said, playing the song.

"What? *NO!*" Meeka yelled.

"Sorry, I didn't get that. Could you try again?" Siri asked

but continued to play the song.

"*JUST TURN OFF THE PHONE!*" Quinn yelled.

Meeka pushed every button on the side of the phone until she found the right one and finally shut Siri up.

Quinn swerved past cars, avoided pedestrians, and nearly missed a few stray cats until he skidded into a dead-end alleyway. Delphi had grabbed hold of the back of his seat, her knuckles white from gripping so tightly. Asher looked about ready to vomit again, and Fitz didn't look much better. They were all breathing heavily from the adrenaline rush of the chase. Delphi came to her senses first.

"What are you doing? You've trapped us in a dead-end!" Delphi yelled.

"Shhhh!" Quinn hushed and turned around to face her. "Just trust me, okay? I know what I'm doing," he whispered.

Delphi looked at him and saw the fear in his eyes. She nodded a bit reluctantly. "Okay."

The sirens that they could hear in the distance grew louder. The FBI was heading right towards them.

"You've got to be kidding me!" Meeka hissed. "How do you know that being *trapped* is going to work?"

"I don't," Quinn whispered back with a hint of a smile. "Everybody, get down!"

The sirens swelled to an ear-splitting shriek. Everyone collectively held their breath and tensed up as the noise grew closer, closer.

The two black government vehicles flew past the alleyway and down the street, their loud sirens fading into the distance. They all let out a sigh of relief.

August's blank face broke into a huge grin. "That. Was. *AWESOME!*"

"At least someone enjoyed that," Asher mumbled.

"Let me guess," Delphi said to August, "you want to go again?"

"Well, *DUH!*" August replied.

Delphi rolled her eyes, and Fitz looked at his cousin like he was crazy, which, in light of recent events, he probably was.

"You people are all deranged," Meeka remarked.

"Come on, I know a place where we can stay for a while. Plus, you have *a lot* of explaining to do." Quinn said, stepping out of the car.

They all got out while Quinn unbuckled Macy from her car seat.

"Hang on." Asher started, "Before, you didn't even want us to know you *had* a car. Now, you're trying to *help* us? And how do we know we can trust you?"

"I just saved your ass from the frickin' FBI. I think I'm trustworthy. Besides, how do I know I can trust *you?*" Quinn pointed out.

"He's right, you know; he did save us," Delphi said to Asher.

"Since when did *you* become the naïve one, Delphi?" Asher asked.

"I'm not being *naïve.*" Delphi argued, slightly agitated, "I'm just saying that it's the only plan we've got. That is unless you have a better idea?" Delphi raised her eyebrows and waited for an answer.

Asher was silent for a moment.

Meeka spoke up, "I agree with Delphi. Considering all of our options, which would include either staying on the streets, turning ourselves in, or going with Quinn, it's the best chance we have."

Asher relented, "Okay."

"Great, now that that's settled, can you grab that tarp by the trash can? We need to cover the car," Quinn said.

They hid the car with the tarp and Quinn led them to the side of a brick building with a fire escape running down its length. Quinn grabbed the ladder of the fire escape and pulled it down. He lifted Macy onto the ladder and followed her. When he got to the stair portion, he looked down to see no one had followed.

"Well, come on, it's perfectly safe," Quinn said.

"A mysterious ascent up the side of a building... I'm in!" August jumped onto the ladder and started climbing.

"Wait, hold on. Why not just use the front door?" Meeka asked.

"It's locked, my parents aren't home, and I forgot my key. Now come *on*," Quinn replied and started clambering up the stairs again.

Meeka looked at Delphi for backup, but she just shrugged and followed August. Fitz went next, followed by Opal. Asher motioned for Meeka to go ahead of him. "Ladies first."

Meeka smiled and grabbed the first rung of the ladder. When they reached the top, Quinn opened a window and climbed through. Once everyone was inside, Quinn shut it again.

They were in a small bedroom. The walls were lined with

bookshelves filled with old CDs, and the wall space left was covered in retro vinyl discs. There was a small bed and desk in the corner, with a lamp, iPod, earbuds, and headphones scattered across it.

"Home sweet home," Quinn said, motioning around the packed room.

"This is your house?" Meeka practically shrieked, "Are you insane?"

"Ummm, I'm gonna go with no," Quinn answered sarcastically.

"They saw your face, those guys from the *FDI* or whatever. The first thing they'll do is go into their database and find out who you are and where you live!" Meeka explained.

"Calm down. It'll take them a while to find anything on me. They don't know my name. All they have is my license plate, but that isn't even my car. And, umm, just so you know, it's FBI, unless you were talking about Foreign Direct Investment, then you got it right," Quinn responded calmly.

"That's not your car? So what did you do, steal it?" Delphi asked.

"No, no, it's not like that. It's my uncle's car, but he lives in Pennsylvania. He's just letting me borrow it until I have enough money to get my own," Quinn clarified. "'*Do me a favor and try not to bust it up,*' he said before entrusting me with it. Oh man, he's going to kill me!"

"Okay, borrowing the car makes more sense, but where is Pennsylvania? I've never heard of it before," Delphi said.

"Just like how you've never heard of New York City?" Quinn asked.

They all nodded.

"Okay, we need to get some things clear right now, but first, I think we should move into the kitchen. It's a little less cramped there."

They all shuffled out of the room and down a short, tight hallway. The kitchen wasn't much more extensive than Quinn's bedroom, but it was definitely better. It was equipped with all the necessities, plus a round kitchen table with four chairs and a vase of yellow tulips. Meeka, Delphi, Fitz, and August each took a chair. Asher remained standing by the window, looking out onto the street. The little girls plopped down on the floor and started playing a hand game. Apparently, either they knew everything about each other already, or they just weren't interested. Quinn leaned against a counter with his arms crossed.

"Okay, now will you please explain to me who you are, what you are doing here, and why the FBI is chasing you?" He listed the questions on his fingers and then stared up at them expectantly.

"Ooh, storytime," August said, criss-crossing his legs on the chair and leaning over on his hands.

"Dude, are you *ever* serious?" Asher asked his friend.

"I don't know, you tell me," August said with a smirk.

"The answer is no. Let's move on." Meeka cut in, "You already know all of our names, so unless you want a list of each of our likes and dislikes, you are going to need to be more specific."

Quinn sighed, exasperated. "Fine, where are you from? Because it certainly isn't around here."

Delphi decided to answer this question. "We're from The Metropolis. Asher, Opal, Meeka, and I have parents in the Empire, so we live in that area. Fitz is just visiting August, who also lives there and—"

"Whoa, whoa, whoa, hold your horses. What the hell is the 'Empire' and similar to you never hearing about New York flippin' City, I've never heard of your 'Metropolis' either." Quinn interjected. "You obviously have North American accents, so you must be from The U.S, which leads me to the point of this making no sense whatsoever." He pinched the bridge of his nose in frustration. "It's also not likely that you *all* have amnesia, and you are kind of freaking me out."

"Really? *This* is the part where you're freaking out. How about when we were nearly killed by a bunch of people we have never even met!" Meeka yelled, making Opal and Macy jump.

Fitz spoke up, "Can we *please* all just calm down and figure this out? I think we're all on edge right now, but we need to know what's going on."

"Yeah, I agree, so let me explain." Delphi continued as if she were speaking to a child, "The Empire is the government that presides over all of Esprit. It's a democracy, so we can vote for the Director and people in other political positions like the Board of Governance, which my parents are on."

Quinn interrupted, "One question. Actually, I have *many* questions, but it's just one for now. What is Esprit?"

There was an almost tangible silence in the air, then August burst out laughing. "Man, you're hilarious. I almost believed you for a second there, but, ha! Not knowing the name of your own planet. That's really funny."

Quinn's glare at August was so deadly looking that it almost rivaled Delphi's.

"Wait, you're being serious? You can't be serious. That was just a joke, right? I mean, you can't get dumber than me, forget me, you can't be dumber than Asher." August spoke a mile a minute.

"Thanks, man. You make me feel all warm and fuzzy inside," Asher said to August, "And for the record, I am *not* stupid. I just fall asleep in class a lot. What can I say? It's boring." He shrugged.

"We're getting sidetracked here," Meeka pointed out. "If you don't know about Esprit, Quinn, then what planet do you think we're on?"

"Um, Earth?" he replied. "In the country of The U.S? In the state of New York and the city also by the name of New York? If you need me to be more specific, we are in the borough of Manhattan, if that helps at all."

"Who names a place New York, New York? It sounds kind of repetitive, doesn't it? I would have gone with something more creative. Maybe Augustville, New York. Has a nice ring to it, don't you think?" August remarked.

Meeka stuttered, ignoring August. "No—n—no, we can't just magically end up on some other planet. That's not plausible. I mean, it can't possibly…"

"Actually, it can," Fitz remarked. "That swirly light vortex thing could have been a portal or some other mode of transport through the universe."

"You mean like a wormhole? And what are you talking

about, some 'swirly light vortex thing'?" Quinn asked.

"What's a wormhole?" August asked.

"Really? Do any of you know anything about space? Astronomy?" questioned Quinn.

"I mean, using my common sense, it sounds like we're talking about a hole for worms, but this little voice in the back of my head is telling me that that really isn't relevant to our lovely little discussion," August replied.

"Translation: No, we don't know much about space. They don't really teach that stuff in school on Esprit," Asher said. "And the swirly light thing vortex thingamajig whatever— God! We need to come up with a better name for that thing!— is what came from this orb when Fitz dropped it in the sink, right before we ended up here."

He took the orb out of his sweatshirt pocket.

Quinn ran his hands through his hair. "You're trying to tell me, that that *thing*," he glanced at the orb in Asher's hand, "brought you to Earth from another *PLANET?*"

Asher chuckled, "Basically."

"Does this normally happen on whatever planet you said you were from?"

"Esprit, and no. Do we *look* like we have any idea what's going on?" Delphi replied.

"All we know is we need to find a way back home," Meeka said.

"So why not just backtrack and do exactly what you did to get here in the first place?" Quinn asked.

"That was what we were going to do, but then Opal went into that candy shop, we met you and Macy, and then the FBI people started chasing us," said Delphi.

"Wait a minute, if you're aliens, then how are we speaking the same language? I mean, English is only spoken in The U.S, England, Australia, Canada; okay, there are a lot more than I originally thought. Still, you get the idea," Quinn said.

"*Excuse* me? Aliens? What's that supposed to mean?" Meeka asked. "And how do you know that we aren't speaking Vernaculus?"

"Uh, because we're on *Earth* in *The United States*, and I absolutely *suck* at languages," Quinn responded.

"Hey, I have an idea," Delphi said, picking up a notebook and pencil from the table. She scribbled something on the paper and set it back down. "Quinn, can you read that?"

"Um, nope," he replied.

"Oh, come on. It just says that Asher is an idiot," August said.

"She's not wrong," Meeka replied jokingly.

Asher grinned. "I mean, compared to your IQ..."

"Thank *you*?"

Delphi continued, "My point was, if Quinn can't read this, then that means that we're all speaking a language that we have never learned before. And the best part is, we didn't even realize it.

CHAPTER 5

ASHER BLOWS IT

After a long discussion and an even longer debate about how any of this happened, everyone was exhausted. Meeka went up to the roof for some fresh air. Asher noticed and followed her up. Macy and Opal had fallen asleep on the floor, and Quinn and Delphi brought them to Macy's room. When they came back, they saw that August and Fitz had raided the cabinet underneath the TV and were now watching a movie about an alien invasion called *Independence Day*.

"Is this really what you think we look like?" August asked, looking at the greenish big-eyed aliens on the screen. "Not gonna lie. I could totally pull it off, but they are definitely mistaken. I mean, do I look green to you?" he looked down at his hands.

"No, I guess the *Race to Witch Mountain* movie was more accurate." Quinn said, "Minus the superpowers."

"Hey, I have superpowers. I'm super awesome," August said.

"And don't forget the fact that Delphi has *actual* superpowers," Fitz pointed out without taking his eyes off the TV.

"Oh yeah," Quinn said. "The flashes, right?"

"Uh, yeah. I guess you could call them a superpower," she replied, sitting down at the table in the kitchen.

Quinn sat across from her. "What exactly happens when you get them? I saw that you got a headache back there. Does it still hurt?"

"No, I'm okay." She let out a sigh. "It's just freaky, you know? The first time it happened was when I touched the orb." She told him about the images she had seen and how real they had felt. "I felt trapped inside my head, then I actually passed out the second time." Delphi filled Quinn in on what happened when she looked at the Empire State Building.

"Is it possible that you're seeing pictures of the, wow, this is going to sound crazy, but pictures of the future?" Quinn asked when she had finished.

"Apparently, teleporting with the use of little orb-shaped objects is possible, so I wouldn't be surprised," she said. "It's just hard to know for sure. Yeah, I saw the Empire State Building before I even knew it existed, but what about the other ones? Those I'm really not looking forward to."

"Let's hope I'm wrong then," Quinn replied. "I wanted to thank you, you know, for trusting me."

Delphi nodded shyly. "Oh well, what else was I gonna do? I had no other choice..." She laughed nervously.

He smiled at her awkwardness. "Well, I'm pretty sure your friend listed a few other choices."

"Yeah, all of which would probably get us killed."

"That's true. Either way, you made the right decision, even if not everyone wholeheartedly agrees."

Delphi gave a small smile, "Oh well, um, thank you." Delphi looked down to the granite kitchen island, running her finger along the marbled design.

"Can I get you something to drink? Tea, coffee...?" Quinn asked, turning around and grabbing two mugs.

"Coffee will do." Delphi looked up. Quinn quickly put together two mugs of coffee and set them on the counter, both steaming.

"Thank you," Delphi added. "Y—you, um, you did a very good job driving today..." she stammered with an unsure look.

Quinn leaned forward over the counter. "You really tried there, didn't you?" he teased. "But thanks."

Delphi turned red, feeling embarrassed and unsure of what else to say.

They both took a sip from their coffee, Delphi avoiding eye contact.

"So, tell me more about yourself, Delphi..."

✳✳✳

While Delphi and Quinn talked and drank enough caffeine to last everyone the night, Meeka and Asher were on the roof, enjoying the city lights. The top of Quinn and Macy's sixth-floor walk-up was mostly bare except for a few randomly placed crates and potted plants. Night had fallen. Between the stars and the city lights, it was a gorgeous sight.

Meeka and Asher were sitting on a crate overlooking the city. Asher took his gaze off the skyline and glanced at Meeka. He noticed how the city light's glow shone on her face, leaving a shimmer in her eyes. He couldn't stop admiring her beauty as she stared into the horizon.

"This is insane," Meeka said, breaking the long stretch of silence.

Their eyes met.

"What I meant was, when I look up at the sky, it's hard to believe that I'm on another planet. Nothing *feels* different, and yet here we are," Meeka whispered the last part as if she were afraid that if she said it too loud, things would get worse.

"Hey, the way I look at it is you can either welcome the craziness or live your whole life in fear of it," Asher replied in a comforting tone. "And personally, being afraid of the past instead of living in the present doesn't sound super exciting."

Meeka laughed, "Well, I don't think I necessarily want to be chased by the Federal Bureau of Investigation."

"You know what I meant, Meeka," Asher smiled as he leaned back.

"Of course I did," she started, "Do you think we will be okay? Or make it home? Or make it home alive, for a matter of fact? Are we —"

"You're rambling. And that's surprising coming from '*Miss Bossy*,'" Asher interrupted while moving closer to her.

Meeka looked to the ground. "I'm just feeling, never mind." She shut down.

"No, go on..." Asher tried making eye contact, hoping to comfort her.

Meeka looked up at the scenery. "Asher, I'm terrified. What if someone gets hurt?"

"I think we're all feeling the same way, but we all have each other, and that's what's most important right now," Asher said reassuringly while moving his hand to Meeka's knee.

Meeka turned and smiled at Asher. She placed her hand on his and rested her head on his shoulder. Asher's cheeks were the color of Fitz's hair, and his stomach was doing backflips.

"I'm exhausted," she sighed.

"Aren't we all..." Asher teased.

They both chuckled.

"I wonder how our parents are going to react..." Meeka murmured, lifting her head.

Asher jumped to his feet and started pacing. "Oh, no, no, no, no, no! I completely forgot about our parents! What if they got home and noticed we weren't there!? What if they're searching for us? They are going to *kill* me! We will never be able to see each other again... you're gonna lose your job and, and—"

"ASHER! Pull yourself together and take a deep breath before you pass out! I'm sure everything will be fine... I hope. But we'll deal with that when we get there. Until then, we have to stay optimistic."

Meeka grabbed him by his shoulders, stopping him from walking back and forth. Asher took a deep breath.

"You're right, like always."

They both smiled. Meeka pulled Asher in, wrapping her arms around him, giving him a comforting hug. Asher acted as if he was frozen in time.

"Hey, Asher..." Meeka laughed nervously.

"O—oh s—sorry," Asher stammered, taking Meeka's hint. Asher put his arms around her as well. He was so overwhelmed with joy that he could barely keep his cool. He had always had feelings for his sister's best friend. They had grown up together, and the two had formed a bond during their many years spent together, even if they thought they were hiding it well.

After their moment, they pulled apart, both smiling awkwardly.

"I think we should go try to get some rest," Meeka sighed.

"Yeah. Keyword, *try*, after today... I don't know if sleep is achievable." They both laughed again.

But as soon as they turned their backs to head downstairs, there was a clattering noise behind them, almost as if someone had dropped something. Their nerves were so on end that they both jumped at the noise. Asher wasn't exactly compelled to turn around to find the source of the sound, and apparently, neither was Meeka. She had grabbed hold of Asher's wrist with a look of terror on her face. Trying to mask the fear that was indeed mirrored on his own face, Asher turned around.

A white rectangular box was sitting on the ground directly in front of the crate they had previously been sitting on. Asher picked up the box. On the face-down side, there was a timer counting down from ten minutes. Asher stuffed his fist in his mouth to stifle a shout. Meeka turned around and came up behind Asher to see what he was looking at.

Her eyes went wide. "Please tell me that's not what I think it is."

They both peeked over the side of the building to see where the box had come from. A pair of headlights glared from a black car parked on the side of the empty street. A blonde man in a black suit got out of the passenger's side. He walked to a spot on the road with a better view of Meeka and Asher on the roof.

"Hello there!" the guy called up. "What are you kids doing up so late?" He spoke casually enough, but his tone had a slightly annoyed sound to it.

"What do *you* want?" Asher practically spat while Meeka reflexively grabbed his hand.

It was clear that these people wanted something from them; they just didn't exactly know what. The sleek black suit, the government vehicle, and the white box that Asher was still holding were all indicators that they were once again dealing with the FBI.

"I believe you have something of mine," said the man.

Asher looked down at what he was holding. "Oh yeah? Well, you can have it back." He made to throw it, but the man spoke up once again.

"I wouldn't do that if I were you. What you are holding in your hand is a time bomb set to go off in ten. No, wait." He checked his watch. "Eight minutes, seven minutes and fifty-nine seconds, fifty-eight seconds, fifty-seven seconds..."

"We get it. Cut to the chase. I suppose you want us to come down and turn ourselves in?" Asher replied sarcastically.

"Well, I did assume that anyone smart enough to outrun my men in a car chase wouldn't be stupid enough to choose to stay in a building that is," he indicated his watch again, "seven minutes and ten seconds from blowing up. And I don't recommend throwing the bomb down here so close to all of these still occupied buildings." He motioned behind him.

"That's sick, all of you," Meeka spoke up. "There are innocent people in this building, including children."

"On the contrary, we evacuated all the current residents on the other floors of this building."

"How the *infernum* did you manage that?" Meeka asked.

"Inconspicuously, my dear. In a way that would not alert them of any danger."

"And a spontaneously combusting building isn't *conspicuous?*" Meeka's voice had raised an octave, betraying her attempt at keeping cool.

"People's minds are really very easy to twist, Miss McBella. For example, a simple gas leak caused the explosion, or perhaps young Quinn Russo was smuggling dangerous weapons into his apartment, but rest assured, he was apprehended by the proper authorities."

"We need to get out of here," Meeka whispered to Asher, gripping his hand harder.

He nodded and dropped the bomb, which was now counting down from six minutes. They ran to the exit and climbed down the steps to get to Quinn and Macy's apartment. Asher and Meeka pounded on the door until Quinn opened it.

"Was wondering when you guys would—"

Asher cut him off. "We need to leave. Now."

Delphi came over and saw the look in Asher's eyes. Something was seriously wrong. "What happened? Are you guys alright?"

"We need to wake up Macy and Opal. We have less than six minutes to get out of this building before it blows," Meeka said to Delphi.

The two girls dashed into Macy's bedroom, Quinn hurried to his room to grab something, and August and Fitz came over.

"Blow? As in blow *up?*" August asked.

Asher nodded. "Yeah."

Quinn came out of his room with Delphi, Meeka, Macy, and Opal following close behind. Quinn tossed a beat-up old backpack to Asher and a black drawstring bag to Delphi. He slung his own book bag over his shoulder.

"Supplies," he said.

They left the apartment and climbed the stairs to the roof.

"While in my room, I took a peek out of the window. This is the only exit that they haven't blocked," Quinn told them. "Hang on a second. What about everyone else who lives here? We can't just leave them!"

"Don't worry, the blonde dude down there helpfully informed us that everyone else from this apartment was already evacuated," Asher replied.

Quinn looked relieved for a moment, and then a serious expression crossed his face once more. "How much time do we have?"

Asher walked over to the bomb. "About five minutes."

"Hold on, I'd like an explanation of how this is our only exit." August said, "Because right now, to me, it looks like we're trapped."

Quinn walked over to a ladder lying on the floor and picked it up. "This should work."

He walked back to the part of the roof closest to the top of the building adjacent to them and extended the ladder over the gap between the buildings.

"Who wants to go first?" he asked.

Delphi spoke up. "I will."

Delphi walked over to the ladder and grabbed the first wrung with her hands. She continued to cross on her hands and knees to distribute her weight. She wobbled a few times and almost lost her balance. The six-story drop down was a nice incentive to stay upright. She cursed herself the entire way, thinking this was one of her more stupid moments. When she finally reached the other side, she stood and gave them all a thumbs up. Opal went next, and Macy followed her with encouragement from either side. Then went Fitz, Meeka, Asher, Quinn, and finally, it was August's turn to go, and he was running out of time.

"Nope, no way, uh uh. Not going to happen." He said in utter defiance.

"Seriously? If you don't move fast, you're going to be a fried August sandwich with sauce on the side!" Asher whisper-yelled, trying not to attract attention from the people lurking below.

"Or I could be smashed as flat as a pancake from falling from this high up!" August retorted.

"Guys!" Delphi hissed. "Can you please stop talking about August food and hurry up!"

They were down to two minutes.

"August, are you afraid of heights?" Asher asked.

"Technically, it's a fear of falling."

"Oh please, did you get that line from a movie?" Asher replied.

"As a matter of fact, I did, and I think it sums up the acid reflux going on over here pretty well."

"Sorry, I can't hear you," Asher said.

August rolled his eyes and bent down. "I said that it describes the fear nicely!"

One minute.

"What?" Asher asked.

"I said that it explains my fear well."

Thirty seconds.

"I didn't quite get that!"

"Oh, come on, are you going deaf or something?" August asked, standing up.

"Do you have any idea what you just did?" Asher questioned August.

"What? Oh." August suddenly realized that he was on a different rooftop. "I did it! I'm— Hey! Are you even listening to me?"

Asher's face had gone slack. He was staring at his watch. "Shut up and run."

"What?"

"Just *RUN*!"

They only made it to the opposite side of the roof when the

explosion sounded. They were all pushed back with a force similar to a Tyrannosaurus Rex sneezing. Quinn's hands were scraped and bleeding from trying to catch himself as he fell. Delphi hit her head and now had a long gash across her forehead. Asher landed on his arm and cried out in pain. Macy scraped her shin, Opal was plopped into a sitting position, and Meeka bit her lip hard as she toppled to the ground. Fitz and August had both fallen but had come out relatively uninjured. As they looked back, they could see a semi-transparent shield glowing around Quinn and Macy's entire building. Well, what was left of it, anyway. The bomb had gone off as expected, but instead of throwing debris everywhere or spreading to other buildings, it had been contained in the bubble that was now dissolving.

"What the—" Quinn started as he saw the bubble finally dissipate.

"No time! We need to move," Meeka cut him off.

They climbed down a ladder on the side of the building and took off down the street.

CHAPTER 6

FIGHT, FLIGHT, OR FALL

They managed to hitch a ride on a relatively empty bus headed to the airport. On the way there, Meeka cleaned up their injuries with a first aid kit that she had found in one of Quinn's bags.

Macy was curled up and trembling next to Quinn; her eyes were filled with tears and drooping with exhaustion. Opal looked just as exhausted between Delphi and Asher. Meeka went over to Macy first and cleaned her scraped-up shin. Macy flinched a little as Meeka patted the scrape with a wipe and put a bandage on it.

"Thank you," Macy whispered drowsily.

Meeka gave her a warm smile and went over to Opal. The most she had were a few bruises that Meeka couldn't do much about and a face dirty with ash and grime. Meeka cleaned the dirt and moved on to Asher.

"Ow!" Asher said when she touched his damaged arm.

"Oh, don't be a wimp," Delphi said.

"It's alright. He hit it pretty hard. There's a slight chance it might be broken," Meeka replied as she took a sling out of the first aid kit.

Asher stopped making faces at Delphi and looked up at

Meeka, who was attempting to put the sling around him. "What? Broken? No, hey, it's not that bad." He tried to move his wrist and yelped in pain. "Okay, so maybe I can't move it, but—"

"'But' nothing. You are going to help me get this sling on your arm, or I'll do it myself in a much more painful way."

Asher couldn't stop staring at Meeka while she situated his arm.

"There, that's better. Isn't it?"

Asher slowly nodded in agreement while Delphi shook with laughter at the look on his face.

Once Meeka had finished her medical rounds, they combed through the contents of the bags. Altogether, they had a wad of cash, a credit card, a first aid kit, matches, a pocket knife, eight small water bottles, and some protein bars between the three bags. They had discarded their phones and *cursors* so that no one could digitally track them.

"When did you pack all of this stuff?" Delphi asked, making sure to keep her voice low because Macy and Opal had fallen asleep.

"When we put Macy and Opal to bed. You came up with the idea of having them wear normal clothes. That way, in case of an emergency, they would be ready. So, I figured we should have some other essentials packed, too," Quinn replied. "Good thing too, or we would be back to square one. I really wasn't expecting them to find us that fast."

"I did," said Meeka. "I told you it was a bad idea to go to your house. I told you they would figure out who you are and where you live."

"It doesn't matter now," said Delphi. She really didn't want Meeka and Quinn to start again.

"Yeah, what matters is figuring out what to do now," Asher said. "For starters, we're headed to an airport, right?"

"Yeah, I think it's the JFK International Airport," Quinn replied.

"Well, then we just catch a flight to somewhere *very* far away from here," August suggested.

"But it's not that simple. For starters, flights are expensive, and none of us have passports," Quinn said.

"Well, we have that card for money, plus that wad of paper. You know, on Esprit, we just have pectos to pay for everything, kind of like your card. It has this screen on it, and when you swipe the screen, you can transfer money anywhere," Meeka explained.

"Okay, okay. So anyway, money's covered, but what about the passports?" Quinn asked.

"What *is* a passport?" Fitz asked.

"It's basically a small book that allows you to travel to different countries under the government's protection and permission," Meeka said, surprising everyone.

"How do you know what a passport is?" Quinn asked.

"There was an airport pamphlet on the seat when we first got on the bus." She shrugged. "I decided to do some research. Apparently, passports are necessary if we are going to get far enough away from here."

"Yeah, and I don't think the people who so obviously want us dead will give us permission, much less protection, in a foreign country," Asher pointed out.

"Is there a way to make false passports?" Delphi asked.

"I'm sure it's possible, but I've never been very good with techy stuff like that," Quinn replied.

"If I can get to a computer and a printer, I might be able to do it," Fitz said.

"Really?" asked August. "I didn't know you could do that kind of thing! Why didn't you tell me? Oh wow! The trouble we could get into…"

"You never asked," mumbled Fitz, blushing at all the attention he was receiving.

"Thank God you didn't tell him," Delphi said, shuddering. "Forget about burning the carpet. You would probably cause some major power outage or something."

"That's not a bad idea," August said, seriously considering it. "The power going off would be a good time to loot some places."

Delphi and Meeka both glanced at August in alarm.

Asher, noticing Delphi and Meeka's expressions, whispered, "Don't worry. It's just a front. He doesn't *actually* ever steal anything."

"Hey, don't go giving away my secrets. You'll make them think the bad boy has gone soft," August replied.

Delphi rolled her eyes. "You're not a 'bad boy,' August."

"Do I need to remind you who got the entire school district to shut down for a day because of a 'freak storm'? I had to pay a kid in my chemistry class thirty pects just to get him to send fake weather alerts to the teacher's *cursors*."

"That makes you a prankster, not a 'bad boy,'" Delphi replied.

"Eh, potato patato."

"Let's get back to the task at hand," said Meeka, redirecting everyone's attention and cutting Delphi off mid antagonized groan. "So, assuming Fitz can make false passports, we can get tickets, and people don't show up to try and kill us. Where will we go?"

They all looked at Quinn.

He massaged the back of his neck. "I've always wanted to go to Italy. It's actually where my parents were..." he trailed off. "It's actually a really nice place. Plus, it's on the other side of the world."

Delphi raised her eyebrows, noticing Quinn's quick subject change when he mentioned his parents, but she didn't say anything.

"Other side of the world? That sounds perfect," said Meeka.

"Do you think the FBI will still be able to find us?" Delphi asked no one in particular.

"I think it's definitely a possibility," said Quinn.

"Well, that makes me feel so much better, thanks," Delphi replied sarcastically and scrunched up her face.

"Just think about it. How did the FBI know you weren't supposed to be in New York City, though? For crying out loud! How did they know you weren't even supposed to be on this planet? They must know about Esprit. How else do you explain all of this and their new souped-up otherworld technology?" Quinn said.

"Otherworld technology?" Asher asked. "You mean the bomb?"

"No, I mean those cool sunglasses they were wearing. Of course, I mean the bomb! That bomb tore my house to shreds. We have bombs on Earth, but not like that one. They don't usually have shields of light."

"That was a light barrier," Delphi explained. "So that the flames don't spread to unwanted places."

"I *knew* that that's what the barrier was for! But how do you explain how the FBI of *this* planet got technology from *yours?*" Quinn said.

"I can't."

✳ ✳ ✳

When they got to the airport, they navigated through the crowded building until they found an internet cafe with a row of computers along one wall and a printer and laminator in the corner.

"Perfect!" Fitz exclaimed, obviously in his element.

He sat down in one of the computer chairs and started hacking away at the keys. "Okay, so I just have to get into the database that makes U.S. passports, copy and paste some of our photos onto passports with our names on them, and print them out."

"Oh, is that all?" Asher asked sarcastically.

"Shouldn't we use fake identities so the FBI can't track us?" Delphi asked.

"That's a good idea. I'll come up with some fake names for the passports," said Fitz, nodding and furiously typing on the keyboard. "And I'll change some of our ages, too. I'm guessing you have to be a certain age to fly alone on any planet."

Quinn gave him a nod.

"Hang on," said August. "I want to make up my own name. What about Sir Barnaby Buchanan?"

"What about no?" said Fitz.

"I don't know. 'No' seems like a long shot. I mean, who would believe *that*? Ooh! And I could wear one of those fake mustaches. "

Fitz just rolled his eyes and kept typing. "I still need pictures of everyone."

"We can just take them here. It looks like there's a camera on the computer." Meeka said, pointing at the screen.

Fitz set up the camera, and they took turns taking photos.

Once both groups had taken their photos, Quinn asked Fitz, "What about the cover? How are you going to make it?"

"I saw a gift shop on the way in here," Delphi said. "I'm pretty sure I saw them selling toy passports. Based on the picture Meeka showed me in that pamphlet, they are pretty realistic. We can just take the paper out of the inside and shove the new stuff in."

"Guys, the waitress is coming over here," warned Meeka.

"I'll go order something. We can't let her see Fitz's computer screen." Quinn walked toward the server and started talking to her.

They huddled closer around Fitz to block any view of the

screen that the waitress might have had.

"Okay," whispered Meeka. "When Quinn comes back, Delphi, you two should take Opal and Macy and get the toy passports from the gift shop." Delphi nodded her head. "Asher, you, August, and I need to make sure the waitress does not see this screen, okay?" They nodded as well. "Fitz, um, just keep doing whatever it is that you're doing."

Quinn came back with two donuts and a couple of coffees. "I see the boss just finished giving out orders."

"Donuts!" Macy said excitedly.

"Hold on a minute. These are mine," said Quinn playfully.

"Aww."

"I'm just kidding. Here's one for you and one for Opal."

"Yay!" They each took a donut.

"What is this?" Opal asked, looking through the hole in the middle.

"Macy can explain it to you, but you should really try it," said Quinn, looking back at Meeka. "So, where were we? Oh yes, you were giving out orders."

"Yes, and you, Delphi, Macy, and Opal need to take a little visit to that gift shop to get those fake passports," Meeka replied.

"Come on, let's go," said Delphi, taking Opal's hand.

Quinn took Macy's hand and followed Delphi out of the cafe.

When they located the gift shop, Delphi spied the passports and retrieved eight of them. They walked up to the counter, and the sales clerk eyed the toys suspiciously.

"And you need *eight* of these?" he asked.

Quinn fumbled for an answer, his cheeks turning a faint shade of pink.

Delphi spoke up, "Our little brother is still with our parents, but you know how little boys are. They tend to break everything they touch. We thought it was best for backups, keeps him occupied on the plane." She gave the clerk her most innocent smile.

"Oh, yeah, yeah. My nephew is just like that. Okay, that will be $28.00."

They weren't entirely sure that the clerk had bought it, but he brushed it off quickly enough.

Once they had paid and returned to the cafe, Fitz was in the process of printing the last fake passport.

"Woah, how did you get them to print like that?" Quinn asked when he saw the passport in each person's hand. The card-like texture of each of them was precisely the same as a genuine passport.

"Well, I may have tweaked the printer a little bit," Fitz replied.

"Now we have to get the covers on them, though," said Delphi.

They slid the play passport papers out of the toy passport covers and slid their fake ones in.

"Okay, and this one is yours, Delphi," Fitz said, handing her the final finished passport.

"Thanks." She slid her cover onto it and opened to the page with her fake identity. "Marjorie Johnson?"

"Yup," said Fitz, "I'm Oliver Brown."

"Hey! I'm a Johnson too!" said August. "Jack Johnson."

"Sounds like a superhero's alter ego name," said Quinn.

"I don't get it, but I will definitely take it," replied August. Quinn just sighed.

"Wait, why does August have the same last name as me?" Delphi asked.

"I thought that if we changed around the number of people we had with the same last name, such as you, Opal, and Asher or me and August, the FBI will have a harder time figuring out who we are if they do end up tracking us down. I just made August part of your family because he has the same hair color as Opal," Fitz answered.

"I guess that makes sense," said Delphi. "What about everyone else?"

"I'm Bailey Garcia," said Meeka.

"Kaiden Johnson," Asher said.

"I'm James Williams," Quinn added.

"I'm Gwenn," Macy piped up. "I like that name."

"My name's Katie," said Opal. "But my name's Opal."

"Hey, you know how you like to play pretend?" Asher asked, crouching down to be eye level with Opal.

"Yes?"

"Well, it's just like that. Right now, you get to play as Katie Johnson, okay?"

She crossed her arms. "Okay, fine, but I still don't like my pretend name."

They continued to go over their fake identities while Fitz bought plane tickets to Italy."

"And. We. Are. Done!" Fitz said, stopping to turn to the group with a smile on his face. "We'll be flying in a smaller scale commercial aircraft."

"Really? How did you manage to get eight last-minute plane tickets to Italy?" Quinn asked.

"I kind of 'rearranged' some passengers on the flight list. I'm pretty sure we need this flight more than they do." He handed them the tickets that had just come out of the printer.

Delphi stuffed her ticket into her back pocket, along with her passport. "Let's hope you're right."

They gathered into their groups; Delphi, Asher, August, and Opal in one; Quinn and Macy in another; Meeka; and Fitz by himself. Then headed to the security checkpoint. Delphi's group got in line first. They made their way through the line and up to security.

The woman surveyed them. "Aren't you a little young to be traveling on your own?"

"Thanks for the compliment, but I'm a big boy. And— oof!" August grunted loudly.

Delphi had jabbed him hard in the stomach and then cut in front of him. "Sorry about that. He has a bit of a cough, nothing serious. The medicine I gave him makes him a little loopy."

August quickly turned his grunt into a fake cough.

"The two of us," she motioned to her and Asher, "are eighteen. I believe that allows us to travel unaccompanied."

"It does. I just need you to tell me your names and birthdays, and then I can let you through."

After everyone had made it through security with few dilemmas, minus August's fat mouth and Quinn's minor lying problem, they boarded their flight to Italy. Meeka and Delphi sat together in one row, Asher and August across from them, and Opal and Macy sat together across the aisle from Quinn and Fitz. Meeka was reading the safety procedure pamphlets, and Delphi was doodling on a piece of scrap paper. Asher and August were talking and laughing, but both Meeka and Delphi noticed Asher was blushing slightly. Delphi wondered why until she saw Asher sneak a glance at Meeka when she wasn't looking. Opal and Macy were giggling and making up a handshake. The minute Quinn sat down, he bought a pair of headphones and listened to music on his iPod. Fitz fidgeted with the seatbelt and then decided to tamper with his TV.

Once all the passengers were settled, and the flight attendants had gone over the safety precautions, the pilot announced takeoff.

August's knuckles turned white as he clenched the armrests of his seat and squeezed his eyes shut. "I don't want to do this. I don't want to do this." The plane hit some turbulence as it got up in the air. "I *definitely* do *not* want to do this!" He made the mistake of looking out the window. "*Stercore*! That's high!"

"Shut up and switch seats with me," Asher said as he climbed over August.

"Really, man! We're doing *this* again?"

Asher rolled his eyes and plopped down in the window seat, pulling the seatbelt across his waist at the same time August did.

Their flight started off well enough. Even Asher wasn't nauseous. Apparently, air travel was the only travel that agreed with him.

Throughout the beginning of the flight, Delphi noticed that Asher wouldn't stop staring in her and Meeka's direction. It eventually got to the point where she couldn't take his ridiculousness anymore and decided to call him out on it.

"Asher, do you *mind*? Meeka and I are trying to have a nice conversation over here, and you making googly eyes at her doesn't help."

"What makes you think I was looking at Meeka?" Asher retorted.

"Well, you certainly weren't making faces at *me*. And unless you have developed an interest in windows, small televisions, or airplane seats that I was unaware of, I'm sticking with my first guess."

Asher opened and closed his mouth a few times, thinking of a reply. "What? I don't— I mean— I wasn't..." He looked at August for backup.

August whistled, "I don't know, bro. She kind of has you there."

Asher eventually gave up and sank low into his seat, putting his headphones back on.

"Did you really have to do that?" Meeka asked, her grin contradicting her question.

Delphi laughed. "Of course I had to do that! He was seriously getting on my nerves. And if there's one thing I'm getting a little sick of, it's you and Asher doing your little dance around each other."

"What dance? There's no dance! We're just friends."

"Mm-hmm, yeah right, and August has never made a flirtatious remark to me." She looked over at him, and he

69

winked at her. "See what I mean!"

Meeka rolled her eyes.

"And don't think I didn't notice you two sneaking up to the roof," Delphi said, raising her eyebrows expectantly.

"I didn't *sneak* anywhere, and Asher followed me. We didn't go up together."

"So you're saying nothing at all happened?"

"Well, a bunch of secret agents wearing sunglasses at night kind of threw a bomb onto the roof, so, unless you're talking about that, nothing happened," Meeka lied.

"Come on, I have a bit of a double agent thing going for me. You can't hide your feelings from me because you're my best friend, and Asher certainly can't hide his feelings from me because one, he stinks at it, and two, I'm his twin sister."

"Since when have you ever been good at spotting romance? And don't use August as an example. Even a cat would know if he was flirting with her."

"Well, I wouldn't have any more examples because no one ever really flirts with me," Delphi replied.

"What about Mr. Reckless Pretty Blue Eyes over there?" Meeka teased.

"You know, given that you seem to hate Quinn, you sure sound eager about him flirting with me."

"I don't *hate* him. We just don't necessarily see eye to eye."

"There you go again with your diplomatic answers."

Meeka chuckled, "You're nuts."

"And you're weird." Delphi laughed.

"And tired. I'm going to take a nap. Wake me up when we

get there." Meeka rested her head on the back of her chair and fell asleep.

A few hours later, things started taking a turn for the worst.

Delphi looked up from her doodles and noticed the lights flickering. She shook Meeka awake and looked across the aisle at Asher and August, who were still enthralled with their televisions.

"What's the matter?" Meeka asked, still half asleep.

The plane jolted, causing most of the passengers to take off their headphones and look around.

"Oh great, just what we need. More problems." Meeka was suddenly awake.

Three dings rang over the loudspeaker, and the pilot made an announcement. "Attention all passengers, this is your pilot speaking. We have hit a little turbulence. The ride should be smooth from here. No need to panic."

So, naturally, everyone panicked.

The plane jolted again, which didn't help anyone's stress levels. Then the lights stopped flickering and turned off completely.

There was a moment of silence when the plane rocked again.

"On second thought," came the pilot again, "be prepared to make an emergency evacuation."

Flight attendants rushed into the cabin and started calmly giving out instructions as air masks dropped from the ceiling. Apparently, the airline provided parachutes on their small aircrafts. People wrenched them out from under their seats and hurried to put them on with the assistance of the cabin crew. The attendants opened the exits and ushered people out in as orderly of a fashion as possible.

The plane was still in a gliding phase and hadn't started to plummet yet.

Loud cursing could be heard in the direction of Opal and Macy's seats. A flight attendant wearing a parachute rushed over to Quinn to see what was wrong.

"It's stuck; her seatbelt's stuck!" he said frantically, trying to pry Macy out of it.

"Calm down and hold on. I have a switchblade we can use," said the flight attendant.

She ran over to a compartment near the door, but before reaching it, she tripped and was sucked out of the aircraft.

The plane shifted more fiercely this time, and the gang was thrown to the back of the aircraft.

"Someone needs to try to steady this thing!" Delphi yelled over the roaring in her ears, attempting to shut the airplane door.

August came over and helped her push it back into place.

"I can try to get it back up and running," said Fitz, running to the cockpit.

"Delphi, there is a pocket knife in my backpack. We need to cut my sister out of this thing," Quinn yelled.

Delphi obliged. The moment she found the knife, Fitz came back. "I think I've bought us some more time, but it won't hold. The tech is going nuts, and it seems the pilot has escaped already."

Asher's voice went up about eight octaves. "Are you trying

to tell us that there is no one on this hunk of metal capable of flying it?"

Fitz nodded and ran back into the cockpit.

"I'll go see if I can help him," said Quinn. "Delphi, can you cut Macy out of the seat?"

She nodded. "You really think you can fly this thing?"

"Hey, I can drive a car at one hundred miles an hour in New York City. How different is it, really?" He gave her a small smile that didn't reach his eyes and ran off.

Meeka crouched next to Macy. "Hey sweetheart, now listen, everything is going to be okay. We are going to get you out of this seat. I promise. I just need you to pinky promise me that you will try your hardest to be calm. You are so brave."

Macy nodded, but you could see the fear written all over her face as Delphi struggled to cut her seat belt. Asher started pacing.

"Oh, this isn't good! Macy's gonna die! We are all gonna die! She's gonna be stuck forever! Oh, no, no, no! We are gonna sink in the ocean and never—"

"*ASHER, SHUT THE INFERNUM UP! YOU ARE NOT MAKING THIS ANY BETTER!*" Meeka screamed, losing her temper.

"I'm sorry, M'lady." Asher's voice was shaky under his breath.

Meeka looked back to Macy. Macy looked more panicked than before. "Don't listen to him. We have this under control! You're going to be just fine!"

"Ugh! This knife is absolute crap," Delphi grumbled, cutting halfway through the strap.

The plane jolted again, and Delphi sliced her hand.

"*Dautor!*" she yelled.

Macy started to struggle.

"You need to stay still, okay, Macy? Please stay still for me," Meeka pleaded with her.

Opal moved towards Macy, trying to get a better look at the seat belt. "Are you guys a million percent sure you are going to get her out?" she questioned.

"Of course we are! One thing I know is I never make a promise I can't keep." Meeka tucked a piece of Macy's hair behind her ear and glanced at the belt.

"Delphi, come on, you're almost there," Meeka said, trying to keep any bit of hope anyone had left.

"Delphi! You're almost there!" Opal repeated with joy.

Finally, the last thread was torn. Yelps and screeches filled the air as everyone's adrenaline skyrocketed. Meeka scooped up Macy and Opal as they rushed over to the boys in the cockpit.

"Oh, thank God!" Quinn ran over to grab Macy. "Thank you, guys. Really."

"Let's finish this conversation later because we *need* to get out of here... *NOW*," Delphi said, looking around.

Everyone started to freak out, unsure of what their next move was.

"Guys, take one of these and put them on immediately." Asher ran over with a bunch of parachutes and began to distribute them.

A massive shudder shot through the plane, pushing everyone to the wall. The aircraft filled with screams.

"I think it's best we jump out now because, looking at it,

this is the safest and shallowest we can jump into without dying," Fitz explained.

"That's cheerful," Quinn mumbled.

"But we don't know how to use these things!" Meeka gestured to the parachute she was helping Opal into.

"There's a first time for everything. The directions are on the bag, and the flight attendants explained everything before takeoff," Asher replied.

"Reading about it and actually doing it are two *completely* different things, Asher," Meeka said.

"Well, we don't have much of a choice, so let's just jump before we crash, shall we? We'll need an older person to go first, so then we can get the children out of here asap!" Delphi said.

"I'll go, but I think it's smart for August to come with me, so there are two people to help," Quinn said as he took a step closer to the exit and pushed the button to open the door.

August looked terrified. "Uhhh, well, I guess my choices are either fall and crash or fall and not crash, sooo..."

"Just *GO!*" Delphi yelled.

August nodded, and he and Quinn jumped out. Opening their parachutes, they landed safely in the water. Meeka took a peek out the exit, then knelt down to the little girls.

"Ready to fly, girls? I need you two to be brave for me, okay? Can you do that?" Meeka asked reassuringly.

Opal nodded, her expression still panic-stricken. Macy brushed her curls away from her face, her eyes wider than ever and filled with fear.

"Hey, don't worry. Just pretend that you're flying. The

water is just a cushion for you to land on, and we'll be here to help you the whole time."

Macy and Opal's tense stances eased up a little. Flying didn't seem as bad as falling.

Meeka and Delphi helped the girls out of the plane. Both landed safely in the water, with the two boys there to assist. Next, Fitz jumped out.

"I'll go now," said Delphi, checking her parachute. Delphi jumped out, landing in the water with ease.

"Okay, you ready, M'lady?" Asher said, looking at Meeka fiddling with a strap on her parachute.

"No! I'm terrified! I don't want to do this!" Meeka panicked.

"Like Delphi said before, I don't think we have a choice. Let's go together! I mean, I do only have one arm to help myself with so..."

They both jumped out. Just in time, because part of the plane caught fire and hurtled into the water. As it sank, the water swirled around it, creating a whirlpool.

Once in the water, it was clear that Asher was struggling. Meeka swam over as fast as she could to assist.

"August, help!" she cried out. August came over to help, but all three of them struggled to bring Asher to shore. The tide was too overpowering. It pushed them further back, away from everyone else. The added whirlpool of the sinking airplane only added to their struggles. They grappled with the water, swiftly moving their arms and legs. It was just too much, and they were running out of energy. Water splashed in their faces, spilling into their mouths and making it harder to breathe.

"This isn't working!" Meeka shouted in between breaths. The shoreline looked like it could have been miles away.

"I need a break!" August said, slowing down.

"There are no 'breaks,' August!" Meeka shouted.

Asher hollered in pain as the wave struck his hand. It wasn't looking good for the three of them.

Meanwhile, Delphi and Quinn attempted to keep Opal and Macy afloat.

"We can't let the whirlpool suck us in!" Quinn yelled.

"Oh, you don't say?" Delphi called back.

Quinn looked at her incredulously.

"Sorry, I get snappy when I'm overwhelmed!" Delphi looked around as much as she could, searching for the rest of the group. "Meeka, Asher, and August are struggling a little behind us. Hang on." She looked around once more. "Where's Fitz?"

A streak of red hair caught Quinn's eye. "Over there!" He pointed.

"What about the others?" Delphi asked.

"No time. They'll have to tread a little while longer. Fitz needs help."

"Go! I'll keep Macy and Opal afloat," Delphi yelled.

Quinn nodded and dove underwater.

Delphi looked back at Asher struggling and bit her lip. Meeka and August wouldn't be able to hold out much longer. There were still fires reflecting off the water's surface from the fuel tanks igniting. The plane sank at a snail-like pace, dragging everything around it down. She brought her attention back to the two girls doggy paddling in an attempt to keep their heads out of the water. Abruptly, Quinn resurfaced in front of her, out of breath and hanging onto Fitz. He was missing his glasses and spluttering water non-stop.

"Come on, buddy, you got to help me out here," Quinn begged Fitz. He turned to Delphi. "How are they doing?"

"Not so good. Asher's arm, or lack of use of it, is really causing problems."

There was movement in the distance. A small, rusted old white fishing boat was coming up to them.

"Look! Over there!" Delphi yelled, pointing. "Hey! Over here! Hey!"

Meeka, Asher, and August noticed the boat too and started waving to attract its attention.

They shouted until their voices were hoarse, and they were way past out of breath. The fishing boat finally got close enough to let Asher, Meeka, and August on. They didn't even think twice about who could be on the boat; they were safe, finally. Everyone was exhausted and coughing up the water they had choked on. The trio crashed onto the bench of the boat. August rested his arm on Asher's shoulder and covered his face from the sun, trying to catch his breath. Meeka practically collapsed her head on Asher's lap. Asher rested his seriously injured hand on her head. Meeka, Asher, and August tried to calm down as the kind old fisherman steered his boat over to Delphi and the other half of the group.

Once aboard, Delphi checked to make sure Macy and Opal had no injuries. Luckily, the girls were perfectly fine, other than being tired and out of breath. Fitz struggled to get on, slipping from his shaky grip. Quinn, once again, had to assist him. Fitz collapsed to the floor, heaving in breaths of fresh air and coughing up water. Quinn stumbled a little from the rocking of the sea and took a seat. Even though everyone was tired, out of breath, cold, and bruised, they were still alive.

CHAPTER 7

WELCOME TO ITALY

"Perché eri in mezzo al mare?" the fisherman asked in Italian.

"Il nostro aereo si è schiantato e abbiamo davvero bisogno che tu ci porti a riva." Asher replied, his teeth chattering.

The fisherman nodded and returned to the wheel of his boat.

"What did he just say? I only caught 'plane' and maybe something about a river?" Quinn whispered to Delphi.

"The fisherman asked why we were in the middle of the sea, and Asher told him about the plane and that we need to get to shore," she whispered back, shivering.

"Okay, so nothing about a river?" he asked.

"No."

"I told you I suck at languages."

"I guess you did," she replied.

The ride to land was a welcomed break for everyone, except Asher, who had found yet another form of travel that nauseated him. The sea sprayed up against the sides of the boat as they skidded across the water, forming rainbows against the sunlight. Macy and Opal shivered under towels. Macy's eyes were wide and terrified, shifting around like some new danger would pop up at any second. Opal looked too tired to be scared. Sitting in the corner, she sucked her thumb and closed her eyes. They stayed silent throughout the trip, primarily because of sheer exhaustion and adrenaline lows.

Some people gave them funny looks when they got to land, but most ignored them. Maybe a bunch of drenched kids in street clothes was normal around here.

"Okay, we need to know our next step," Delphi said while wringing out her shirt.

"I personally think we should get Asher to the hospital. His hand is practically falling off," August said dramatically.

Fitz departed from the group and found a map of the area.

"Okay, so I think, if I'm seeing this correctly, and it's possible that I'm not because I lost my glasses, but if I'm seeing this correctly, the nearest hospital is about a mile away. We can walk!" Fitz handed Delphi the map so she could navigate.

The group walked the few blocks to the hospital, asking locals for any shortcuts to speed up the trip and even stopping to purchase some cheap new clothes and a pair of glasses for Fitz. The Esprit kids had to do all the talking with the language difference.

After changing and a walk that felt much longer than a mile, they made it to the entrance. Luckily, the nurse at the front desk spoke English, so the Russos could understand.

"I just need you to sign a few things before a doctor looks at you," the nurse said, handing them a stack of papers attached to a clipboard and a pen.

"Thanks," Meeka replied, grabbing the clipboard and pen and heading over to a couple of chairs in the waiting room.

"Great. Paperwork," Delphi said sarcastically. "Nice to know this is being documented."

"As long as we keep using our pseudonyms, we should be fine," Fitz said.

"But aren't they tied to the plane crash now?" Quinn asked.

"I guess, but if they ask for ID, the passports are all we've got," Fitz replied.

"Not to mention, my passport says I'm eighteen, so no parent or guardian *bovis stercus* required," Asher added.

"Asher!" Meeka scolded, "Just because Quinn and Macy don't understand what you're saying doesn't mean Opal can't."

"Sorry, I curse when I'm in pain," he replied sarcastically.

Meeka did her best to hold in a laugh as she rolled her eyes and finished filling out the papers. She went back up to the desk and handed the nurse the clipboard.

Meeka returned with a bag of ice for Asher. "He said that there's a good chance that we'll have to wait a little while."

After forty-five minutes of eternity, a nurse in blue scrubs called out, "Kaiden Johnson?"

Quinn decided to stay behind with Macy and Opal in the waiting room while the rest trailed behind Asher and walked to the Vital's room. "Now, how did this happen, sweetie?" The nurse asked.

"Oh, um, I tripped and fell on my hand," Asher lied.

Once the lady finished his vitals and his x-rays, she directed him to his room, where he waited for the doctor.

"Guys, I'm starving," August complained while holding

his stomach.

"How about you and Fitz go back to the waiting room, where Quinn and the little ones are, and raid the vending machine or something?" Delphi suggested.

The two boys ran out of the room as if it was a race.

Delphi closed the door behind them. And turned to Asher. "How are you feeling?"

Asher shrugged, "Hungry."

"I meant your wrist, idiot."

"Doesn't change the fact that I want food."

"Maybe August will bring you back something," Meeka said.

"He might think about it, but the chance of it actually getting here without it being eaten is slim to, give me a second to do the math." Asher pretended to count the fingers on his left hand. "Yeah, none."

"You'd think we'd be in shock after crashing a plane on the coast of Italy," Meeka said.

"We had that entire slightly uncomfortable boat ride with the fisherman to be in shock," Delphi replied.

"You call being soaked, broken, bruised, and freezing cold 'slightly uncomfortable'?" Meeka asked.

"I mean, only one of us was *broken*."

"Guys, right here and not a malfunctioning robot, so stop saying I'm 'broken,'" Asher said.

"Ok, what would you call yourself then?" Delphi asked.

"Hi, I'm Asher. Nice to meet you. By the way, we're twins and have lived in the same house for sixteen years."

A knock on the door cut off Delphi's response.

A big man holding a clipboard walked in. "Hello, Mr. Johnson. How are you doing today?" he asked kindly.

"I'm doing just fantastic!" Asher said sarcastically, gritting his teeth and lifting his arm in reference.

The doctor laughed, "Well, clearly you have broken your wrist. I think we all knew that. The worst part is that we will have to reset your wrist to cast it. I won't sugarcoat it; it will hurt. But it will be over quick. First, before we do that, I want to take a look."

The doctor touched Asher's wrist in different places. Asher hissed in pain.

"I'll be right back with my supplies, and we will get you all set up," the doctor said while walking out of the room.

Moments later, the doctor was back with a cart and his assistant.

"I'm sorry, ladies, but we are going to have to ask at least one of you to step out for a moment. We don't want to overwhelm our patient, and we need enough space," the assistant said, setting up a medical station next to the bed.

"Oh, for Heaven's sake. Just go hold his hand, so he stops crying like a baby!" Delphi said to Meeka with a face of playful disgust,

"Ew, no, that's weird," Meeka said with a huge grin while walking over to Asher's side, where his hand was already waiting to interlock with hers. Delphi stepped out of the room. Asher looked at Meeka with a nervous pout. She lightly moved his hair out of his face. "It can't be as bad as what you've been through in the past few hours," she whispered.

Asher nodded with a half-smile, gripping her hand harder.

"Okay, Kaiden, we are going to have you look away, and on the count of three, we will do our thing," the doctor explained. "One—two—three!" a loud snap came from his wrist with a loud yelp in pain.

"*FAEX!*" Asher hollered. He started breathing heavily as his eyes teared up. He was so tense; he looked like a statue.

"Fantastic job, young sir. The worst is now over. We are just going to patch you up, and you can go on with your day," the doctor said as he took out his tools to cast him up. Asher finally opened his eyes and looked at Meeka.

"*Dautor stercore!* That hurt like a—"

"Oh, I can tell!" Meeka interrupted before he could curse anymore.

The doctor finished wrapping his arm as Delphi was welcomed in. "You are all set now. We will need you to come back in a few weeks to take your cast off. The people at the front desk will clarify dates," the doctor said.

Delphi looked at her brother's hand interlocked with her best friend's, and she had to roll her eyes.

"You two *bother* me," Delphi said sarcastically, laughing.

Asher glared at his sister while Meeka stood there, smiling. They both helped Asher up and headed back to the waiting room to meet up with the rest of the gang.

"Good, you're not dead," August said when they entered the waiting room.

"Uh, thanks, I guess," Asher replied, chuckling.

They went up to the front desk to schedule Asher's next appointment.

"Okay, we will see you in seven weeks to remove your

cast," said the lady at the counter.

"I highly doubt that," Delphi mumbled to herself while Meeka and Asher politely nodded to the woman.

They left the waiting room of the hospital through the glass doors that led outside.

"Now we need a game plan," Meeka said. "I suggest we start by finding a place to stay and lie low for a few days. Maybe we'll finally be able to catch our breaths and, with any luck, those FBI psychopaths might even think we died in the plane crash."

"That is if we had any luck," Delphi replied.

"Okay, Miss Negative, not helping," Meeka teased.

"What about a B&B? I think I saw one on the way here," Quinn said.

"What's a 'B&B'?" Fitz asked.

"You know, I thought it would eventually stop being weird having to explain normal things to you people, but nope, still weird. A B&B is a bed-and-breakfast, like a hotel. You have those, right?"

"Of course, we have hotels," Meeka said.

"Great, well, let's go then," Quinn said, walking back in the direction they came from.

They walked about a half mile before Quinn stopped in front of a beachfront house. "Here we are."

They found a payphone, and Meeka called the number on the sign outside the house.

A woman answered the phone in Italian. "Ciao questo è Spiaggia Letto e Prima Colazione come posso aiutarti?"

"Hello, we would like to rent your bed-and-breakfast for

two nights, please."

"You speak English? Okay, two nights starting tonight?"

"Yes, please."

"What time will you be coming?"

"As early as possible," Meeka replied.

"Well, the rooms are all ready now."

"Then we will be there in less than a minute," she laughed. "Thank you."

Meeka hung up the phone, and the gang walked up to the front of the beach house. The house was a light ocean blue with yellow window panels. There were two doors in the front of the building, one side labeled with the number '216' and the other '217.' A lady in a red and purple floral dress walked outside the side numbered '217.'

"Hello guests! Welcome, welcome!" the woman said with a smile and shook everyone's hands. "My name is Ms. DeLuca. You will be staying at my son's house, 216. He travels so much that we figured we would just rent it out. Not a bad idea either. It helps me keep up with the taxes. Oh, and look at me rambling now. Here are the keys. I live in 217, so if you have any questions, feel free to knock on my door," Ms. DeLuca said kindly.

The gang headed inside, greeted with a colorful, beachy setup. They all split up to explore. It was a two-bedroom home with a cute kitchen and a divine view to complement it. It also had a rather large living room area, but the size of the two bedrooms made up for that space.

"How are we all going to fit into *just* these two small beds? Both rooms only have a twin-sized bed in them!" Delphi whispered to Meeka while standing in the mint green painted room.

"I have no idea. This house seems to only accommodate two people," Meeka said, stepping aside as Opal and Macy darted into the room. "I'll give up sleeping on the bed to the little ones. They've been through enough. I think getting to sleep through a night on a comfy bed is well deserved." She picked up Macy and stood her on the bed. "And they are small enough, you can join them. You can easily fit two people on one of these, and both of them put together barely equals one person."

"You don't have to," Delphi argued.

"I insist." Meeka walked out of the room with Opal and Macy.

The boys were in the living room messing around with the T.V. channels. Meeka walked in and rolled her eyes at the boys, whose eyes were glued to some cartoon.

Delphi stayed in the bedroom and laid out some wet clothes to dry. Exhausted, she walked over to the bed, but before she got there, her head started to throb in pain, and the world around her blurred. She lost feeling in her legs and collapsed onto the bed in a heap, blacking out.

"*Crap,*" I thought.

I knew I was in another one of those flashes. I slowly opened my eyes, silently pleading that no one was waving a gun at me this time. Nope, no guns, at least not that I could see. The lights were blinding me, but I kept my eyes open in search of a clue of where I was this time. I attempted to sit up because I realized I had been staring at the ceiling, but I was met with resistance.

"*What the heck?*" I thought.

I turned to look at my right wrist. I felt the cool metal of a handcuff digging into my skin.

"*Ouch,*" I internally grumbled.

I was chained to a bed rail. I looked next to my arm and saw a tall stand with a bag filled with water hanging from the top. Why was I hooked up to an IV?

I heard a noise, footsteps coming this way, and quickly closed my eyes. A tugging sensation in my gut told me I was traveling back to the present. Good, I didn't want to know any more about what I had just seen.

***

Delphi awoke with a start. Her head still hurt, just like the last time she had gotten a flash. She stumbled out of the bedroom, her hand on her head.

"Delphi," Meeka noticed her. "What's wrong?"

"I got another flash. It didn't make much sense." She

groaned. "I just need to clear my head."

She walked towards the door, but Quinn stopped her. "I'll go with you."

"No, I'm fine, really." She tried to push past him.

"Come on. What if you get another flash and you faint or something? Someone needs to go with you."

She couldn't argue with his logic. "Okay, fine. Does anyone need anything while I'm out?"

"Good thinking. You two should pick up some groceries. The kitchen isn't stocked, and while Delphi and Quinn are out getting stuff, the rest of you boys are going to help me hang up our wet belongings," Meeka instructed.

"Aw, come on Meeka! We literally have been running away from death for the past thirty-six hours! Can we just rest?" Asher complained.

"We can all rest later. After we get everything situated. Now, stop complaining and come help."

Asher rolled his eyes jokingly but stood up to help.

"You guys head out. Asher, Fitz, and August get started. I'm going to put Opal and Macy down for a nap before dinner," Meeka said.

CHAPTER 8

BIG DECISIONS

Delphi and Quinn left the house and started walking up the street. Meeka had handed Delphi an ice pack for her head before they left, and Quinn had brought along the map and was now looking for a grocery store.

"So we're here." He pointed to the map. "So the grocery store is right around—"

"Here." Delphi pointed to another spot on the map.

"Yes, great. Let's go." Quinn folded the map and put it back in his pocket.

They stayed silent until Delphi tripped over an uneven part of the sidewalk and would have fallen on her face if Quinn hadn't stabilized her.

"Thanks."

"Anytime," he smiled at her, but she had already started walking again.

"So, what's with you?" Delphi asked.

"'What's with me,' what?" Quinn asked, a little caught off guard by the question.

"I mean, what's your story? You seem kind of cut off," she replied.

"I'm not cut off."

"Really? There's one thing I pride myself on: my ability to read people. You are a little harder, but I've gotten the gist. You're extremely protective of Macy and almost seem like a bit of a loner, but not exactly by choice. What's up with that?"

Quinn looked at her curious expression and took a moment to study her eyes. They were different from anything he'd ever seen before. Her left eye was blue, but her right eye was gray. It was an interesting combination that could easily make her look intimidating, but right now, they were wide open and curious.

"Quinn, you clearly live alone, other than your sister. There were no signs of parents around at your house. And the second you mentioned them, you shut down," Delphi added, trying to ignore his blank expression while he looked into her eyes.

"That's not—I don't want to talk about it."

"You're lying. You obviously haven't had anybody to talk about this with. What's going on?" She looked pleadingly up at him.

"I-my parents weren't home because," he paused, "well, because they're never coming home." He sighed.

"So they're..."

"Yeah. They were in the army, both of them. My mom was a general, and my dad was a sergeant major. It happened in Afghanistan. There was an explosion and..."

Delphi sat down on a bench, and Quinn followed suit, sighing.

"And?" Delphi asked.

Quinn's expression turned angry. "And they died. They

went and got themselves killed in an explosion and left Macy and me to fend for ourselves. Do you want to know what I was doing in that candy shop two days ago? It was Macy's birthday, her second birthday without her parents. I just wanted to get something fun for her." He looked defeated. "And, of course, my dad's brother wanted nothing to do with us. He said we were old enough to live on our own now. That wasn't true. I've spent the past two years avoiding foster workers and working my ass off in different jobs. My uncle helped a little, I guess, with his stupid money. I didn't want to take it at first, but... we got desperate."

"You've been living alone this whole time?"

"We didn't have a choice. The foster system would have split us up."

"That's... cruel."

"I know, but it's just how things work here."

"What about those flowers that were on your kitchen table? Is that your own personal touch?"

Quinn gave her a half-smile. "My mom used to always make sure there were flowers in the house. Macy used to love it, so I kept it going... for her."

Delphi couldn't tell who he was referring to by 'her.' "Are you sure you're angry with your parents?"

"Angry? Of course, I'm angry! Do you have any idea how hard it's been without them?"

"You have to stop lying to me... and to yourself. You care about them, Quinn. Anyone can see that."

"No, I don't." There were tears in his eyes now. "Not anymore."

"Then why did you want to come to Italy? You were about to say something on the bus about your parents and Italy. What was it?"

"They grew up here and got married here. I thought coming to Italy might make me feel closer to them, but they feel farther away than ever. And I hate them for it."

"Quinn—" Delphi started.

"Does your head still hurt?" Quinn asked abruptly.

"A little, I guess, but that's not—"

"Well, then we should go get those groceries and get you home so you can rest." Quinn stood up, but Delphi grabbed his arm.

"This conversation doesn't have to be over." She tried pulling him back down, but he resisted.

"Yes, it does. Now, get up, and let's go," he said sternly, shaking her off and walking away.

"What do you mean? You can't keep something like that bottled up forever."

"I don't have a choice."

"There's always a choice! I'm your choice. Just talk to me, please."

"I told you, I don't want to talk about it."

"But for just a moment, you opened up, and I could tell it was a relief. Why are you hurting yourself like this?"

"Because this pain makes me who I am. You don't understand. Without it, I don't know how to cope with any of this."

"Let me help you."

"I don't want your help. I don't want anybody's *help*."

"Just—"

"No, Delphi. Let's just go to the store and go home. I'm done talking."

They shopped in silence, only speaking when needed. When they did speak, it was sharp, like knives. It was obvious Delphi was hurt, and Quinn was beyond upset. Quinn's attitude eventually started transferring to Delphi, creating a tense atmosphere, and the walk back home wasn't any better.

When they got back to the house, Meeka and Asher came over to help with the groceries.

"What took you guys so long?" Asher asked.

"Nothing," Quinn said sharply.

Meeka looked back and forth between Delphi and Quinn. Noticing the tension, she changed the subject. "Let's get these groceries into the fridge and then make some dinner."

Delphi nodded and rushed into the kitchen.

After dinner, they turned on a show for Opal and Macy and sat around the kitchen table.

"We need a plan to get home," Meeka said.

Delphi looked up from her hiding place behind her hair. "What? No! We can't go home!"

"Delphi, we can't just stay here! We don't belong on this planet. We aren't safe," Meeka said with a worried look.

Delphi stood up, sliding the chair back behind her. "And we can't just leave either!"

"What the *infernum* is going on? Why can't we go back to Esprit? We have nothing to gain from staying here, except maybe a coffin. We can't stay. We just can't," Meeka said.

"Maybe you guys should calm down..." Asher started, but

they both acted like they hadn't heard him.

"If we leave, we are putting both Quinn and Macy in danger. You think leaving will stop the FBI from hunting them down?" Delphi retorted.

"I can protect Macy," Quinn said, his voice dripping with venom.

Delphi violently slammed her hand on the table. "*WELL, WHO'S GOING TO PROTECT YOU?*"

Quinn glared at her, getting up from the table and storming out of the room and into the boy's bedroom without saying a word. After Quinn left, Delphi stormed out of the kitchen and into the other bedroom. Everyone else was left speechless.

"Well, that escalated quickly," Asher said, breaking the silence.

"No kidding," August said. "What's up with them?"

"You two are clueless," Meeka said.

"Clearly, they had an argument during their outing..." Fitz jumped in.

"Really? I didn't catch that. Did they tell you?" August asked.

"No, they didn't *tell* me. You're just oblivious," Fitz retorted.

"I think we should all head to bed. It's been a rough day. Go get some sleep. We can finish our conversation in the morning," Meeka suggested.

✳✳✳

Everyone parted ways. The boys went to their room while Macy and Opal met Delphi in bed. Meeka stayed in the living room, reading a book and doodling on a piece of paper. It had to have been around eleven o'clock when Meeka's attention was grabbed by someone walking into the living area.

"What are you doing up out here?" It was Asher.

"Well, for starters, I gave the bed up to the other girls. And other than that, I can't sleep." Meeka gave a half-smile, signaling him to sit down. "Now, why are you up?"

"Quinn fell asleep in a recliner. I was sharing the bed with August and Fitz until August pushed him off the bed and onto the floor. So I thought that before I get attacked, too, I should leave."

"That is quite a reason if you ask me." Meeka laughed as Asher got comfortable. He grabbed a blanket from the hassock in front of him and gently spread it across both of them.

"Crazy day, am I right?" Asher asked.

"Almost too crazy. I'm so exhausted, but my brain is spiraling with thoughts that make it difficult to fall asleep." Meeka moved closer to Asher, fixing the blanket along the way.

"I don't think reading and doodling are helping either. You should just let yourself rest," Asher said comfortingly and took the book, paper, and pencil away from her.

"I guess. Doodling is Delphi's strong suit, anyway," Meeka replied.

Asher's face turned red as he placed his arm around Meeka, creating a more comfortable seating position. He put his feet up on the coffee table. Meeka looked up at him with a smile, then rested her head on his shoulder and curled her legs onto the couch. Asher moved his head onto hers, both of them closer than ever. With the long day and fighting the adrenaline keeping Meeka awake, she finally drifted off to sleep in the warm embrace of Asher's arms.

Asher noticed Meeka passed out cold. "Finally. You deserve a peaceful rest, M'lady," he whispered, quiet enough so she didn't wake.

After some time of soaking up the moment, Asher drifted off to sleep too.

A few hours later, someone padded into the living room.

"What do you think you're doing?" Delphi hissed, waking Asher up with a jolt. "You've got to be kidding me."

Meeka was still fast asleep.

Asher put his finger to his mouth, signaling Delphi to be quiet.

"What? No, I'm not shutting up about this!" she whispered.

"Fine, just sit down and be quiet."

"Don't tell me what to do. You have some serious explaining to do." She moved in front of the couch but didn't sit down.

"Why are you even up? And what's there to explain?"

"I needed a glass of water, and don't play dumb with me. What the heck is all... this?" She waved her hands, motioning around them on the couch.

"We were talking, and we fell asleep. That's it."

"So it has absolutely nothing to do with the fact that you both are seriously crushing on each other?"

"First of all, do not *ever* say the word 'crushing' again, and second, we are *not* crushing on each other!"

"That's exactly what Meeka said."

"She said that?" Asher sounded hurt.

"See! You *are* crushing on her."

Asher gave her a look.

"Oh, please! I can say whatever I want, thanks very much. If you're not 'crushing,' then you love her, plain and simple."

"Excuse me? So suddenly, you're okay with the 'L-word'?"

"I'm not okay with it. I'm just stating facts. The only people who don't notice it are you two."

"Let's just pretend you never saw this, okay?" Asher said.

"Well, what do I get in return?" Delphi asked.

"I hate you." Asher glared at his sister, then looked down at Meeka.

Delphi shrugged with a mischievous smirk. "I have a proposal,"

"Oh, Lord, what could it be?" He rolled his eyes.

"It's simple and easy. Admit you are in love with *my* best friend." Delphi smiled darkly.

Asher stuttered, "Oh, uh..." He laughed nervously, "Any other proposals?"

"Nope! That or I will never let you live this down." Delphi crossed her arms.

"Fine. I don't dislike Meeka." Asher turned his head, looking away.

"Not good enough. Come on, Asher, just say you love her and I'll shut up and leave."

"Oh my God, Delphi! You get on my last nerves! I really like Meeka! Okay? You happy?" he whisper-shouted, annoyed.

"Very." Delphi smiled, turning to walk out of the living area, "Goodnight, Asher... and Meeka," she teased.

Asher rolled his eyes, bringing his other arm around Meeka and drifting back to sleep.

✳✳✳

"OOOOOO, someone's being naughty!"

Asher was awakened yet again, this time by August staring him right in the face. His hair was messier than usual, showing that he had just woken up.

"Uhhh, wha—what?" Meeka had just woken up and was shielding her eyes from the sunlight streaming in from the windows. Her eyes widened. "We fell asleep! Oh my God, we fell asleep! And now everyone is gawking at us like we are in a display case or something." Meeka scrambled out from under the blanket and off the couch.

"Actually, I sent Fitz back to our room because he is too innocent to see you two right now," August said with a smirk.

Fitz yelled from the other room. "You didn't send me away. I walked away by choice because I was exhausted, and you pushed me out of bed in the middle of the night! I'm going back to sleep!"

"Delphi!" Asher yelled.

She walked out of the kitchen, clearly enjoying herself. "Hey, don't blame me. You should have been prepared to get up before everyone else did and saw you two."

Opal and Macy walked out of their bedroom, rubbing their eyes and yawning.

"What's for breakfast?" Macy asked.

"Food, I hope," August said.

Delphi glared at August. "Stop being an idiot."

"But I'm so good at it."

Delphi ignored August and turned to Meeka. "Can you come help me with breakfast?"

"Definitely," Meeka said quickly, thankful for the distraction.

She followed Delphi into the kitchen.

"Okay, so some of this food looks familiar and some others I have no clue about," Delphi said, pointing to a jar of pickles.

"Let's just stick with what we know. Eggs, for example," Meeka replied.

"Works for me," Delphi said.

They scrambled the eggs and put them on the stove.

"About last night..." Meeka started.

"What about it?" Delphi asked, smiling.

"It's just, I didn't *mean* to fall asleep," Meeka said.

"Go on."

"I don't entirely know where I'm going with this, so I'd rather not." Meeka turned the stove off and dumped the eggs into a bowl.

"As long as you don't try to apologize, you're all good,"

Delphi said, taking plates out of a cupboard.

"I'm sor — hang on, what?" Meeka asked.

"I'm glad that brain of yours has started catching up," Delphi teased. "You two bother me more when you pretend you don't love each other."

"Love? Wow, Delphi. Don't you think that's a little premature?"

"It's been eleven years, so no, I don't think that's early, and jeez, this is like déjà vu. I had the same conversation with Asher at one in the morning," Delphi replied, piling utensils onto her stack of plates.

"So you're not mad?" Meeka asked.

"Nope, at least not at you. Him: I like making antsy. Hope you had fun last night." Delphi winked and walked out of the kitchen.

Meeka stood there for a moment, holding the bowl of eggs and contemplating what had just happened.

Delphi walked across the room to go and put away the blankets, passing Asher in the process.

"If I ever catch you falling asleep with my best friend again, you're dead," Delphi threatened Asher jokingly.

Chapter 9

Goodbye

Once breakfast was over, the gang reconvened to figure out how to move forward.

"Anyone have any ideas on how to get home?" Meeka asked the group.

"Again, not leaving," Delphi interrupted.

"Delphi, we have to. We have no other choice." Fitz surprisingly jumped into the conversation.

"Well, if you guys want to go home, then okay. But I'm not going," Delphi said stubbornly. The room went silent in shock.

"You're leaving. I'm not going to let you stay here," Quinn spoke up.

"You aren't going to *let* me do anything," Delphi said. "I make my own decisions whether or not you like them."

"I already told you I can take care of myself and Macy," Quinn grumbled.

"Yeah, and you can tell that to the FBI when they are holding you at gunpoint," Delphi said sarcastically.

"Guys, we need to agree on *something*," Meeka reasoned. "And if you guys don't either change your attitudes or tell us what your problem with each other is, we're going to have an even bigger problem."

Delphi said, "I'm not going." At the same time, Quinn said, "You aren't staying."

"Okay... anyone else?" Meeka asked.

"What if we vote on it?" Asher asked. "All in favor of staying?"

Delphi and Opal raised their hands.

"Leaving?" Asher asked.

He, Meeka, Fitz, August, and Quinn raised their hands.

"See, you can't stay," Quinn said to Delphi.

"Shut up. You don't even get a vote," she countered.

"Seriously! What is *up* with you guys?" Meeka asked.

"It's not as if you like Quinn much anyway, Meeka," Delphi said.

"Okay, don't turn this on me," Meeka replied.

"I'm just saying that Quinn seriously needs to work on letting people in, that's all," Delphi said.

"Because you're so good at letting people in, Delphi," Quinn retorted.

Delphi looked as if she'd been hit.

"You've already pried into my personal life. Why don't I get to hear more about yours?" Quinn said.

"I didn't pry into anything. You told me!" Delphi countered.

"What did he tell her?" August asked Asher.

"You think I know what's going on?" Asher asked August.

"She asked about my past," Quinn said with a sharp glare at Delphi.

"And here I was thinking you didn't want anyone to

know," Delphi retorted.

"Oh, I'm not giving out any details. I'm just giving everyone else a better idea of what's going on," Quinn said.

"You know what? Forget I asked," Meeka said. "We already voted, and we need to get ready to leave."

Delphi glared at Quinn. "Fine. You know, I think I'm starting to feel better about leaving. I just need some air first." Delphi stormed off.

Quinn followed her. They walked out onto the beach, Delphi walking far up ahead of Quinn and looking out into the water. The wind blew her hair around, framing her face in a captivating way.

"Delphi, can you stop?" Quinn called out, but Delphi ignored him. "Delphi, come on. Where are you even going? Delphi, Delphi!"

Quinn continued to call Delphi's name out to her until she finally stopped.

"You didn't seem to want me to listen to you before when you confided in me. Why should I listen to you now?" Delphi asked, still refusing to face Quinn.

"Because you are the ones who dragged me into this mess. If I never met you guys, my house wouldn't have exploded, I wouldn't have crashed a plane in Italy, and my little sister wouldn't be in constant danger."

"*I DIDN'T ASK TO BE HERE EITHER, QUINN*! I would be home enjoying my summer! It's not my fault we're here!" Delphi snapped.

Quinn pinched the bridge of his nose, which Delphi noticed he did when he was overwhelmed. "Well, whose fault is it?"

"Honestly, Quinn! You can't just blame one person for all of this! And if you really want to blame someone, blame the FBI. They tried to *kill* us!" Delphi started walking away again.

"Delphi, stop!"

"No, I said I needed air, and right now, you're suffocating me."

"Please."

"Oh, so we're trying new tactics now, are we? Trying to be nice, Quinn? Well, it's a little late for that." She walked faster, kicking up sand under her shoes.

"I'm sorry," Quinn said.

Delphi ignored him.

"Has anyone ever told you how stubborn you are?"

"It's been mentioned once or twice," Delphi mumbled.

"You know, you're very pushy."

"Did you just come out here to try to insult me? Because, if that's the case, you're going to have to try harder than that."

"No, I came out here to apologize."

Delphi finally turned towards him. "What?"

"You're going to make me say it again, aren't you?" he asked.

"Well, I'm still mad at you," she replied stubbornly.

"I said I was sorry. You're the first person I've told about my parents, and I guess I was just so used to being closed off about it. I got nervous. And I don't want you leaving while you're still mad at me."

"It's not like I *want* to be mad at you," Delphi said. "I'm just worried about you. Keeping all of that to yourself it's— it's just not healthy."

"You don't think I know that? That's why I told you. It gets harder and harder to hold all the anger together. Sometimes I'm even afraid I'll lash out at Macy."

"Quinn—" Delphi started but was cut off by Meeka yelling at them from the house.

"Guys! It's time to go!"

They walked back to the house together in silence. When they got inside, the rest of the gang was crowded around the sink in the kitchen. Asher was holding the orb over the sink filled with water.

"Are we all ready?" he asked.

They all nodded.

"Maybe you and Macy should go into the other room. That way, you don't accidentally end up coming with us," Asher suggested to Quinn.

He nodded and tried to usher Macy out, but she moved towards Opal instead.

"I don't want them to leave," she said.

"Mace, they won't be safe here. They have to go home. We'll see them again." Quinn looked up at Delphi. "We'll see each other again, right?"

"I really don't know. I don't think it's entirely likely that we will go on vacation to Earth or anything," Delphi replied.

"Oh, so this is a 'forever' goodbye..." Quinn hesitated.

Everyone looked upset as they nodded.

"Thank you for everything," Meeka said with a smile.

They shared their goodbyes. Macy and Opal hugged each other, and Quinn awkwardly shook their hands. When he got to Delphi, he paused.

"Well, goodbye, I guess," she said.

"Yeah, goodbye." He put out his hand, and she shook it.

Quinn and Macy left the kitchen and went into one of the bedrooms.

"Okay, let's do this," August said, eagerly rubbing his hands together.

Asher dropped the orb in the sink and fished it back out. They collectively held their breaths as the orb opened, and he pushed the button...

Nothing happened.

"What? Why are we still here?" August asked, his voice echoing the panic around the room.

"We did all the same steps! How is this possible?" Asher asked examining the orb.

Meeka walked over to take a peek.

"Is- Is that a crack?" she pointed out.

With further examination, they confirmed the orb was broken.

"Does this mean...?" Delphi asked in fear.

Asher finished her sentence, fear written all over his face. "We're stuck here, indefinitely."

CHAPTER 10

FBI

"Let's go, people. Let's go. Keep up the research. We need to find these miscreants." A tall blonde man in a black suit yelled and rapidly clapped his hands at a group of researchers at computer desks.

"Looks like someone's struggling. Did you lose your kids again, Spencer?" A woman with jet black hair pulled up into a bun, brown eyes, and espresso brown skin walked into the room.

"First of all, it's Agent Smith to you. And it's not my fault they got away. They couldn't have gotten far," Spencer replied.

"Since I'm the General, I can call you whatever I want. And it is, in fact, *your* fault. What did you expect kids to do when they found out you threw a bomb at them? They're not going to run *to* you. They are going to run *away* from you," she said.

He scowled. "Oh, well, if I seem to do everything wrong, what might you have done differently that night, General Brooks?"

"Easy. Walk up, knock on the door, and have a *civil* conversation. Again, they are teenagers who probably have no idea what they are doing."

"It's not that simple," Spencer practically growled.

"Maybe not for you. You never were very good at conversing. It always had to be action," General Brooks pointed out.

"Are you here for a *reason*, General?" Agent Smith asked, irritated.

"Yes, actually, I came to offer my help with the case."

"What makes you think you can come in here and take over *my* case?"

"These kids aren't your average teenagers. It just so happens that this specific threat is also under my jurisdiction."

Spencer rubbed his hand down his face in an exasperated way. "Cassidy, I—"

General Brooks's eyes flashed dangerously. "Don't you *dare* call me that."

Agent Smith opened his mouth to respond, but one of his researchers interrupted him. "Hey, boss, I think we've found something."

Spencer and Cassidy rushed over to the man and looked over his shoulders.

"A credit card was used in the JFK International Airport, a credit card that belonged to Mr. Carlos Russo," the agent said. "Further research shows that Mr. Russo and his wife, Ava, passed away two years ago in a bombing in Afghanistan."

"What's your point?" Spencer asked.

"In their passing, they left their two children in the care of Carlos's brother, Antonio. Those two children are Quinn and Macy Russo."

"Well, damn, why didn't you just start with that? Track that card. I want to know everything it has bought in the past forty-eight hours," demanded Agent Smith. "And look into the Uncle. We might be able to dig up something in that family's past that can help us."

"So much for them 'not getting far,'" Cassidy mocked.

"Those kids know how to cover their tracks. The credit card was used for a flight to Benevento, Italy, but they must have used fake names because the name tracker isn't picking up anything on them on the flight list," another agent said.

"Well, what names were they under then?" General Brooks asked.

"Oliver Brown, Marjorie Johnson, Jack Johnson, Kate Johnson, Kaiden Johnson, Bailey Garcia, James Williams, and Gwenn Williams," a researcher answered, pulling up the passport scans and looking at the pictures. "And somehow they got ahold of passports, too, but it's definitely them."

"Uh, sir? Their flight never reached Benevento. These logs say it went down somewhere in the Tyrrhenian Sea off the coast of Western Italy, but there is no direct record of how. It just says they were having technical problems and ordered an emergency evacuation," a woman at one of the computer desks said.

"How many casualties?" Agent Smith asked.

"There were only thirty-eight people on the plane. Thirteen have been counted unharmed. Sixteen were injured, one confirmed death, and..."

"And?" Agent Smith asked.

"And eight missing."

"That can't be a coincidence," General Brooks said. "These kids just happen to get on a plane, and it malfunctions for no apparent reason, then they disappear?"

"Luckily, I don't believe in coincidences," Agent Smith replied. "Check all of our resources in Italy. I want proof that these kids are dead."

"Sir, if they're dead, then that means—"

"I *KNOW* what it means!" Agent Smith yelled at the agent. "Just search everything. Find concrete proof."

"I don't buy it," General Brooks said, still pondering the plane crash. "Are there any reports by who last saw them?"

"Not all the crash victims have been bombarded by the press yet. Most are still recovering either from shock or injuries," said a woman at one computer.

"Well, are there any statements by anyone?" General Brooks asked.

"The pilot, who escaped from a latch in the cockpit, and a few passengers who got out first. But none of them mention the kids at all."

"I found something!" called an agent, pulling up a video on his computer and projecting it on the larger screen at the front of the room.

Agent Smith and General Brooks moved closer to the screen.

"This is an interview with one of the flight attendants. Just watch."

The interviewer on the display was holding a microphone up to a woman, the same woman who tried to help the gang before falling out of the plane. She was a little cut up and had a sling around one of her arms from the fall.

"Can you tell us about the eight people reported missing in the crash, ma'am?" asked the interviewer.

"Yes, yes. There were eight kids still left on the plane when I fell out. Well, actually, two were little kids, and the others were all teenagers. One of the little girls was stuck in her seatbelt. When I went to get something to cut her out of it, I was sucked out of the plane," said the woman.

"Did you see any of them actually escape the plane before it crashed?" asked the interviewer impatiently.

"No, I was occupied with helping other passengers stay afloat in the water. I do know that the plane continued to glide for several more minutes before actually crashing, though. They may have had enough time to escape."

"So, no bodies have been found?"

"Oh, goodness no! At least, I hope not. I know about as much as you do about what happened to the missing group."

The interviewer pursed her lips. "There have been other reports of technological problems during the crash. Do you have anything to say about that?"

"Well, the lights were flickering a lot, and there was plenty of—"

The agent paused the video. "They go on to talk about a bunch of safety measures and repeatedly ask if anyone had any more information on the kids, but no one says anything useful. Practically everyone just says the same thing about being clueless about the topic."

"DAMN IT! One of them is dead," Spencer yelled.

"Calm down. How do we know that they didn't get the

little girl out? Those teenagers are extremely resourceful. If they can outrun your agents in a car chase and escape from a building you blew up, what's a plane crash?" said Cassidy, smiling as Agent Smith's expression turned bitter.

"Sir, there are medical records under one of the fake identities from Salerno, Italy," a researcher said.

"So one of them's hurt? How badly?" Cassidy asked.

"A broken wrist, but it doesn't mention anyone else, so we can't tell who else is alive."

"Get people in Salerno and block all exits out of the city. We need to get these kids contained before they go and blow up another plane."

"I guess we're going on that vacation to Italy after all, Spencer. Oh, sorry, *Agent Smith*," General Brooks taunted, walking out. "I have to go prepare my troops. I'll see you in the jet."

Once she had closed the door behind her, Agent Smith let out a long sigh, rubbing his forehead.

When he looked up, he saw everyone staring at him. "Okay, show's over. Back to work, people. I want you to pinpoint their exact location. They can't have made it very far from that hospital."

The agents returned to furiously typing on their keyboards while Spencer walked over to the coffee pot and poured himself a cup.

"Nothing else is coming up. No more medical records, phone calls, or plastic is showing up. Hold on. One kid used the credit card again to pay for a bed-and-breakfast called Casa De Luca. It's located right on Crestarella beach," said a researcher.

Spencer almost choked on his coffee but regained his composure before anyone noticed. "Damn these kids. Are they deliberately *trying* to push my buttons?" he mumbled. Out loud, he said, "Well, what are you waiting for? Get some information on the owner and direct it to me. I need to catch a flight."

He hurried out of the room and towards the jet's landing pad.

"Was wondering when you would show up," Cassidy said, already suited up and ready to go.

Spencer walked past her and up the jet's entrance staircase. "I had some actual work to attend to before departing."

Cassidy just smiled mockingly and followed him up the staircase. Once inside, they took their seats, and Agent Smith debriefed his agents.

"Okay, boys, we are headed to Salerno, Italy. Your job is to find the kids and get them on this plane. General Brooks will have her men —"

"And women," she cut him off.

"Yes, anyway, they will be stationed around the entrances to the city."

"Where are these kids?" asked one agent.

"Crestarella Beach," Agent Smith replied.

"Crestarella Beach?" Cassidy asked. "That sounds familiar. Spencer, why does that seem familiar? Oh, yes! That's where you booked the bed-and-breakfast we were going to go to."

"They booked the same bed-and-breakfast as well,"

Spencer said grumpily.

Cassidy laughed. "Well, well. We need to be careful. I may start rooting for them."

CHAPTER 11

PLAN B

"It—It didn't work," Meeka said as everyone stared at the orb in utter shock.

Asher handed her the orb, and she stuck it in her pocket.

"Somehow, repeating that same thing over and over again doesn't seem to fix the problem," August replied helpfully.

Delphi glared at him and walked out of the kitchen. "We obviously need a new plan. And we need to tell Quinn and Macy about this new... development."

"No need," said Quinn, attempting to hide his relieved smile and walking out from behind the living room wall.

On the other hand, Macy made no effort to hide her squeal of glee. "You don't have to leave!" She rushed out from behind Quinn.

"We heard it all. What are you guys going to do?" Quinn asked.

"We need a new plan. We have to think of something and soon." Meeka said, panicking.

"Do you guys know if you can fix the orb?" Quinn questioned.

Delphi shrugged in response. "No, we don't even know how this contraption works."

"Okay, I say we at least get out of Salerno. We literally crashed a plane here. Who knows what kind of attention that's received?" Meeka said.

"But where do we go?" Fitz asked. "Why don't we see what we can find online? There must be a map or something. We just can't stay here," he suggested as he slowly walked over to the computer. "We have to go somewhere far enough away from our current location but close enough to take a taxi. We can't just take another flight." Fitz fiddled with the keys for some time as the others watched.

"I recommend somewhere with fewer people. Fewer crowds will probably make it less likely for mass searching," August added while leaning over Fitz's shoulder to see the screen.

"Yeah, the FBI can find us at any minute since we've been in this location for over twenty-four hours," Delphi said as August flirtatiously glared at her.

Delphi rolled her eyes.

"We could go to Castelluccio, Umbria. It's a small town only about four and a half hours from here." Fitz pulled up a picture of the town to show everyone.

"Works for me. We can leave tomorrow morning. Asher, go call a taxi company and try to schedule someone to pick us all up at six a.m. tomorrow morning," Meeka instructed.

"Hold on. I don't think it's smart to go straight to Castelluccio. I think we should find somewhere before the town and walk the rest of the way. You know, so it's harder to track us down with the taxi record?" Quinn proposed.

"That's a good idea. I'll do more research and print a

mapped-out plan," Fitz replied.

As Fitz continued working on their plan of action, the rest of the gang prepared for their departure. Meeka and Delphi packed up the dried clothes into a couple of backpacks they had purchased on their way to the hospital from the boat docks.

"Hey, Asher," Meeka called from across the room. "Why don't you, Quinn, and August run to a store and get some new essentials like a first aid kit, portable food, etc. We only came with practically wet clothes and money. If we are going to leave, we need to have supplies."

Asher nodded. "Sounds good. We'll pick up another bag or two as well."

Asher, Quinn, and August headed out with the dried-out wad of cash. Meeka and Delphi continued to work in the peace and quiet without the noisy boys, except Fitz being present. Macy and Opal were watching T.V. as they jumped around on the couch.

"Well, I guess you're getting your way after all," Meeka said to Delphi with a laugh.

"I told you we shouldn't leave. Besides, this plan seems more concrete. What were we going to do when we got home, anyway? We would be grounded for all eternity for disappearing, and the follow-up questions of where we were aren't exactly believable," Delphi replied.

"I guess you're right, but your parents have just as much explaining to do. I mean, what were they doing keeping a teleportation device in their bedroom?" Meeka thought out loud.

"It's crazy! And what's even more confusing is I've never seen it in their bedroom before the incident."

"They must have brought it home more recently. I guess we won't know until we're back on Esprit." Meeka sighed as she walked over to the couch to sit with the rambunctious girls.

"Hey Fitz, it's been a while. How are you doing with the plan?" Delphi asked as she walked over to him.

"Actually, pretty good. I mapped out just about everything. Here, take a look," Fitz said, waving a piece of paper. "So, we are going to have the taxi driver drop us off at this gas station so they can't track us to our official destination. The downside to being dropped off here is we have to walk about eight miles through all this forest." He pointed to the vast patch of green on the map. "Then about five miles through a lot of flatlands. We should be walking for four or five hours, give or take. It's the only way to make it to Castelluccio without being dropped off in a place giving away where we really want to go, though."

"Jeez, that's far and it will probably take way longer than that because of the little girls. Do we have a Plan B in case something goes wrong? You know, since anything that *can* go wrong probably *will*." Delphi gave a half smile.

"Not really. This is kind of already 'Plan B' since the orb didn't work," Fitz replied.

"So we have to get up before the sun *and* walk forever in the woods? Why would I want to do that?" Opal sassed.

She jumped off the couch, then crossed her little arms, making a pouty face.

120

"Only choice, kiddo," Meeka glared, with an already exhausted look on her face.

$$* * *$$

After a few hours filled with Meeka and Delphi taking the little girls to the beach, making lunch, and taking small naps, the boys returned.

"Guess who's back!" August called out, waking up Delphi and Meeka, who were resting on the couch.

"Honestly, I wish it wasn't you," Delphi groaned. "What did you guys get?"

"Well, we got the food, bags, and first aid kit, but that's unimportant!" said August.

"Unimportant? That was the entire purpose of you leaving," Meeka said.

"Yeah, yeah, yeah, but look at this!" Asher said excitedly as he dumped a shopping bag filled with camouflage attire. "Then look at this stuff! Quinn showed it to us! It's called eyeblack!"

"I don't know how I should take in this situation. Should I be mad you purchased useless items or match your excitement?" Delphi retorted while she rolled her eyes. "So... what's the point?"

The three boys stood in front of her with huge grins on

their faces.

"To disguise ourselves and blend into the environment! We found a map of Italy in the store, and there are a lot of forests where we're going," August said.

"Yeah, we know, but —"

Meeka cut Delphi off. "But I'm not putting dirt on my face. No way!"

"It's not *real* dirt," Asher answered.

"Sure looks like it. Do you seriously want us to look like we rolled in mud for hours on purpose?" Delphi snarled.

"But this could come in handy! You might not even have to do it! It's only for an emergency," Asher replied excitedly.

"And you're all in on this, too?" Delphi asked Quinn.

He shrugged and grinned. "You'll probably look great in dirt."

Delphi glared at him. "I'll get you for that."

"Come on! We probably won't even need to use it," August interrupted.

"Fine. We can pack it with us, but there is no way I'm going to be caught dead in that," Meeka said while she stared at the pile of greens and browns on the floor.

"What if we don't die while we wear them?" Asher smiled, knowing the reaction he would get out of the girls.

Meeka and Delphi both glared at him.

"I want pizza!" Macy jumped up randomly.

"Huh?" Quinn said.

Everyone was caught off guard by the topic change.

"I said, 'I want pizza!'" she repeated.

Everyone looked around and nodded at each other.

"Sounds good to me," Delphi said.

They all got ready to leave and headed out to walk to the restaurant down the street. It was a beautiful beachside Italian restaurant with flowers, vines, and lanterns. The walls had old artwork painted on them, filling the place with a fancy rustic feeling. It was around sunset, and the place was packed. The group was seated at a table in the corner of the deck. The sun setting behind the mountains made for a perfect view, like a scene from a movie. Chatter filled the air as the smell of freshly cooked food teased everyone's noses.

"This place is breathtaking!" Meeka said in awe.

Opal and Macy wanted to sit on the end closest to the water. Meeka sat between Opal and Asher, with Delphi right across from her. Quinn sat in the shade next to Delphi, away from the blinding light of the setting sun, and August sat next to Asher. Fitz sat across from August, next to Quinn, the light from the sun making his red hair glow.

"Ciao! What can I get you folks to drink tonight?" A waiter in a black suit and white apron asked with a cheerful smile.

Everyone ordered their drinks, iced tea for the older kids, Shirley Temples for the little girls, and their pizzas because they already knew what they wanted.

"I'm starving! When is our food going to get here, Delphi?" Opal whined.

"We just ordered. Be patient. It will be here before you know it," Delphi assured her.

"I feel like I'm beyond underdressed for this place," Meeka said while looking around.

"Me too. It's kind of classy looking." Delphi smiled.

"I think you look fine," Quinn said to Delphi.

Delphi froze for a second. "Oh, uh, thanks."

Quinn casually rested his arm on the back of Delphi's chair. She looked down at it and back up at him.

"Oh, sorry, is this bothering you? These chairs without armrests are really annoying," Quinn said, smiling at her.

"Oh, no, it's fine," Delphi replied, turning back towards Meeka and Asher.

When she looked away, Quinn palmed his forehead, mouthing 'idiot' to himself.

Asher and Meeka both gave each other a look after seeing the interaction with Quinn and Delphi. Delphi's glare at the two of them didn't stop the looks, though.

"Hey, Delphi, are you comfortable?" Asher teased.

"Shut up, Asher," Delphi said through gritted teeth.

Quinn laughed and turned to Delphi, giving her a comforting smile. Delphi eased her posture.

A few minutes later, the waitress came back with their food. Setting the warm, delicious-looking pizza in the center. Opal and Macy were eager to take a look.

"Finally!" August said, reaching for a slice and taking a huge bite. "Thes es rearry goo!" he said with his mouth full.

Delphi made a disgusted face at him and picked up her own slice. "So, what do you guys want to talk about?"

"It feels like we have a lot to talk about, but it makes me exhausted just thinking about it. I feel like we finally have a moment to catch our breaths," Meeka replied.

"Why don't you guys tell me more about Esprit?" Quinn asked.

"Well, what do you want to know?" Delphi asked.

"It's a whole other planet I just learned about. I want to know everything."

"Let's start at the beginning, shall we?" August said in mock seriousness. "So there's this tree in the middle of the planet. What's in the middle of yours?"

"Molten hot lava, and metal," Quinn replied.

"We have a tree, and you get *lava*?" August asked, pouting.

"Unless you have reason to believe that the *Journey to the Center of the Earth* movies are real and there is a whole other world under us, yup, just hot rocks," Quinn replied. "So besides the tree, what else is different about your planet?"

"We don't have an FBI working for the Empire," Fitz said.

"Do you have any secret services?" Quinn asked.

"Not that we know about," Meeka replied.

"Well, I guess that just means yours is better at being 'secret' than ours," Quinn replied, making a few of them chuckle.

"Besides a few things, Earth doesn't seem that much different from Esprit. Maybe just smaller, more united, and with more advanced technology," Asher pointed out.

"And maybe a few different foods," said Delphi. "What's that jar of green stuff back at the house, anyway?"

"You mean *pickles*?" Quinn asked, laughing. "They're just pickled cucumbers."

"They looked kind of small to be cucumbers," said Delphi, laughing too.

"That's because they're fermented in jars. We had to do that for a project in my foods class at school once. My group just ended up smashing the jar when one kid got it stuck. Long story short, we failed the assignment." Quinn smiled reminiscently. "That memory just seems so ordinary now that all of this has happened."

"Okay, but back to the pickles. What other things do you ferment and why?" August asked.

"Uh, I'm pretty sure you can pickle ham too," Quinn said.

August's face quickly switched to a look of disgust. "*Why?*"

"I don't know why!" replied Quinn, laughing at their discussion topic and turning to look at Delphi, whose laugh lit up her face.

She met his gaze, her smile still glowing. "Any other strange foods we should be wary of?"

"In some parts of the world, they eat bugs," Quinn said.

"There goes my appetite," Meeka said, setting down her pizza crust.

"Hey, you don't know until you try it. I wouldn't recommend cow tongue either, though, but that's just my preference."

"Yuck!" Macy said, sticking out her tongue.

"Do people on Earth just eat anything that moves?" Asher asked.

"Pretty much, although you aren't allowed to hunt endangered species," Quinn said.

"What are those?" Asher asked.

"Animals that have been over-hunted or are losing their habitats," Quinn explained. "You don't have that kind of thing on Esprit?"

"No, compared to Earth, I think we have a pretty small

population. Plus, we don't have as many wild forests as you do. We mostly just fish and keep farm animals, not much hunting," Meeka said.

"Seems to me like Esprit is more advanced in more ways than technology," Quinn said.

"Yeah, it seems so," said Delphi.

***

As soon as they finished their dinner and paid the bill, they returned to the bed-and-breakfast.

"We have an early morning tomorrow. We should get to bed," Meeka said with a yawn.

"Oh, well, we all know who you'll be sleeping with," August teased while nudging Asher's arm.

Meeka glared at August out of embarrassment.

"You know what, everyone? Sleepover in the living room. Get pillows and blankets," Delphi instructed.

Quinn and Meeka pushed back the couch and moved the coffee table. Opal and Macy took the cushions off the couch and threw them on the floor. They emptied the hassock and sprawled all the blankets across the floor. Delphi went into the other rooms to get more pillows.

"You really didn't have to say anything, dude," Asher whispered to August.

"Oh yes, I did. You know I did," he replied with an

annoying grin.

Everyone situated themselves on the floor setup. The little girls both helped pick out a movie for everyone to watch. Halfway through the film, most of them were out like a light.

"Meeka?" A faint whisper came from Asher.

Meeka turned around and saw Asher sitting up.

"What? Go to sleep," she whispered back.

Asher mouthed the words, "I'm sorry." Meeka gave a quiet laugh, assuring him that everything was fine.

"Want to go for a walk?" he added softly.

"What? It's late. Where would we go, anyway?"

"Um, the beach..."

She hesitated a second and then nodded in agreement.

They got up quietly, careful not to disrupt everyone else who was fast asleep. The two stepped out the back door and walked down the walkway to the sand.

"August is such a *cane*," Asher said while smiling at Meeka.

"I was expecting it." Meeka laughed. "Race you to the water." Meeka took off towards the sea. Asher quickly trailed behind.

"This is my favorite part about Earth, I think. It kind of reminds me of home," Meeka said as she admired the waves in the moonlight. She smiled and kicked the water.

Asher stood admiring Meeka just as she was admiring the water.

"Stop staring at me like that," Meeka teased as she looked at Asher.

"What do you mean? Like what?" he asked cluelessly.

"Like the way you always do." She smiled.

"And is that a bad thing?" Asher asked.

Meeka kicked the water at Asher's feet. "You look at me the same way Delphi looks at baby owls in the pet shop."

"Oh, Delphi loves owls," Asher pointed out.

"Exactly, my point made," Meeka said proudly.

"Meeka, did you tell Delphi... never mind. It was stupid." Asher's demeanor changed.

Meeka picked up a shell. "Tell Delphi what?"

"Delphi told me that when she said you had feelings for me, you denied it. Did you mean that?" Asher said uncomfortably.

"You are really dumb sometimes, Asher. Do you know that?" She handed him the shell and continued walking along the beach.

Asher followed. "Just making sure I'm getting the right messages."

Meeka stopped in her tracks. She turned around and locked eyes with Asher.

"Do I need to put my messages in caps?" Meeka asked sarcastically. "I don't need to keep deleting the messages now because Delphi is okay with all this. I hope you are catching on to what I'm saying because I'd say, metaphorically, you're getting a notification."

Meeka gave him a grin and turned to the water. Asher stood in shock. He took a moment to process, then looked at the shell Meeka had placed in his hand. It was a perfect ladder horn seashell. He inserted it into his pocket with a smile. He walked over to Meeka's side, placing his arm around her playfully. Meeka looked up at him and subsequently to the water.

"Like you said earlier, M'lady, it's late. We should head back and get to sleep."

Meanwhile, back inside the beach house, Delphi had awakened to a sizable gap next to her. She sat up and noticed who was missing.

"Those two..." Delphi whispered, rolling her eyes. She laid her head back down, hoping to fall back to sleep.

A few minutes passed before Asher and Meeka returned inside. They both went back to their spots on the floor.

"Goodnight, Meeka," Asher whispered.

"Night," Meeka replied as she rested her head down.

"Had fun, Meeks?" Delphi groaned teasingly.

"Delphi! What the *infernum*?" Meeka whisper-yelled.

Delphi chuckled before drifting off to sleep.

Chapter 12

A Long Walk

It was lightly drizzling when they woke up the next morning. Rubbing the sleep out of their eyes, they all got up and got ready to leave. August took a bit more coaxing than the rest.

"But I need my beauty sleep," he whined.

"And *we* need to stay alive. For all we know, the plane crash grabbed the attention of the FBI, and they're on their way here now," Asher retorted, nudging August with his foot. "Come on, just get up."

"Five more minutes," August said, closing his eyes again and turning over onto his side.

"Not a chance," Delphi said, walking over.

She snatched the pillow out from under August, and his head banged onto the hardwood floor. She hit him with the pillow until he sat up.

"Okay, okay. I'm up!" August said, putting his hands up in mock surrender. He imitated a whisper directed towards Asher, "Someone woke up violent today."

Asher rolled his eyes and nudged August again with his foot. "Get up."

They got their few belongings together and walked over to the adjacent house of the owner to return their key.

"I hope you kids enjoyed your stay!" Ms. De Luca said, taking the key from Meeka.

"Yes, very much, thank you," Meeka replied, as the rest nodded in agreement.

"I'm so glad. Enjoy the rest of your trip! Arrivederci!" She waved goodbye and returned to her house.

"Okay, time to get that taxi," said Asher.

They called the taxi company on the payphone and requested a taxi to fit eight people. Ten minutes later, they were sitting in a van converted into a taxi. Quinn was up front with the driver. Opal, Macy, Fitz, and August were in the row behind him, and Delphi, Asher, and Meeka were in the far back.

Asher leaned closer to Delphi and Meeka and whispered, "If we have to walk through the woods for a really long time, can we wear the camo?"

They each shot him a look that doubly shut him up, but not for long.

"Come on. It will keep us safe, and Quinn said it will probably stop us from being mistaken for a bear or something by hunters... if we come across any," Asher pleaded.

"Maybe," Meeka said. "Maybe, but I will probably regret saying this later."

"You're only giving in because you like him!" Delphi pointed out.

"No, that's not why. It's as a safety precaution. Imagine coming all this way only to be mistaken for a wild goose or something. What then?"

"A wild *goose?*" Delphi asked, noticing her friend was

grasping at straws.

"Among other animals," Meeka said, trying to salvage her argument.

"I can tell I'm outnumbered, aren't I?" Delphi asked.

"Yup!" said August, turning around in his seat to face Delphi.

"Oh, just shut up," Delphi said. "And stop eavesdropping on our conversation."

"And how do you suppose I do that?" August asked, wiggling his eyebrows. "You're sitting right behind me, and I can feel your warm breath on the back of my neck."

"You're such a drama queen," Delphi said.

"What? I thought it was hot," August replied.

This caught Quinn's attention, and he turned around in his own seat to face everyone behind him. "Hey, cool it." He gave August a pointed look.

"No, I said it was hot, not cool," August said to Quinn and turned back toward Delphi. "Honestly, I think he's a little confused."

"I think you're the confused one," Delphi replied.

"Wait. What do I have to be confused about?" August asked.

"Did you have something helpful to add to our conversation, or did you just turn around to torment me?" Delphi asked August.

"It's not just you being tormented, Delphi," Meeka said, shaking her head. "He has a gift. One where everyone around him just wants to shrink away when he opens his mouth."

"No kidding," Delphi agreed.

"Hey, that wasn't nice," said August, mockingly clutching the part of his chest where his heart was. "Your words cut deep, you know."

"Oh, give me a break," Meeka said, rolling her eyes.

"I think all of this eye-rolling that you are making people do is going to make us all dizzy, August," Asher said.

"Stop agreeing with your girlfriend. Remember, pals before gals," said August.

"I'm not—" Asher started.

"Don't you dare," Delphi threatened before he could finish his sentence. "Don't you *dare* deny it."

Asher decided against saying anything at all.

"Ooh, I told you someone was violent today," August said to Asher.

"You better watch yourself too, August," Delphi said.

"Or what?" August asked, smirking.

"I wouldn't encourage her if I were you," Asher warned.

August shrugged and plopped back into his seat.

"When we get out of this car, I need to borrow Quinn's pocket knife," Delphi said.

"Oh, crud. August better watch his back," Meeka said.

"And his front," Asher added.

Delphi stared daggers at the back of August's head. She was so transfixed with attempting to actually burn holes there that she didn't notice August turn around again to look at her.

"I know. Take it all in, beautiful. I'm just gorgeous," said August, tousling his hair.

Delphi blinked rapidly. "What? No!"

"*No*, what? I saw you staring." He wiggled his eyebrows again.

"I was attempting to burn holes in the back of your head, not, you know what? I'm not explaining myself to you. You're hopeless."

"So I've been told," August said and, with another flirtatious look, turned back around.

"I hope he gets a crick in his neck from turning around so much," Delphi mumbled.

"I can hear you talking about me," August said in a sing-song voice.

"Ugh!" was Delphi's only reply.

"I feel the need to clarify. Asher and I are not a thing," Meeka said, with her hands up.

"You feel nothing," Delphi answered with her signature death stare.

"Violence. Right. She chose violence this morning," Meeka said.

After some time, Asher informed them that he was feeling car sick. Meeka handed him a blue emesis bag as a 'just in case.'

On the other hand, the swaying of the vehicle was causing others to doze off to sleep. Unsurprisingly, Meeka fell victim to that, especially with the late night she had had the night before. She gently rested her head on Asher's shoulder and peacefully slept.

"Don't you dare throw up on her," Delphi hissed.

Asher rolled his eyes at his sister. To his surprise, Meeka was helping with his motion sickness and replacing it with butterflies.

When they reached a gas station several hours later, Quinn asked the driver to stop.

"What? You want some snacks or something because stopping for that will cost you extra," said the driver.

"No, this is where we're getting out," Quinn corrected. "How much?"

Quinn paid the driver, and they all got out. All that was left was a trail of dust following the van as he sped away.

"So what now?" August asked.

"Now, we walk," Fitz replied.

"Wait, wait, wait! The camo!" Asher said excitedly.

"And the dirt," August smirked.

"No, no, no, no, and again no!" Delphi said, crossing her arms.

"Meeka said we could. For safety," Asher reminded everyone.

"Correction, I said 'maybe,' not yes," Meeka corrected.

"But still. Let's just do it," Asher pleaded with Meeka.

Meeka looked to Delphi, who stood with her arms crossed, glaring at her.

"Sorry, Delph. I'm gonna give in."

"Ugh. I knew you would," Delphi replied.

Everyone walked into the gas station and headed to the bathroom to change. All the girls went in first. Opal and Macy put on their camouflage jumpers while Delphi and Meeka were given pants and jackets. They quickly changed and walked out. Opal and Macy walked out as if they were runway models in a fashion show. Delphi and Meeka walked out next.

Delphi had a drawstring bag with all their old clothes inside, and Meeka walked out with the jacket tied around her waist and her white tank top on. The boys went in next. They exited with the eyeblack already on their faces.

"Time to put the finishing touches on," Asher said, walking up to Meeka with the eyeblack.

Meeka grabbed his wrist before he could put the line on her cheek, "Absolutely not. I'm not putting dirt on my face."

"Oh, come on, Meeka. *You* voted for the *whole* attire," Delphi said sarcastically.

Meeka rolled her eyes and let Asher put the eyeblack on her cheeks. He then tossed it to Delphi, who applied it to herself and the little ones.

"We look sick," August announced.

To Meeka's bewilderment, she saw a necklace around Asher's neck. It looked oddly familiar to her.

"Where did you get that?" Meeka asked Asher, pointing to his necklace.

"Oh, this?" He held it up like a trophy. "It's the shell you gave me last night. While you guys were changing, I purchased some string and made it into a necklace."

"That is *so* stupid, dude," August interrupted.

"If anything is stupid, it's you," Meeka retorted. "I find it rather meaningful. Take some notes, August."

"Asher sucks with the ladies. So, no thank you," said August, swollen-headed as ever.

"Yup. You are so right," Delphi jumped in sarcastically.

"Guys, we should start walking," Quinn said.

The group walked across the street and into the woods. It

wasn't as pleasant of an experience as hoped. Some spots were slippery because of the gloomy weather, making it harder to progress.

"I'm tired," Macy complained.

"Me too. And my feet hurt already," Opal added.

"We've only been walking for about an hour. Let's keep going a little more before we take a break," Meeka said.

The girls groaned but trudged on.

"Only a few more hours, guys," Fitz called out from ahead of the pack.

They walked a little farther before taking a break in a small clearing.

"How do you know we're going the right way, Fitz?" Asher asked.

"I bought a compass at that gas station. They had a lot of random junk in there," Fitz replied, sitting down and taking a swig of water from his canteen.

"You know, that's great and all, but who brought the toilet paper?" August asked. "Because from my point of view, that is the *most* important thing we could bring."

"*Toilet paper?*" Fitz asked.

"Yes, toilet paper. I mean, we are in the middle of the woods. No bathrooms, at least as far as I know." He turned to Quinn expectantly.

"Yeah, no. We don't normally build stuff like that in the middle of the forest."

"See? Toilet paper is a *necessity,*" August said.

"Could you stop repeating the phrase 'toilet paper' over and over again?" Meeka asked.

"Don't worry, I took some from the bathroom of the gas station," Asher said, unzipping his pack and chucking it at August.

It struck August in the stomach, but he was able to catch it before the roll fell to the ground.

"Now go do your business before you start another rant about toilet paper," Asher said.

August rolled his eyes and walked away, only to come back a couple of minutes later without the toilet paper.

"Did you actually use *all* of it?" Asher asked.

"No, there was a fuzzy little jerk over there who kept 'accidentally' dropping acorns on my head."

"A *chipmunk*?"

"A very *angry* chipmunk," August corrected.

"You seriously have the ability to even make wildlife annoyed with you?" Delphi asked.

August grinned. "Hey, maybe it was pissed off that I was pissing on his tree."

"This was all an elaborate ploy just to tell that joke then, wasn't it?" Meeka asked.

"It wasn't *all* a ploy," August said, taking the toilet paper out of his pack and throwing it to Asher. "There really was an angry chipmunk. He was going *nuts*."

Delphi let out a loud groan.

"Let's just keep moving," Fitz suggested, taking the compass back out of his pocket and standing up.

They trudged on for what felt like forever before they decided they needed to rest again. Opal and Macy were out of breath, and August complained that his legs had turned to jelly. Everyone was sweaty and exhausted and nearly collapsed against the trees at their next rest stop.

"How much farther do you think we will have to go?" Quinn asked.

"No clue. This rocky terrain and the ever-growing steepness of it all are really slowing us down," Meeka replied.

"Well, how many hours have we been in the forest for?" Delphi asked Meeka, who looked down at her watch.

"Three, so we're about halfway to the town," she replied.

Fitz called out from up ahead, "Guys, we have a slight issue!"

Everyone rushed up to him.

"A *slight* issue?" Asher asked, looking out at the rapids of the rushing river.

"Well, I didn't want to alarm you," said Fitz.

"Well, this *is* alarming!" Quinn said, picking up Macy.

"Piggyback ride!" Macy yelled, delighted.

Asher followed Quinn's example and picked up Opal. "Okay, I know you think you're too big to be picked up, but I need you to just deal with it. Whatever you do, just don't hit my broken wrist."

The people in the group with the backpacks tightened them across their shoulders, and they all waded into the water.

"Is anyone going to offer to carry Fitz? Because we all know he can't swim," August asked.

Everyone looked over to Fitz, who was still standing on solid ground and staring at the water like it would swallow him whole at any second.

"No one is going to carry him. It's not that deep," Quinn called out, a quarter of the way through the river. The water rose to his torso, and in certain places, it was even higher.

Fitz slowly got into the water, the force of the rapids causing him to stumble. He grabbed onto a branch that was hanging over the river.

"Come on, Fitz. Just take it a step at a time," Quinn yelled in hopes of boosting his confidence.

"Guys, we are going to be here all day unless someone goes and helps him," said August as he pushed through the rapids.

"Hey, August, your cousin, your problem," Delphi said. "No offense, Fitz."

Fitz slowly took another cautious step. "Yeah, um, okay."

August turned his back on the opposite river bank to assist Fitz, even though he didn't think he could be much help.

"Grab my arm and get a move on," August instructed.

Fitz did as he was told, and the two attempted to trudge across the river.

About halfway through, Fitz slipped on a rock and was suddenly pulled under. He did all he could to get his head above the water, but it was no use, and he was starting to be dragged away by the rushing rapids. Luckily, August grabbed Fitz's arm in time. In an attempt to pull Fitz back to his feet, August dug his heels into the dirt below the water's surface and pulled as hard as he could. Meeka turned around to help and grabbed Fitz's other arm. Together, they managed to get Fitz across safely.

"Finally!" August gasped, soaked and lying on the ground on the opposite river bank.

Despite the warm day, Fitz was shivering. If not from the cold water, then from the unpleasant experience.

"We really need to teach you how to swim, dude," August said to Fitz, who had sat down on a rock, gulping in air.

***

They kept hiking for what felt like an eternity until they made it to the forest's edge.

The view was breathtaking. The sun had come out and was shining brightly over rolling green hills as far as the eye could see. Puffy white clouds lined the sky, providing the occasional escape from the rising temperature. They found the road again and made sure to keep it in sight as they trekked through the grassy plains.

The sun mostly dried their soaked clothing, but the stifling heat didn't help their exhaustion. With a little over an hour left to go, they had already ditched the jackets.

Delphi stuffed hers into her backpack and rolled up her pant legs. "Remind me again how *necessary* the camo was."

Quinn, Asher, and August grinned at her sheepishly. She rolled her eyes and stood back up, slinging her backpack over her shoulders.

Meeka finished braiding her hair and shielded her eyes from the sun, trying to see farther into the distance. "Fitz, you've got the map. How much farther?"

"Uh, about four and a half miles."

"Let's just get this done and over with," Delphi said and started walking again.

A few buildings started popping up along their route, and they kept walking. Finally, they reached the outskirts of the town.

"Look. We made it," Asher said, out of breath and leaning over with his hands on his knees.

"Yup. Probably should have stretched first," August said, cracking his neck. "Okay, I'm good. Sooo, we made it this far. Now what? No one specified what would happen after the million-mile walk."

"If I'm being honest, I didn't think we would get this far," Fitz said while trying to catch his breath. "But looking back on our past experiences, this one isn't necessarily the worst."

"Let's try to get a cheap motel or something," suggested Quinn. "We need a place to stay, at least for the night. I have one question, though. What is our goal at the end of this?"

"To come out alive," Delphi mumbled loud enough for Quinn and everyone else to hear her.

"Maybe we can see if we can purchase any Earth electronics that can be used to fix the orb. At the very least, I could try," Fitz suggested.

"But that just brings us back to the problem of Macy and Quinn running for their lives while we escape," Delphi pointed out.

"If Fitz ends up being able to fix the orb, we can worry about the technicalities and problems then. Right now, I just want a warm bath in that motel that Quinn was talking about," Meeka said.

Before they got into town, they did their best to wipe their faces clean of the grungy makeup with the water from their water bottles, but that didn't stop them from drawing unwanted attention.

"I guess camo isn't in style right now," August whispered to Asher.

"Or, you know, it could be that we are a bunch of teenagers who just walked out of the woods looking like we were chewed up and spit out by a grizzly bear," Asher whispered back.

They eventually found a motel and being as exhausted as they all were, they didn't immediately notice how dingy it was. Only when they had been shown to their room did they realize that the place was a dump.

"This is disgusting," Meeka said, looking at the stained carpet and bedding.

"That's a massive understatement," Delphi replied, looking into the bathroom. "I don't think you want to take a bath in there, Meeka. It's practically a crusty rust bucket."

"Sadly, this is our best option for the time being. I don't think any of us are up for another walk, especially when our clothes attract so much attention," Quinn said.

"This has to be the world's grossest motel ever, though," Meeka remarked.

"Meh, I've stayed in worse," Quinn replied.

Everyone gave him a look of disgust, but he just shrugged and took off his backpack.

"I'm going to change into some dryer clothes and get cleaned up. We all should." Quinn walked into the bathroom and shut the door.

After they had all changed and cleaned up a little, they took out some of their packed food and ate in relative silence.

"Alright," Asher said after swallowing his last bite of food. "Sleep is probably mandatory now."

"Sleep? On those beds? Good luck with that. I'd rather sleep outside," Delphi said.

"Maybe they aren't *that* bad," Meeka pondered. "What if we just flip the mattresses and the sheets over?"

She attempted to do just that but to no avail. Everything was stained equally, if not more, on the opposite side.

"That didn't work," August observed.

"No kidding," Delphi grumbled. "There has to be something we can cover the beds with."

They searched the room until Opal and Macy found a pile of relatively unsoiled towels under the bathroom sink.

"That should work," Asher said, taking the towels and laying them across each bed. He took a few extra pillows and laid them out on the floor with a towel over them. "And now we have one extra bed."

"I'm still sleeping outside," Delphi said, taking the last of the extra pillows and her own towel and opening the sliding door to the 'pool area.'

There wasn't actually a pool, just a large empty hole in the ground that someone was bound to fall into if they weren't careful. Delphi did the same thing that Asher did inside for her own custom bed.

"You really want to sleep outside?" Meeka asked behind her.

"You really want to sleep *inside?*" Delphi retorted.

"It's not ideal, but Asher made it doable," Meeka replied, sitting down next to Delphi and dangling her legs over the ledge of the pool hole.

"I guess. I think I just need some air, though. Time to be alone and clear my thoughts," Delphi said, sliding to the edge of the pool as well.

"Have you gotten any new flashes recently?" Meeka asked, with a worried crinkle in her brow.

"Not since we first got to Salerno, no."

"You'll tell me if it happens again, right?"

"Of course! None of this has stopped me from trusting you or confiding in you. You're my best friend, Meeka. Why else would I bother you so much about Asher? Hmm?"

"Ugh, can we not bring Asher into everything?" Meeka cringed

"Sorry, Meeka, but you and my brother; I can't let you live that down."

Meeka rolled her eyes with a smile, "I don't want him and me to get between you and me. For crying out loud, this entire trip has revealed a lot about ourselves. It definitely opened up a lot of doors."

"I don't think it's possible for Asher to get in the way. We have always seen each other like sisters. Now I guess we really are." Delphi nudged Meeka.

"Woah, woah, woah. Let's not go *that* far."

They both laughed, but within seconds, their expressions changed.

"Meeka, do you think we are going to get out of this

mess?" Delphi asked, her voice filled with concern.

"I really wish I could give you a straightforward answer. I want to say yes because we always find a way out of our messes, but I'm not sure. This clearly isn't an easy cleanup."

"I've been thinking about what happens when we get home, well, *if* we get home. This is big stuff we wound up in. Discovering a whole other thriving planet, it's crazy. Why would Esprit hide such a beautiful place if they knew about it?" Delphi looked around at her surroundings. "Well, mostly beautiful."

Meeka chuckled at Delphi's sarcastic remark. "I really don't know. I guess all we can do is enjoy it while we're here."

Meeka and Delphi both gave each other a sympathetic look.

"We should get to sleep," Meeka said, breaking the silence.

"Yeah, if that's possible," Delphi added.

"I hope you don't mind, but I'm going to sleep inside. The one perk to this dumpster is it's air-conditioned." Meeka laughed as she stood up.

She walked over to the sliding door and stepped inside. She was greeted by everyone else messing with the T.V. August was arguing with Macy on whether they should watch the mystery or the baking channel.

"Hey, August, quit arguing with a seven-year-old," Meeka chimed in.

"No, just because she's seven doesn't mean she wins the argument." August crossed his arms.

"Man, you're acting like a child," Asher interrupted.

August jokingly glared at Asher, then at Macy.

"Next time we go to a *faex* motel while trying to run from the FBI, *I* get to pick the television channel," sassed August.

"Whatever," Macy said triumphantly.

Everyone sat in silence as they watched a man in a white apron decorate an enormous cake.

"So, Asher, are you going to go over and cuddle with your girlfriend?" August said out of nowhere after he glanced at Meeka, noticing she was half awake.

"Totally uncalled for," Asher replied.

"August, I might not be as intimidating as Delphi, but I will smash your face into a wall," Meeka threatened, with her eyes closed.

"You need to keep her under control!" whispered August to Asher.

"She does and says as she wishes. Again, not my girlfriend, so I have no say in her actions," Asher retorted.

"You would have no say even if we were together, *buddy*," said Meeka, eavesdropping.

"Buddy? Damn, sorry, bro. You just got *friend-zoned*." August nudged Asher.

Asher rolled his eyes and turned his back to August, hoping to fall asleep.

Macy sat at the foot of the bed on top of a towel, mesmerized by the baking show, while an unconscious Opal leaned on an equally passed out Meeka. Asher and August were both trying to fall asleep on the other bed. Quinn was lying adjacent to them at their feet, his legs dangling off the edge of the bed.

"I feel bad that Delphi is outside by herself," Quinn said

while staring at the ceiling.

"Oh, so you're saying some dashing young man should go out and give her some company?" asked August, clearly talking about himself.

"Exactly. That's why I'm going to go out there while you stay inside and not bother her."

Quinn turned around and shot August a sarcastic smile. Then he got up, grabbed another towel and pillow, and walked to the sliding door. He quietly opened it enough to peek out and see if Delphi was awake. To his surprise, she was sitting up and looked like she was watching the stars. He stepped outside and walked over to her.

"Hey, what are you doing up?" asked Quinn.

"Can't sleep. Should I be asking the same?" Delphi replied.

"I thought I would give you some company. Felt bad that you were out here alone."

Quinn laid out the towel and pillow. He made himself comfortable as Delphi watched.

"You don't have to be out here. I made the choice to sleep outside," she assured him.

"And it was *my* choice to come outside and join you." Quinn gave her a friendly grin. "I want to let you know that it's not that bad inside."

"I'm sure it isn't, but it's enough for me to spend the night next to this," Delphi signaled to the empty pool hole. They both laughed. "Anyway, anything interesting happening inside?"

"If you mean other than August arguing with Macy over the T.V., then no," Quinn answered.

"Not surprised. He's a handful," Delphi said. "Before I forget, I wanted to apologize for dragging you into all this."

"What do you mean?" Quinn questioned.

"What do *you* mean? We practically hauled you across your planet, involuntarily, for a matter of fact. And when, or if, we get back to Esprit, your whole life is practically destroyed," Delphi said.

"My life isn't destroyed, Delphi—"

"Realistically, yes, it is. We destroyed your uncle's car, blew up your house, spent half of your money, and constantly put you in danger. So, if you don't think your life is destroyed, get help," Delphi interrupted him.

"I don't need you guys feeling bad for us. Are you kidding? You guys aren't even on the right planet. It took me some time to realize that I shouldn't be mad at you because we're struggling in different ways. Besides, everything that's been destroyed is replaceable, and it's a much better alternative to losing something that isn't."

"Our lives, you mean." It wasn't a question. The minute they had all gotten into Quinn's car for the first time, they knew they were in mortal danger.

Quinn solemnly nodded and unfolded two pieces of paper from his pocket. "I've noticed you like to draw, and you're pretty good at it." He brought out two pencils.

"It's calming, especially when I have a lot of built-up energy or when I need to focus. I just put it all on the page and clear my head," Delphi replied, taking the pencil and sheet that Quinn handed to her.

"Maybe you could teach me. I'm not much of an artist, but

I'm willing to try," Quinn said.

"Sure, okay. So there are two ways you can draw. Actually, I'm sure there are more, but this is just how I think about it. You can either decide what you are going to make beforehand, or you can let your pencil decide for you. Normally, it's easier to start by copying something in front of you rather than just trying to make it from memory."

Quinn nodded.

"Here. For example—" Delphi looked up at him and down at her paper. She started sketching what looked like a face. She added eyes, a nose, a mouth, ears, eyebrows, hair, a neck, shoulders, and a shirt. After a while of sketching, she added some shading and held it up.

"Woah, is that me?" Quinn asked.

"Yeah, so when you think about what things look like, they're often different from what they actually look like in real life. That's why it's easier to copy your subject face to face rather than from memory. When you..." She trailed off after looking up at how Quinn was staring at her.

"What?" Delphi asked.

"Oh, nothing, just got a little lost," Quinn said.

"Do you want me to repeat anything?"

"No. That's not what I meant." Quinn smiled.

Delphi looked at Quinn for a second and then cleared her throat. "Oh, well, do you want to try?"

"Um, yeah, sure," Quinn replied, looking down at his paper. "How exactly should I start?"

"Probably with finding a subject to draw," Delphi said, looking around for something.

"What about you?" Quinn asked.

"Me? I don't know. Why would you want to draw me?" Delphi asked.

"You drew me," Quinn replied.

"Fair point," Delphi said. "Okay, now that you know what your subject is, you need to choose where to start. I like to start with the eyes. That way, you can fit them to the size of the face."

Quinn looked at Delphi and then started scribbling circles onto his page.

"No, no," Delphi said, grabbing Quinn's hand to stop him from drawing. "Look at my face. Look at my eyes. Try studying the shape of them instead of trying to memorize it."

Quinn studied Delphi's face and flipped the paper over to try again. This time, the eyes looked a little better, but not by a lot. He attempted to draw the nose next. Then the mouth, trying to follow Delphi's instructions. After about half an hour of "No, those lines connect there, not there," and "Wait. What the heck is that supposed to be?" Quinn finished his drawing and held it up.

"You weren't lying when you said that you weren't an artist," she said, looking at the distorted picture of her. "Am I supposed to be winking?"

"No, I couldn't get the eyes to be even, and before you ask, the right arm isn't a saxophone."

"Okay, let's just chalk it up as abstract."

Quinn laughed. "But I *am* an artist, just not the drawing type."

"Well, what type then?" Delphi asked, still shaking with

laughter at her portrait.

"I'm a musician, sort of," Quinn replied. "Music is for me what drawing is for you. It's calming."

"So, you play an instrument?"

"A few, actually. I'm pretty good at piano and guitar. I went through a drummer phase, but that didn't really end well. Don't laugh, but my best is probably the violin since it's also the instrument I've been playing the longest. I loved it. Not anymore, though. Life got in the way, and I had to give it up. I haven't picked up an instrument in over a year."

"Did you ever perform for an audience?"

"Actually, the funny thing is, I never tried. You see, in fifth grade, we had to get up in front of the school to do a graduation ceremony type thing. When my name was called to get my certificate, I passed out on stage."

"Jeez."

"Yeah, it's a pretty scarring experience for an eleven-year-old. After that, I never got up in front of a crowd again."

"Has anyone ever heard you play?"

"Not besides my immediate family and this one guy lurking in the alley next to my house who yelled up at me to tell me that I sounded like Chopin himself. Although, I'm pretty sure Chopin didn't play the violin."

"Well, even though I have no idea who Chopin is, he sounds like he was an excellent violinist."

"Oh, forgot, totally different planet."

"We had a lady named Nerwren, who played the violin. She wrote so many famous pieces. I learned about her from

Meeka. Her parents loved listening to Nerwren's music. Maybe she is Esprit's 'Chopin.'" Delphi adjusted her position on the towel and laid down.

"Maybe," Quinn responded, getting up. "I think I'm going to run inside and check on Macy."

"That's probably a good idea. You don't have to sleep out here either, by the way."

"Are you sure?" Quinn stood up and picked up the towel and pillow he had brought outside.

"I'm positive. I actually would like to be alone for a little."

Quinn nodded with a smile and yawned. He headed inside and situated himself at the foot of the bed Asher and August were sleeping on. Soon enough, he, along with everyone else, was fast asleep. Macy and Opal were curled up next to Meeka, Fitz was on the floor, Asher, August, and Quinn on the other bed, and of course, Delphi, who was bundled up outside.

CHAPTER 13

FBI PART II

The car hit a bump and shook the passengers inside.

"We're almost there, sir," said the driver.

"Good, I hope we haven't kept them waiting too long." Agent Smith said. "They may start to miss us."

The driver drove up to the Casa de Luca bed-and-breakfast and let the agents out. A second car drove up behind them, and General Cassidy Brooks got out, along with a few of her troops. More cars arrived, and more agents and soldiers got out of them.

"Squadron A, surround the left side, Squadron B, the right. Don't give them any exits," General Brooks ordered the troops.

"What is going on?" Ms. De Luca had just walked out of her house to find the swarm of FBI agents and military troops surrounding her building.

"Please stay back, ma'am," General Brooks said.

"Agents, move in," Agent Smith said once the house was surrounded.

An agent kicked open the door, and they swarmed inside. The agents all had their guns out and pointed in front of them as they scoured the rooms for any trace of the gang.

Agent Smith walked in behind them, and an agent addressed him, "Sir, they're not here."

"What do you mean 'they're not here?' No one could have tipped them off that we were coming!" Agent Smith yelled and then into his earpiece, "Find them."

"Yes, sir," was the reply from the receiving end of the earpiece.

The researchers back at the offices were desperately looking for a clue that would lead them to where the kids went.

Agent Smith walked back outside the house and up to Ms. De Luca. "Where are they? Where are the kids? They're gone."

Ms. De Luca put her hands on her hips. "Well, I could've told you that. Instead, you went and busted open my door."

"I'm sorry, ma'am, but this is a very delicate situation, and we are going to need your full cooperation. Why don't we go inside and ask you a few questions?" Spencer said, attempting to be polite.

"Sure, welcome yourself into my house. Maybe I can even get you some tea and cookies," Ms. De Luca said in a huff, walking inside. "You American police think you're so high and mighty, breaking into people's homes and welcoming yourselves inside." She continued to grumble until they reached the kitchen.

Ms. De Luca, Agent Smith, General Brooks, and four other agents occupied most of the space in the room.

"So why are you after these children, anyway?" Ms. De Luca asked General Brooks, choosing to ignore Agent Smith altogether.

"Right now, they are a few of the most wanted people in the world," General Brooks said, going through the pre-planned reason for the kids being a threat.

"Are you saying they're dangerous?" Ms. De Luca questioned.

"Ma'am, though this may be an interrogation, we are the ones interrogating you, not the other way around," Agent Smith said.

General Brooks shot Spencer a look and answered Ms. De Luca's question. "Yes, they are potentially dangerous, and we will appreciate any information you have on them. For example, do you know where they went?"

"I wish I could be of more help, but they never told me where they were headed."

"How long ago did they leave?" Agent Smith asked.

Ms. De Luca looked at General Brooks, continuing to ignore Agent Smith. "They left early this morning."

"Is there anything else you can tell us about them?" General Brooks asked.

"One of them had a broken arm, and they used a credit card to pay for their stay. I'm also pretty sure that more than one of those kids spoke fluent Italian as well as English. They stayed two nights and used the payphone just outside quite a few times. Last I saw them, a large taxi picked them up and sped off."

"I'll have agents do a more thorough sweep of the house and see if we can find any clues as to where they went. They will also check the computer's search history," Agent Smith said to General Brooks, who nodded in agreement.

They left Ms. De Luca inside, and Spencer sent agents into the bed-and-breakfast. When the agents came out, the agent carrying a USB port walked up to Agent Smith.

"They left nothing behind but an empty pack. As for their search history, they looked up a map of Italy, presumably to find a new place to hide, but there was nothing specific," the agent informed him.

"So there is nothing in that house to indicate where they went?" Agent Smith asked.

The agent shook her head.

"Told you these kids were good," General Brooks said to Spencer.

"I don't need your input, Cassidy. Someone get in touch with that taxi company. I need a break," Agent Smith stormed off in frustration.

General Brooks sighed, "Okay. Well, let's get back to work," she said to the agent.

"Yes, ma'am." The agent went off to instruct the others.

A few minutes later, an agent walked up to General Brooks. "General, we were able to contact the taxi driver. I would like to start by saying he was a very stubborn man. He was very vague with his answers, but we managed to get out of him that he had just dropped off eight people at a gas station about four hours from here. He was on his way back to Salerno as we spoke. He gave us the exact address of the gas station, but that was all the help he was to us."

"Interesting. Did he see them do anything at the gas station?" asked General Brooks.

"No. Unfortunately, he said he drove off as soon as the

group got out and paid."

"Damn it. Okay, well, we will have to work with what's given. Gather everyone and send them to this gas station."

The agent walked away and did as he was told. Soon enough, all the cars were filled up once again with agents and troops alike. Everyone set off for a long ride, but this time, General Brooks and Agent Smith were in the same vehicle to discuss their plan.

"What's your idea once we arrive at our destination? You clearly have communicated no information with anyone since your 'hissy fit,'" General Brooks said.

"I'd appreciate it if you didn't give me a hard time, General Brooks. Once we arrive, we will go inside and check their cameras, check their system to see their purchases, and ask the employees questions. Got it?" Agent Smith said in a pointed tone.

"Yes," General Brooks replied. "And I'd like to ask why you stormed off."

"And I'd like not to answer," snapped Agent Smith.

"Clearly, you have a problem with me. What is this attitude for?"

"Maybe it's because you won't stop dictating what I do. I know how to do my job, so stop making little comments about it. I don't need your help with this case. And for your information, I left to go and clear my mind. You know it's frustrating having a serious case like this and then having someone like you point out every little apparent detail." Agent Smith rolled his eyes.

"What's frustrating is working with someone who clearly

doesn't want them there. You let our past and personal lives impede our jobs. Just calm down and do your job."

"Our past has nothing to do with this. You just piss me off in general. And why be calm when there is a group of kids *not* from this *planet* roaming around? They could be here to kill us. We were given zero information concerning them. This could start a war between planets, and you don't seem to care. Do you not understand how serious this is?"

"They are *kids*. They seem harmless. Have you ever thought that they might be here by accident and just as terrified as we are of them? They haven't killed anyone yet."

"The plane crash? Someone died in that," Agent Smith pointed out with his arms in the air.

"They didn't cause the plane crash. They clearly were trying to get away from us. I don't think those kids would put their lives at risk."

Agent Smith remained silent and turned his back to General Brooks.

***

Hours later, night had fallen. They finally arrived at the gas station, where the driver said he had dropped the kids off. General Brooks and Agent Smith both got out of the vehicle and gave instructions to everyone else.

"Gather over here," General Brooks called out.

The agents and troops gathered around as told.

"Listen up. Agents from squadron A will follow General Brooks and me inside to question the manager and any other employees that were present while the kids were here. After that, I will join Squadron B to check CCTV," Agent Smith announced.

"My troops will remain stationed outside," General Brooks added.

Cassidy and Spencer entered the station, followed by Squadron A, and headed towards the counter where the cashier awaited them nervously.

"Can I help you?" he said in a small voice.

"FBI," Agent Smith said, holding up his badge. "We just need to ask you a few questions about a few of your customers from earlier today."

The cashier nodded.

"Did you notice a group of eight kids come in here?" Agent Smith asked.

"Um, yes. Most of them were teenagers, right?" the cashier answered.

"Correct. And did they speak to you directly?" General Brooks asked.

"Yes, they bought a few things, although I can't remember what exactly," the cashier replied.

"Well, you can't have too many customers out here in the middle of nowhere," Agent Smith said. "But that is unimportant since we can see what they bought on the CCTV footage. What we are wondering is if they said anything to you or you overheard them saying anything that can tell us where they are."

"They didn't say anything to me specifically, but I did see them go into the bathrooms and change into camouflage clothing," the cashier said.

"So what? They're going hunting now?" Spencer practically yelled, flinging his hands up in exasperation.

Cassidy gave him a pointed look and turned to the cashier. "Thank you for the information. Were there any other employees here who saw them and could give us more details?"

"No, it's just me today."

Cassidy nodded.

"We also require access to your CCTV footage," Spencer said to the cashier.

"Sure. Follow me."

General Brooks led squadron A outside while the agents of squadron B, including Agent Smith, were brought to the gas station's CCTV footage in the back room. They rewinded a couple of hours back until something caught Agent Smith's eye.

"There," he said, pointing.

The agent stopped the footage.

"Fast forward a little," Agent Smith said.

The agent did as he was told and stopped as he saw the black smudges that must have been the gang entering the gas station.

"Zoom in," Agent Smith said.

As they zoomed in, the image became a little clearer. You could see the blurry faces of the gang.

"Now play it," Agent Smith ordered.

The recording ran, and they watched as the group walked into the gas station, went into the bathrooms, came out in their camouflage attire, bought a few things, and walked out. The outdoor CCTV footage showed them head across the street and disappear out of view of the camera.

"And there they go, off-camera," Agent Smith grumbled.

"Well, you can see them walking in this direction." An agent pointed to the screen. "Why don't we go check out what they could have possibly walked to?"

"Might as well," Agent Smith grumbled.

Agent Smith walked out of the station with a few other agents. They scoped out the direction they saw the kids walk to on the cameras.

"Woods. Just woods." Agent Smith scowled in frustration.

"Go across the street and scout the area," General Brooks instructed one of her squadrons.

They followed her instructions and went over to the edge of the forest. They searched the area with their flashlights until one man poked his head up.

"We've found footprints!" he yelled to General Brooks. "It looks like eight people headed straight into the thick of the forest, General."

A voice in Agent Smith's ear stopped him from yelling any profanities.

"The credit card has been used again. A transaction in Castelluccio, Umbria. They're still in Italy. It paid for a cheap motel near the outskirts of town," said the researcher.

"We've got them," Spencer said. "Contact the owner of the

motel and tell them to not let those kids leave."

"Yes, sir," the researcher replied and hung up.

"Castelluccio, Umbria?" General Brooks asked, having overheard Spencer talking.

"Yes, and we need to get there fast before they decide to pick up and leave again. I left an agent with orders to contact the motel manager, but I don't know how much help they will be in keeping the kids there."

"Right, especially since you couldn't do that yourself," Cassidy replied.

Spencer ignored her, opening the car door and ducking inside. He rolled down the window and looked back at Cassidy. "Coming?"

They were on the road again, discussing their new plan of action now that they had finally located the gang.

"My troops will be stationed at all the exits to the motel, including their front door," Cassidy said. "We'll take the same approach as we did in Salerno, just with the right information."

"Exactly. My agents will be ready and armed. We'll get these kids to cooperate one way or another," Agent Smith said.

The agents and troops in the other cars were notified via walkie-talkie of the plan.

Eventually, they made it to the *Motel of Castelluccio* and parked in an adjacent parking lot, hoping the kids wouldn't catch on to what was happening until it was too late. The troops fanned out around the motel, and the agents headed straight to the door of the gang's room. Agent Smith pushed past the other agents, who had their guns pointed right at the door, and aimed his own gun at the handle.

CHAPTER 14

EAT MY SHORTS

Delphi woke up in the pool area of the motel. She sat up and blinked a few times to get the sleep out of her eyes, yawning in the process. Her eyes started to refocus on her surroundings.

A cry of alarm barely escaped her lips before a hand clamped over her mouth and a pair of brawny arms hoisted her up from behind.

She struggled and fought, her eyes wide with alarm. Delphi looked towards the sliding glass door of her room to find that everyone was still passed out cold. She continued to fight as the men, one holding a gun to her forehead and the other holding her arms behind her back, dragged her to the front of the motel.

Before they got to the front, though, she bit the hand clamped over her mouth as hard as she could. The man loosened his grip but didn't let go. She took her chance and kicked the agent hard on his kneecap. He let go of her mouth but didn't stop holding her arms.

"You *irrumators!*" she shouted. "Let me go!"

Like that was going to do much to help. The agent holding the gun pointed it more threateningly at her, but she refused to let that intimidate her.

"Let me go!" she repeated.

The agents said nothing. The man whose kneecap she kicked recovered, and instead of putting his hand back over her mouth, he tightened both hands around her arms.

"Help!" she screeched as stubborn tears swelled up in her eyes, but she refused to let them flow. "Help!"

A loud bang, a gunshot, rang in her ears.

"NO!" she yelled, terrified that someone had been hit. The tears started flowing. "No!" she said again, more meekly.

✳✳✳

A gloomy morning settled outside the windows as the rest of the gang groggily awoke. Birds could be faintly heard chirping to each other in the trees.

"What time is it?" August asked as the others started standing up and walking around.

"Uh, it's 5:30 a.m," Asher said.

"Why are you all up so early, then?" August asked, laying back down.

"It's not like we could really sleep—" Meeka was cut off by the sound of a gunshot right outside the door.

August jolted up.

"GET DOWN!" Quinn yelled and then suddenly remembered Delphi was still outside.

Quinn and Asher looked towards the sliding glass door simultaneously, but Delphi was gone.

"DELPHI!" Asher yelled in anguish.

The door handle turned, and everyone's heads snapped back just as it opened, revealing Agent Smith in the doorway.

"Don't worry, she's in safe hands," he said tauntingly.

"What have you done to her?" Quinn asked, standing up from his crouched position on the floor.

Everyone followed suit as Agent Smith answered. "She's right outside, waiting for you."

"You lowly piece of *faex*!" Asher screamed.

"Now, now. No need to yell," Agent Smith said, grinning menacingly. "Just come with me, and no harm will come to you."

"You want to talk about no *harm*?" Meeka yelled. "All you have been doing is trying to harm us!"

"I see we are doing this the hard way. Very well," Agent Smith touched his earpiece and said, "Come in."

Armed agents swarmed in through the glass and front doors, each grabbing the arms of one of the kids. Macy and Opal were each picked up by an agent, and they were all pushed outside.

The minute they exited the door, they spotted Delphi struggling and doing her best to make the lives of the two agents holding her difficult. She saw them too and breathed a sigh of relief, but that relief was short-lived as she remembered the guns pointed in their direction.

Quinn and Asher fought the agents holding them. Quinn elbowed one in the face, and Asher kicked at their shins until more came to the aid of the ones they fought off from pure adrenaline. They were overpowered and forced into compliance.

"Hold on, hold on," August said, his hands up in surrender as an agent pushed him. "Would you cut that out?" he yelled at the agent. "Gee, you people need to learn some hospitality. I mean, what is this? You FBI people— Remind me, what does FBI stand for?"

An agent rolled his eyes but answered nonetheless. "Federal Bureau of Investigation. Now keep moving."

As they were pushed into a line, shoulder to shoulder, August said, "Federal Bureau of Investigation, you say? Sounds more like Federal Bureau of Injustice to me. Anyway—"

"Shut it!" a man holding a rifle yelled, cutting him off.

August shut up, and Delphi stopped struggling, glaring daggers at the people surrounding her.

"Trust me, hurt any of us, and you will regret it," Meeka threatened.

"You guys look pretty roughed up already. There will be no need to hurt you if you just cooperate," General Brooks warned, looking at the split lip that an agent had just given Quinn and the bruises and scratches the gang had accumulated on their journey to that point.

"*Bovis stercus,*" Asher cursed.

"I'd like to make a small amendment to what the General just said," Agent Smith remarked. "We *will* hurt you if you *don't* cooperate. I sensed some confusion on the subject."

Delphi took that moment to break away from the agents

restraining her. Spencer was standing right in front of Delphi. He grabbed at her, but she quickly curled her hand into a fist. All her adrenaline and frustration built up into that one moment. She punched him square in the face. There was a small *crack,* and he stumbled back ever so slightly. Quinn's jaw dropped as he looked back and forth between Delphi and Spencer.

Blood streamed from Agent Smith's nose as he grabbed at her again and caught her arm, squeezing so tightly she was sure it would leave a mark. She looked up at his face to see how much damage she had done. His nose looked a little crooked, and blood was still flowing out of it. Her knuckles were red from the impact, but she didn't care. She was sick of this guy. They all were.

The rest of the gang stood there, stunned.

"Damn," Meeka said, impressed.

"And this, folks, is why the bully transferred schools," Asher said, smiling slightly while still struggling against the agents holding him.

"*Vescere bracis meis!*" Opal cursed at Spencer.

"*Opal!*" Meeka said, surprised.

"What did she say?" Quinn asked Asher.

"Eat my shorts," he answered.

"What?" Quinn asked incredulously.

"It's a much worse curse in Vernaculus," Asher replied.

"No more funny business!" Agent Smith yelled, holding the crooked bridge of his nose to try to stop the blood flow.

He pushed Delphi back towards the two men who were previously holding her. She fell into them with a grunt. They caught and steadied her before taking out a pair of handcuffs and clamping them around her wrists. The rest of the agents followed suit, and each fastened a pair of handcuffs on one of the kids. The cool metal cut into their skin the more they resisted, but that didn't stop them from refusing to submit entirely.

"How did you even find us?" Quinn asked.

"You really should be leerier of the kinds of transactions you make," Agent Smith said, holding up Quinn's credit card.

"Won't be making that mistake twice," Quinn practically growled.

"Get them into the car," Agent Smith ordered. "And make sure they ready the jet. We'll be there in about five hours."

The group was prodded into the back of a large black van. Once they sat down inside, the door was slammed shut. The driver climbed into the front seat and closed his own door. The vehicle gave a jolt as it started down the road, back to Salerno, where the jet was waiting to bring the kids back to the U.S.

"*Ita et nos sumus damnatorum,*" Asher cursed again.

"English, please," Quinn grumbled.

"We. Are. So. Damned," Delphi repeated in English, sounding defeated.

"We can't just sit here and not do anything," Meeka said while comforting Macy and Opal.

"Well, we're a bit tied up at the moment," August replied, holding up his bound wrists.

"What *can* we do? They caught us. It's over," Fitz sighed.

"It can't just be over," Meeka said. "It can't."

"I'm scared," Macy said, looking up at Meeka and then towards Quinn. "I want to go home."

"Me too," Opal agreed, curling up between Asher and Meeka.

"If it's not over, what do we do?" Asher asked.

"You'll do nothing," an agent said from the row in front of them. "You will sit there like good kids and do as you're told."

"We have to keep our voices down," whispered Delphi so their babysitters couldn't hear her.

"Anyone got a plan?" Quinn asked, looking around.

Everyone shook their heads, but an idea dawned on Meeka's face.

"My hairpins," she whispered. "If we can get them out of my hair, we can pick the locks on these handcuffs."

"Assuming that works, what then?" Quinn asked.

"It worked on the chest holding the orb, so it should work on these," Meeka said, and then a look of concentration crossed her face. "And then... I don't know what to do then."

"Okay, so we get free hands and then jump out of a moving van," August said. "Ooh, that rhymes. *Free hands then jump out of moving van*," he whispered in a sing-song voice.

"That's not necessarily a complete rhyme," Delphi pointed out, but August kept humming his tune anyway.

"We can't jump out of the van. Those guys up front will surely catch on before we can all get out, plus we would also need to unlock the door. Not to mention, Macy and Opal would have trouble jumping out of a *stationary* van, and we're moving about sixty miles per hour," Meeka said.

"Well, we have to stop eventually, right? Maybe we could

make a break for it then," Asher thought out loud.

"But there's no way these people are going to take their eyes off of us for one second," Delphi countered.

"Knock out the driver and borrow the van?" August whispered.

"You watch way too many movies," Asher replied. "They are all armed, and the minute this van veers off course, we'll find ourselves in yet another car chase."

"But we beat them last time," Quinn said.

"Yeah, but you knew the area. This is a whole other country," Delphi contended.

"Fitz could hack the plane?" August guessed.

"With *what*?" Fitz asked.

"And if he did hack it, we would go down with it. Let's please stop trying to repeat our past experiences and figure this out," Meeka said.

"We *might* have a way of getting out of these handcuffs, we can't jump from the moving van, we can't steal the van, we can't hack the plane, we can't sneak away, and they will have eyes on us this whole time. That about sums it up, right?" asked Quinn.

"You forgot the part where they're armed, and we're not," Asher added.

"Oh, yeah, that too," Quinn said.

"I hate to admit this, but I think we're at a dead-end," Meeka said with a worried expression.

"We can't be. We did not come all this way to be at a 'dead-end.' We have to keep fighting!" Delphi exclaimed.

"If we keep fighting, we're putting ourselves in more

danger. Our priority right now is to make it out alive. I won't let us put ourselves, let alone the little ones, in any more trouble," replied Meeka.

"I'm not giving up," Delphi said sternly.

"I'm done putting Opal and Macy in danger. I don't want to risk them getting hurt."

"They're in danger already! You think if we cooperate, they are just going to let us go live happily ever after?" Delphi retorted.

"No, I don't think that. But cooperating is better than having a gun held to a seven-year-old's head. Even if it's just to intimidate us, accidents happen, and I won't let one of those accidents injure us any further," Meeka said.

Opal and Macy shivered at the thought of going through any more hurdles.

"I just want to go home," Opal repeated quietly.

"Delphi, Meeka has a point. At least we all will be alive rather than lose someone while trying to fight back," Asher jumped in as he comforted Opal.

"What the heck do they want with us, anyway? We know we don't belong on this planet, but how do they? And wouldn't it just be easier to kill us on the spot instead of dragging us all the way back to the U.S? They must need us for something. Maybe that's where we can find a foothold. That might be where we have a little power over them," Delphi pondered.

"Not to freak anyone out anymore, but what if they don't need *all* of us? What then? That's when we lose any power we think we have," Quinn said. "Macy and I aren't from Esprit like you guys are, and don't forget that there are six of you. How hard could it be for them to use us against each other?"

Delphi groaned. "I'm really getting sick of all of these 'what ifs.'"

"Me too. Our only option is to yield," Meeka said.

Delphi gave her a look.

"At least to buy us some time," Meeka added.

They stayed silent for a while, listening to the few cars on the road whiz past them. There were no windows to look out of and nothing much left to say. They just sat there as hours passed, the illusion of peaceful quiet washing over them like the waves on the beach. But the tide could be deadly.

When the car stopped, it knocked them out of their stupor. The doors were opened, and they were each forced out and onto the jet.

"Let's get a move on," Agent Smith hastened, pushing Delphi forward.

She slapped his hand away. "*Ede faecam!*"

"Pipe down, missy," Agent Smith said. "And don't get any more stupid ideas." He gestured to his nose.

"You'd be surprised," she retorted under her breath. "I've done worse."

"No one cares about your little antics."

"Man, he's asking for another shiner," Asher mumbled.

"What did you say, punk?"

"I said you should probably bite your tongue before you regret it."

"And you should hold your tongue before you lose it. Keep moving."

After being pushed into the bench seats lining the walls of the aircraft, they took off. None of them were too happy to be back in the air again, especially after what happened last time. August broke out into a cold sweat, and Macy's face was panic-stricken when they hit the turbulence of takeoff.

Quinn, noticing his sister's fear, pulled her closer to him. "Hey Mace, it's going to be okay. We're going to be okay."

Delphi turned towards Quinn. What he had just said sounded so familiar; she just couldn't pinpoint why.

The plane finally got to a stable height and stopped shuttering from turbulence. Just like in the van, there were no windows for them to look out of. Probably a good thing. August would have been much worse with a reference point for how high up they were.

The group sat in silence for a while. They were sick of sitting, sick of traveling, and sick of these people. Opal and Macy were getting really antsy, and no one else was any better. They didn't know what to do; they had nothing to say, no plans, absolutely nothing.

The jet flew over the North Atlantic Ocean for hours before it finally reached the U.S. They landed in the middle of a dense forest on a remote landing site. The gang was pushed around and dragged out of the plane and onto solid ground. They were on the roof of a five-story building that reached the height of the trees surrounding them. It blended in so well that they doubted anyone would be able to spot it from the air, and they were so far into the middle of nowhere that they were pretty sure no one would randomly stumble upon it either.

"Where are we?" Fitz asked.

"That is classified information," General Brooks said. "And from here on out, we need you to put these on." She gestured to the blindfolds that an agent was coming forward with.

"What? No way!" Asher said.

"Why do you need to blindfold us?" August asked.

"So that we don't know how to get around the building," Delphi guessed. "So that we don't know how to escape."

"Exactly, and don't forget to cooperate," Agent Smith said before they were each blinded and trapped in darkness.

As they walked through winding corridors and down long halls, they tried to keep their bearings and map out the place. Still, it was almost as if they were following the most obscure and long paths to their destination.

Eventually, they came to a stop. The group could hear the clicking of keys on a keyboard and a few other noises before being prodded back into walking forward.

"This definitely feels illegal," August said as he was pushed into the chair closest to the door and relieved of his handcuffs and blindfold. His blonde hair was angled in odd directions as the fold was taken off.

Fitz was prodded into a chair next to August, followed by Macy, Opal, Meeka, Asher, Delphi, and Quinn. They were also alleviated of their bindings and blindfolds.

August played with his hair a little while Fitz nervously wrung his hands. Macy was curled into a ball in her seat, and Opal was swinging her legs over the end of hers, trying to distract herself. Meeka and Asher both rubbed their wrists, the metal having made dents in their skin. Delphi gripped the edges of her chair to stop herself from lashing out and getting them into more trouble, and Quinn rubbed the back of his neck, trying to think of something to do.

Agent Smith walked over to Quinn. "Nervous, kid?" he whispered.

Quinn kept his head down in an act of defiance.

"Hey, kid. You look at me when I'm talking to you," Spencer said menacingly. He hit Quinn's shoulders.

Quinn stayed silent.

"I asked you a question."

Quinn still said nothing.

"You know, kid, your parents were the same way, always so stubborn, those two."

Quinn slowly raised his head. "What did you just say?" Quinn asked, unable to be silent any longer.

"Oh, you mean the part about your parents? Yeah, I knew them. Great people, incredibly brave. The day your parents died was a painful day indeed. Remington and Ava, they fought so hard, but in the end... How would they feel if they knew that you had dragged not only yourself but also your little sister into this mess? If I may speak for them, I would say they would be pretty disappointed."

"*YOU BASTARD! SHUT UP!*" Quinn shot to his feet, now at eye level with Spencer. "*SHUT UP! YOU HAVE NO RIGHT TO SPEAK FOR THEM! MY PARENTS WERE GOOD PEOPLE WHO WOULD NEVER ASSOCIATE THEMSELVES WITH AN ASSHOLE LIKE YOU!*"

"Sit back down!" Agent Smith demanded, pushing Quinn

back into his seat.

Quinn stole a glance at Delphi's anxious expression. Her eyes were wide, and her expression was a mix of 'please beat him up' and 'be careful, we don't want to make things worse.' The latter seemed to win out, and Quinn obligingly slumped back into his seat.

"Stay here and be quiet. I will be back in a moment," Agent Smith said, grinning at the reaction he had gotten from Quinn.

The moment the door closed, Delphi felt like screaming. This was her flash, except this time, she wouldn't be sucked back to reality. This *was* reality. Quinn had been right. Her flashes *did* show scenes of the future. Everyone else shuffled uncomfortably. They must have recognized the room from the picture she drew.

Suddenly, an urge of panic arose over Delphi. It felt almost like déjà vu, but worse, more profound somehow. Her breathing intensified, her thoughts running rampant. The room felt warmer than before.

"I can't do this," she whispered.

"Delphi, what's wrong? Are you okay?" Meeka asked as she looked over to Delphi. She saw her struggling to control her emotions, enhancing Meeka's concern.

"Stop! Stop! Stop!" Delphi repeated as she felt an unwanted presence in her mind.

She shook her head in a failed attempt to dislodge her inner turmoil. Something was wrong. If she focused hard enough, she could feel this one blurry spot in the back of her mind, an impenetrable barrier where no thoughts flowed. It was just... dark.

"This can't be real..."

"Delphi!" Meeka called out, trying to get her attention. No luck.

"Her flash! Meeka, this is her flash. This is real," Quinn interjected. "I think she's having a panic attack."

"Make it stop! I want to go home!" Delphi continued to panic, shaking her head.

Quinn, who was sitting closest to Delphi, grabbed her hand. "Focus on my hand. It'll be okay. We will be okay."

Delphi's demeanor instantly changed, regaining control over herself. She remembered back to her flash and this exact moment. She had replayed it over in her mind thousands of times since it had happened. Every word, every gesture was memorized. It was Quinn, the one who calmed her, made everything seem okay. He was the one in her flash. Somehow, she relaxed as she focused on his hand. She went from hyperventilating to calm, slow breaths. She loosened the tension in her body as she looked around the dark room. Delphi could only glimpse everyone's concerned, scared expressions through the shadows. Soon enough, she locked eyes with Quinn but was left speechless as she tried to collect her thoughts.

"So, it was you?" she asked, her voice cracked and quiet.

"What?" Quinn replied, giving her a concerned but soothing expression.

"It was *you*." Delphi repeated.

"Delphi, we need you to explain," Asher jumped in with utter confusion.

"I—I didn't think—I thought my imagination was just—I mean, I knew I was a little crazy, but... I can see the future?" Delphi stuttered. "But it's all so... *cynical.*"

"Well, we aren't exactly going through a period of sunshine and sparkles, now are we, beautiful?" August remarked.

"Not now, August," Meeka interjected, barely noticing what he said and focusing more on Delphi. "Maybe if you could control it, you could see whatever part of the future you want. Maybe you could see a way we can get out of here."

"I don't think that's how it works. At least it doesn't feel like that. It comes so randomly and without warning. I feel so disconnected from it, like it's not even... I don't know how to explain it," Delphi replied, still squeezing Quinn's hand.

Quinn looked up at her. She had a tighter grip than he had imagined, but he didn't want to pull away. "You don't need to explain it. I just need you to be okay." He spoke in a hushed tone that instilled something in her; determination, maybe.

Quinn's eyes were like endless pools of black in the darkness of the room. Instead of finding this daunting, though, Delphi found safety hidden there, someplace to escape and hide, a place to be okay.

He looked back at her, the blue in one of her eyes barely visible, the gray in the other misty, swirling almost in concentration. Delphi was the first to break away, and remembering how Quinn had winced from her tight grip in her vision, she also released his hand. Something in his face changed the minute she let go. He actually looked disappointed.

Chapter 15

Shoot

After a long stretch of silence, the group noticed movement from the guards watching over them.

"Listen up. We will be locking you all in here for a short period to interchange guards," one agent said as he opened the door to step out into the hall.

The other guard followed and locked the door behind him.

"Plan, plan, plan, *now*," rushed Meeka.

"Uh," Quinn said, standing up. He looked down at his chair. "What if?" He bent down and broke two legs off the chair and tested them out in his hands. "What if we knock the next two guards out with these?" He handed one to Delphi and kept the other.

"Great! That gets us out of the room, but what then?" August asked.

"We split up," Fitz said.

"Okay, Fitz, you need to handle surveillance. Make it so that no one knows we're missing. Quinn and August should go with you to handle any security there."

"Macy needs to come, too," Quinn said. "She'll be safest with me."

"Fine. We'll also need supplies. Asher can come with me to

do that. Meanwhile, Delphi and Opal should find the exit, the best one, the first one. It doesn't matter. After Asher and I gather supplies, we'll split up. I'll go and try to find a pattern to the way the guards move, find an opening to get us out of here. Asher will do the same and join Delphi and Opal in search for exits."

"The guards carry a few helpful items, too," Delphi pointed out. "We knock them out and take their key cards, guns, and radios."

"Okay, Fitz and Delphi will take the keycards, Quinn and Asher will take the guns, and Delphi and I will have walkie-talkies. Once you guys," Meeka pointed at Quinn, August, and Fitz, "conk out the guys in the surveillance room, you can take their walkies. We'll turn ours to channel three and hope that these agents don't accidentally tune in."

They heard a shuffle of footsteps, and Delphi and Quinn ran to their places by the door. There was a beep, and the door swung open. Meeka turned Opal and Macy around to shield them from the violence. Quinn hit the first guard right on the forehead, knocking him out as planned. Delphi hit the next guard with a loud crack, snapping the leg of the chair over his head. Together, they dragged the guards into the room and retrieved the already discussed items. Meeka found an extra keycard in the pocket of one of the guards and shoved it into her own pocket.

The group rushed out of the room and closed the door behind them. It automatically locked them out into the brightly lit hallway, a stark contrast to the dark room. They blinked a few times to regain their eyesight and, without a word, split off into their teams.

Delphi and Opal went one direction to find an exit, Quinn, August, Fitz, and Macy another, and Meeka and Asher went down the last hallway.

✳✳✳

Quinn, Fitz, August, and Macy rushed through the halls, hiding from cameras and maneuvering their way around guards to try to find the surveillance room. Quinn skidded to a stop behind a wall, hearing the voices of two agents conversing with each other. August and Macy stopped abruptly behind him. Fitz almost toppled over into the other hallway, right in front of the agents, but Quinn stopped him first and signaled for them all to be quiet.

"Has the park been closed?" asked one agent.

"Yes, except..." the other agent started.

"Except?"

"Except the team of scientists running tests on the ecosystem of the park."

"Why haven't they been directed out with everyone else?"

"They are refusing to leave, and we can't exactly tell them that the weather isn't looking too good; they are testing climate rates."

"Find another way to get rid of them, then."

"They are on the other side of the park, they haven't been

permitted access to any of the restricted sections, and we don't want to arouse any kind of suspicion."

"Just make sure they stay away from this area; we —"

A voice turned on over the walkie-talkies. "Agents Carlyle and Jacobs to the surveillance room."

"Great, I'm on surveillance. We'll talk more about this later," said what must have been either Carlyle or Jacobs, walking away.

"Jackpot," August whispered.

The other agent nodded and walked in the direction of the group hiding behind the wall.

Quinn mouthed a few curse words before pushing the rest of them into a room that Fitz quickly opened with his keycard.

Nearly escaping, August opened the door and peeked outside. "All clear."

They exited the room and went into the hallway that the two agents had been talking in. There was one camera high up on the wall that they stuck close to, avoiding being seen.

"He must have gone this way," Fitz said, pointing in the direction the agent had just left.

"Then let's go," Quinn replied.

They ran down the hall and saw the agent at its end, turning into another corridor.

"How big is this place, anyway?" August grumbled as they snuck behind the agent.

Eventually, the agent turned into a room labeled 'Surveillance' and shut the door behind him.

"Here we are," Quinn said.

Fitz opened the door with his key card, and everyone got

out of the doorframe.

The security in the room all looked towards the doorway.

"Who's there?" one of them asked, his hand closing around the gun in its holster.

The man walked into the door frame, and Quinn knocked him out with the butt of his gun. August took the agent's gun, and they both stepped into the room. Two other agents were sitting in chairs in front of the surveillance televisions.

"Stand up," Quinn commanded.

The guards did as they were told, hands up. One of them glanced at his occupied holster.

"Don't even think about it, or I swear I'll shoot," Quinn said sternly.

His eyes were a vivid blazing navy blue, his expression dark, but there was something unsure about it. The agents sensed his uncertainty and rapidly pulled out their guns. They shot, but August dragged Quinn behind the chairs for cover. They both fell to the hard ground, August slamming his head in the process. His face twisted with pain and his vision went blurry. He blinked it away and sat up.

"I think this guy is starting to wake up!" Fitz yelled from the corridor.

"A little busy!" August yelled back.

He leaned out from behind his chair and shot at one of the guards. He missed the first time but nailed him in the foot on the second. Quinn followed suit and shot the walkie-talkie that the other guard was reaching for, breaking it.

Out in the hall, the agent groaned and opened his eyes. Fitz did the first thing that came to mind and kicked the agent in the groin. The man groaned louder and hit his head back onto the ground.

Inside the room, August kept his gun pointed at the guard he had shot in the foot while Quinn got out from behind his chair and shot the gun that the other agent was holding. The agent dropped it but didn't retreat. Instead, he pursued Quinn, striking him hard in the stomach. Quinn doubled over but didn't back down. He returned it with a punch to the face, dazing the guard. The guard struck back and elbowed Quinn in the head. The guard went to hit Quinn again, but Quinn deflected the hit, turning it onto his opponent. He kicked the agent's kneecap, and the man fell to his knees. Quinn took out his gun and knocked the agent out like the one still lying in the doorframe. August came over and unarmed the other wounded guard.

"What the heck, dude?" August asked, looking at the knocked-out guard.

"My parents were—" Quinn broke off but regained his composure fast enough for it to go unnoticed, "were in the army. Taught me a few tricks."

"I'll say."

"You can come in now!" Quinn yelled to Fitz and Macy outside the room.

They walked in and took in all the damage.

"Are you okay, Quinn?" Macy asked her brother, looking at the grimace of pain on his face.

"Yes, I'll be okay and nice shot, August," Quinn said, turning towards him.

"Yeah, well, I was aiming a little higher, but this works,

too," August said, smirking. "And I've watched enough movies to know that you don't have to shoot to kill to render them useless."

They dragged the unconscious agent out of the doorframe and into the room, shutting the door behind them. Quinn and August kept watch over the incapacitated guards while Fitz sat down in one of the chairs and started typing on a keyboard. They didn't know if there was another way to access the camera feed, so Fitz found a way to take videos of the halls as they were now and kept them replaying.

Quinn grabbed the guns and holsters from the guards, handing one to August, keeping one, and giving the other to Fitz. "You're going to need something to protect yourself."

Surprised, Fitz looked up at him and took the holster, securing it around his waist. "Thanks." Then he pulled up the fake video on the last screen. "We're all set, but we won't be able to see anyone."

Quinn took a walkie-talkie off one guard, turned it to channel three, and spoke into it, "Cameras are offline."

✳✳✳

"Asher, let's go," Meeka said, listening to Quinn's message over the walkie-talkie.

Grabbing Asher's hand, she sprinted down the hall. They found a door labeled 'Supplies' at the end of the next corridor and whipped it open. Hustling inside, they quickly closed the door.

"Grab those plastic bags," Meeka instructed, pointing at a box full of them.

They filled the bags with flashlights, rope, water bottles, duct tape, and anything else that they could carry. Their adrenaline pumped fiercely as they rushed to find any last-second items.

Within about three minutes, they had everything they could take. They were set to fulfill the next step of the plan. It was time to split up.

Asher went to step out the door, but Meeka stopped him, grabbing his hand.

"Asher, wait," she started. "What if this goes wrong? We might end up—"

"I have no clue how this will turn out, but we'll see each other soon," Asher said.

He repositioned his hand so that he was grabbing Meeka's pinky finger with his own. "Promise me one thing, Meeka. Be careful. I know you're going to try to protect everyone else, but make sure you protect yourself, too. I can't risk losing you."

"I'll do my best, but with everything going on, I can't make that kind of promise," Meeka replied.

"You better promise. I can't actually be with you to make sure you're safe, so I kind of really do need you to make that a promise."

Meeka sighed, "I promise to try my best. I can't 'be careful' when we're the ones instigating the danger."

Asher laughed nervously. "You're right. Just, I don't want, you know—"

"I know, Asher." Meeka adjusted her hand to be fully secured with his.

"Every time I think about it, it makes me sick to my stomach." He winced, trying to block the wave of negative thoughts flooding his mind.

"I couldn't let that happen to any of us." Meeka looked to the ground. "I just want to go home."

"Me too, but I don't think home will feel the same once we get there." He looked around the room, then back to their intertwined hands. "Some of it might feel worse—" He squeezed her hand. "But some of it could possibly be better."

The moment was over too soon. There was a change in energy in the room as they realized it was time for their departure. Meeka quickly put down the bag of supplies in her other hand and swiftly wrapped her arms around Asher. Asher reacted almost instantaneously, this time not awkwardly hesitating.

"Everything will be okay," Asher said reassuringly as he held Meeka tighter.

Meeka finally pulled away and raised herself to the tips of her toes, placing her hand on Asher's face. Leaning in, she gave Asher a quick kiss on the cheek and slowly brought her heels back down to the floor. An eternal pause filled the room as they locked eyes. Asher's mouth was slightly ajar, but his facial expression quickly switched to a look suffused with radiance and motivation.

"That's a 'just in case' for all of our 'what ifs.' Please stay safe," Meeka said.

"Until we meet again, M'lady," Asher smiled and opened the door.

✳✳✳

Delphi and Opal skidded to a stop in front of a large door.

"Let's try this one," Delphi said, opening it a crack.

She looked through it to find yet another room.

"Ugh!" she groaned. "We've checked about twenty doors already!"

"We have to keep going," Opal encouraged, grabbing Delphi's hand and walking towards another hallway.

They walked up to another door. Delphi went to grab the handle, but the door flew open. She grabbed Opal, and they squished behind the open door. Holding her breath, Delphi listened to the agents' footsteps disappear to another part of the building.

She let out a long sigh. "That was close."

Opal nodded in agreement.

They raced down six more corridors and tried thirteen more doors before reaching one at the end of the hall.

"Cross your fingers," Delphi said to Opal, swiping the key card and cracking the door. This room, unlike most of the others, was occupied. It was filled with computers, but only a couple of researchers. In one corner, there was a screen showing the feed from the security cameras. Delphi quickly closed the door.

"Good thing Fitz hijacked the cameras," Delphi mumbled.

"Yeah, or we would have been screwed."

Delphi jumped and almost shrieked but stopped herself when she turned to look at who had spoken.

"Holy," she hissed. "Asher, you jerk."

"Nice to see you, too. Took me forever to find you. How's it coming?" Asher asked.

"Oh yeah, it's going great. Searched about thirty different halls already and haven't found a single exit."

"Oh man, we just have to keep looking. This place is a building, not a maze. It probably has more than one way out," Asher replied.

"I'd probably be better at a maze," Delphi grumbled.

They walked down the next corridor and checked a few more doors. When they opened the third door down the hall, they found a staircase.

"That might explain the 'no doors' thing," Asher said, closing the door behind them as they entered the room.

"But there aren't any windows. Of course, we could be in a basement, but maybe this building just doesn't have a lot of windows in general," Delphi thought aloud.

"So, which is it? Up or down?" Asher asked.

"Or split up again," Delphi added.

"I don't know if that's a good idea. Sure, we might be able to cover more ground, but what if we run into trouble?"

"Meeka's alone right now," Delphi pointed out.

"Yeah, and I really wish she wasn't. Please, Delphi," Asher

pleaded.

"Fine. Come on. Let's go up."

They started to sprint up the steps.

"Hey, guys," Delphi said into the walkie-talkie. "We found a staircase. It looks like there are a few more floors to check."

"Copy that," Quinn replied.

"Is Asher with you?" Meeka asked.

"Yup, right here," Asher said into the walkie-talkie.

"Good, just making sure you made it," Meeka replied

"Sweet, we'll check in soon," Delphi said, ending the conversation.

They made it to the next floor and stopped.

"I still don't see any windows," Delphi said, peeking down the corridor.

"Let's try one more level," Asher said, turning back to the steps but stopping abruptly when he found someone blocking his path.

"I don't think so." General Brooks stood there, as solid as a brick wall. "I don't *want* to hurt you, you know."

Asher and Delphi scoffed at the same time.

"I can tell you don't believe me."

"You think?" Delphi asked as Asher backed up, shielding his sisters and reaching for his gun.

"You don't understand. We just want to help you. You just don't make it easy." Cassidy watched as Asher's hand slowly crept towards his gun.

"How exactly is this helping us?" Delphi asked, pushing down her brother's protective arm in front of her and moving towards Cassidy. "All you've been doing for the past *week* is trying to hurt us."

"I do not agree with Agent Smith's methods, nor do I enact them. Let me ask you this: have any of my troops actually hurt you?"

"That doesn't mean you won't hurt us in the future," Delphi pointed out.

General Brooks's mouth set into a grim line. "I think it's time for you kids to return to the safety of that room."

"*Safety?*" Asher asked.

"If one of Smith's agents finds you out here, you can be sure that you won't come out of it unharmed. Meanwhile, all I'm asking is for cooperation."

"But what are we cooperating with? You haven't given us any information, yet you expect us to trust you," Delphi said, covertly turning the dial on her walkie-talkie to change the channel. If they got caught, she didn't want these people to be able to communicate with her friends.

"Not trust, cooperation," General Brooks corrected. "They are two different things."

"Thanks for the vocabulary lesson, but there is no way in *infernum* we are that stupid," Asher replied, grabbing Delphi's arm to pull her back.

She stepped back a few spaces and whispered to Asher, "I believe this is the part where we run."

They gave each other a knowing glance before whipping around and sprinting straight into a wall of agents. The collision knocked them back as they skidded to a stop. The determination on their faces was replaced by disbelief and then anger at their horrible luck.

"I feel like a complete idiot right now," Delphi whispered. "All that talking was just her waiting for backup."

"Actually, it wasn't," Cassidy said, crossing her arms and glaring at the row of agents.

Agent Smith broke through the line. "Sorry, am I interrupting something? Giving out some motherly advice to some kids, maybe?"

General Brooks glared at him. "Here's some advice. You and your faulty circus troupe stay out of this."

"No can do. The delinquents got out of the room. We're here to bring them back. Hope you don't mind if we skip the chit-chat session, then." Agent Smith lunged for and grabbed Opal.

"Ow! Let go of me! Ah!" Opal screamed and kicked as Agent Smith dragged her away from the murderous glares of Asher and Delphi.

"You're hurting her!" Cassidy yelled at Agent Smith. "You act like some barbarian instead of a professional."

"A professional what? Murderer?" Delphi asked, moving towards her sister, with Asher close behind.

"If that's how you need to see me, then go ahead. If you don't follow orders willingly, maybe you will out of fear," Spencer replied.

"Do you hear yourself, Spencer? You sound like some deranged lunatic. Put the child down and handle this in a civilized manner," General Brooks said.

"What do they know about our 'civilized' ways? They're *aliens*, dammit!" Agent Smith retorted while Opal continued to struggle in his grasp.

"You're mad," Asher spat, not moving any closer out of fear of what might happen to Opal if he did.

"Well, maybe that's just what we've needed. It's working, is it not? Now, I'll hang on to little Opal for a while. You two just follow us back to the room." Agents moved around Delphi and Asher to escort them back.

"Oh, and, just for safety measures, drug them," Agent Smith commanded.

Two agents walked up behind Asher and Delphi with wet rags so quickly that they had no time to react. The cloth had a terrible, cloying smell, and, in seconds, they had suffocated in its scent. They collapsed to the floor, absent from the world around them and oblivious to Opal's screams of terror.

***

Meeka dashed from hall to hall, trying to scope out the guards' patterns. She hid in corners when necessary and ran as fast as possible to get to other spots. She carefully observed which guards stood where and where they would move to.

Meeka kept tabs on when she thought would be the safest moments to access specific halls, relaying the information back to the surveillance room on her walkie.

"Okay, guys. There seem to be a lot of blank spots on patrol throughout the hallways. Establishing a pattern is proving difficult. Still haven't found any windows; going to try another floor."

"Sounds good," Quinn replied.

It took a few turns before Meeka found a hallway with a staircase. She ran down a few flights and opened the door. Meeka gasped as she saw the number of people patrolling the hallway. She quickly closed the door as quietly as possible.

"I think I might have found something," Meeka whispered into her walkie-talkie. "Hall E5, lots of security, still no windows. I'm going to check it out."

"How do you suppose you are going to do that? You can't just walk in," Quinn replied.

"Impersonate a guard?" Meeka suggested.

"Uniform?" Quinn retorted.

Meeka groaned quietly.

"Crawl through the air vents?" August asked.

"None and no," Meeka replied. "Not doing that. Why don't I just wait it out and see if there are time intervals on the switch of the guards?"

"That could take hours. We don't have that kind of time," Quinn replied.

"It's our best plan," Meeka retorted.

Quinn hesitated before answering again. "Okay, yes, fine, do it."

"Didn't really need your approval, but thanks," Meeka said, ending the conversation.

She stayed hidden behind the door to the stairway for a few minutes before she heard faint footsteps pounding on the stairs far above her.

"Aw, crud," she mumbled.

The footsteps were getting louder.

She opened the door a little more to see if the guards had moved at all. They shuffled a little, and a few checked their watches, but no one left.

Seconds turned into minutes as she waited, waited.

The footsteps stopped on a floor above her, and she heard a shout of orders.

"Come on," she whispered. "Come on, get a move on, let's go."

Finally, one of the security guards spoke up. "It's time to switch. We need to move to the third floor."

He rounded up all the guards, and they went down a corridor and disappeared from Meeka's view.

She breathed a sigh of relief and quickly opened the door to step out. The halls were now empty and eerily quiet. She took out her keycard and started checking the doors. A wave of fresh air hit her on the second try as the door opened. She had found the exit.

Suddenly, there was a voice barking commands. Meeka had been so caught up in her search that she hadn't heard the footsteps resume. She rapidly closed the door and burst down a different hallway.

When she could hardly hear the voices of the new guards, she stopped and caught her breath.

Panting, Meeka clicked the button on her radio. "Guys—the exit—I found it—I found the exit," she said between gulps of air. "It's on the bottom floor. There's no basement. Just follow the stairs down, and you'll be there. Depending on which stairwell you use, you may end up on the other side of the building. Just find hall E5."

"Okay, we're on our way," Quinn replied over the walkie-talkie.

✳✳✳

A few minutes later, Quinn, August, and Macy were dashing across the hall towards Meeka.

"Have you guys seen —" but Meeka was cut off by a herd of guards starting to enter the area. "Out, now!"

Quinn, August, Macy, Fitz, and Meeka ran out of the building. They sprinted towards the woods but stopped for a second when they heard a guard yelling.

"Hey! Stop!" he said and then spoke into his walkie-talkie. "The kids are escaping. What are our orders?"

Inside, Agent Smith heard the question. He clicked on his walkie-talkie and spoke a single word. "Shoot."

CHAPTER 16

AKIKO

The guards heard the order, and bullets began to fly as the kids started to run again.

They ran as fast as their legs could carry them. Panting, sprinting.

Faster, faster.

Bursts of adrenaline coursed through their veins.

Faster, faster.

General Brooks burst through the facility's doors, followed closely behind by Agent Smith.

"*HOLD YOUR FIRE!*" General Brooks ordered.

Her troops stopped shooting.

"What are you *doing?*" Agent Smith yelled. "They're getting away! Keep firing!"

"*THEY TAKE ORDERS FROM ME, NOT YOU!*" General Brooks yelled at Spencer.

"Well, it seems their *General* is getting cold feet," Agent Smith retorted.

"Stand down!" General Brooks ordered her troops. She turned to Spencer. "I didn't sign up for any of this crap. You are literally battling kids! And guess what? They're winning."

Agent Smith stared General Brooks dead in the eye as he

lifted the walkie-talkie up to his mouth.

"Agents, fire."

Swarms of agents filled the area and started shooting their guns.

"You know our orders," General Brooks growled.

"To hell with the orders," Agent Smith retorted. "If we are going to win this battle, we have to fight dirty."

"You may win this battle but you'll lose the war," General Brooks signaled to her troops to follow her.

They walked into the building, and a few moments later, the sound of a plane taking off filled the air. General Brooks was gone.

Bullets flew through the sky in the direction of the forest. One whizzed through the air and hit a tree trunk, blowing sections of it to bits right next to Meeka.

She looked back in shock. More gunshots followed, and they all glanced at each other in silent agreement, faster.

Faster, faster.

They panted, breathing in and out, their lungs stinging for air. Fear haunted every excruciating step. Macy started to stumble while tears filled her eyes, causing her vision to go blurry. Meeka gave her a slight push to encourage her to move forward while still shielding her from bullets. Soon enough Macy started to sob as she ran faster, her adrenaline kicking in again. She had reached her breaking point, filled with fear, anger, and pain. There was so much pain in her expression.

More shots fired.

Quinn reached to pick Macy up. His fingertips had just touched her shoulders when a bullet came hurtling towards him. It whistled past his ear, narrowly missing him.

He grabbed onto Macy's shoulders but was struck by a sudden flare of pain in his shoulder. He let go of Macy and fell to the ground, yelling in agony. The world seemed to stop spinning.

He didn't want to look down, didn't want to see the blood.

He looked down.

The sleeve of his shirt was completely blown off. His arm was grimy with dirt from the fall, and there was way too much blood. He squeezed his eyes shut and swallowed the lump forming in his throat.

There was a gaping hole in his left shoulder.

The bullet had blasted through him instead of lodging itself inside him. The full force of the pain finally hit him. Tears welled in his eyes as he cried out. Why keep going? After everything, what was the point? A million thoughts rushed through his head, overwhelming him. He was going down an inner spiral. Down, down, down into a dark hole in the back of his mind. He could hide there, away from the pain. But a single thought brought him back to reality; a single thought brought him to his feet.

Make it out alive, get everyone out alive. He thought.

A scream pierced the air as Macy noticed Quinn's blood smeared across his shirt and arm.

Everyone whipped around to see what Macy was screaming at.

Quinn's face was ashen. There was so much blood.

"*BEHIND THE TREES, NOW!*" Meeka yelled.

Everyone pressed their backs against a tree trunk,

shielding themselves from the passing bullets.

"Quinn! What happened?" Meeka yelled over the roaring in her ears.

"He's been shot," Macy said, tears flowing from her big eyes.

The color had drained from Quinn's face, and he was breathing heavily, holding his shoulder to stop the blood flow. He slumped against the tree he was using to obstruct the oncoming bullets.

"We need—" Meeka started but was cut off by the splinter of wood as a stray bullet hit the tree next to her.

"We need to keep going!" Fitz yelled.

August's mouth was set in a grim line, looking at Quinn, but he nodded in agreement with Fitz. Quinn seemed almost ready to pass out as Meeka looked at him again.

"Okay!" she agreed.

Meeka picked up Macy, and they started running again, Quinn lagging a little behind. They kicked up dirt and leaves under them as they ran. Brambles cut at their legs, and branches tore at their faces, but they kept running. Still, their adrenaline rush would only keep them going for so much longer.

Make it out alive. Make it out alive. Keep going. Run, run, run, Go!

They could hardly breathe, could hardly think.

Faster, faster.

They stumbled over logs and ran down hills and through ditches. Out of breath, losing hope, running mechanically. They were numb to the world around them as shots, guns, and bullets seemed to fade.

Everything seemed to fade. The world was quiet. Fitz tripped over a log and fell into the dirt, lacking the strength to pull himself back to his feet.

August stopped to help him but froze. "Listen."

Meeka stopped and put Macy down.

"It's quiet—they stopped—stopped shooting," Meeka said through gulps of air.

Quinn stumbled over to them and crumbled to the ground, coughing up blood.

"*Faex*! Quinn needs help!" Meeka yelped, running over and crouching down next to Quinn.

She gently touched around his wound, which was still gushing blood. He winced and reflexively cried out in pain.

"This is really bad," Meeka muttered. "He's losing so much blood. We need something to wrap his arm in."

"I got this," August said, whipping off his shirt. He walked up behind Meeka and nudged her with his hand. "How about this?"

She snatched the shirt out of his hand, rolled her eyes, and tore a long piece off of it. She handed what was left of it back to August, who put it on again.

"Okay Quinn, I need to apply pressure, so this might be a little uncomfortable," Meeka said.

Quinn's eyes were halfway closed, but he managed a smile-like grimace directed at Meeka. "So—" He groaned and shifted uncomfortably, "What you're saying is that—" He groaned again. "This is going to hurt a lot."

"Pretty much," Meeka said. She put the homemade

bandage under Quinn's arm and brought it up to his shoulder. "On the count of three, I'm going to tighten it, okay? One—" She pulled the bandage tight before she even got to two, and Quinn hollered.

"Sorry," she said softly. "Hey, Delphi, can—" and then she remembered. "We left them," she whispered to herself. "We ran and, oh my God."

The full force of that one sentence hit them.

"No—This can't be—happening right now." Quinn forced the words out in between panting breaths.

"They must have gotten captured. There is no other explanation. What if they got shot down by sir psycho?" Meeka rambled as her panic started to set in. "The worst-case scenario is, is now our reality. Asher was so worried about making sure I was safe, and now he isn't! They could be—"

"Don't even think, let alone say that, Meeka," August interrupted.

"What do you expect? How else do you want me to think? I'm done being *optimistic* because, at this point, that's impractical. This is so damn tiring. Start thinking logically. Our best friends are probably enduring so much agony right now, or worse. Open your eyes, August." Tears started to fill her eyes.

"Meeka," August started.

"The one person who stuck by my side through everything, absolutely everything, might not be alive anymore. The little girl I've been taking care of, protecting, and practically helped raise—"

"That's enough. Stop it right now, Meeka. None of us need

this," Quinn interrupted as he looked over at Macy's terrified expression.

Meeka ignored them. "And him. The one I let in. I let my guard down for the first time. I've been in love with Asher since I was eight. Even through all the danger and risks, I still felt safe with him by our side. He was so worried about not being able to stay with me to make sure I was safe, and here we are. The roles are reversed. I don't know what to do. They were my motivation."

Meeka's eyes stung with overflowing tears as she pulled her knees close to her chest.

There were a few moments of silence, and then, "Him of all human beings in the universe? Him? You know, you were my second choice, but now? Now, I'm a little worried about your mental stability," August said.

"I think we're all worried about her mental stability," Fitz said, looking worryingly at Meeka.

"Excuse me?" Quinn retorted while holding his arm and leaning to look over at August.

"You're excused," he said.

"*Excuse me?*" Quinn repeated.

"What? Got a problem other than your arm?" August asked jokingly, but the usual humor in his voice seemed a little strained.

Meeka looked up from her crouched position on the ground. "Wha—what?"

"I'm just saying you could do a lot better," August said, then mockingly whispered, "If you didn't get the hint, I meant as in me."

Meeka's sorrow turned into anger as she advanced toward August. The fire in her eyes seemed to be battling with the tears.

"How could you just —"

"Woah, woah, woah, easy there, Meeka," August said, cutting her off. "I'm just trying to lighten the mood. I know this stinks, and I mean stinks like *si in cumulum stercore* stinks. You're forgetting Asher's my best friend. We aren't just going to leave them there, we can't, and we won't."

Meeka's eyes were wide with surprise. She never expected August to be the most level-headed person at a time like this.

"Yeah, okay.'' She took a few deep breaths and wiped the tears from her eyes. "Quinn, can you walk?"

"It's my shoulder that's been obliterated, not my legs," Quinn replied stubbornly.

He tried to push himself up but made the mistake of putting weight on his injured arm. He yelled and collapsed back to the ground, lurching over and coughing up everything in his stomach, which wasn't much since they hadn't eaten anything since the night before.

"Okay, looks like mister tough-guy needs some help," August remarked.

"I'm fine, I'm fine," Quinn said, taking deep breaths. "I'm—" He groaned, his face turning even paler.

"You aren't fine, and you need help. I just wish we had a first aid kit, but Asher has the one from the storage room," Meeka said.

"We overheard about some scientists still in the park or something like that. If we can find them, Quinn can get medical help," Fitz suggested.

"Looks like *I* found *you*," said a voice as a man walked out from behind a tree.

He looked about twenty years old, with jet black hair, beige skin, thin almond-shaped mocha brown eyes, and a scar running down one side of his face. Light shone off of his glasses as he walked up to them.

Everyone jumped in surprise at his sudden appearance.

"Aren't you supposed to be on the other side of the park?" Fitz asked.

The guy shrugged. "Technically, yes, but I've never been much of a rule follower. Who are you guys?"

"We're the reason the park is shut down," Meeka replied absent-mindedly.

"What did you do? Blow up a mountain?" He laughed.

"A plane, yes. A building, yes. But not a mountain quite yet. I'll add that to the bucket list. Although the building wasn't technically our fault... Come to think of it, neither was the plane..." August explained.

"What the?" The man said as he looked at the group in shock. Then he spotted Quinn on the ground, bleeding through his makeshift bandage. "He needs serious medical attention. Follow me. I set up camp not far from here." The guy walked over to assist Quinn by holding his arm to restrict movement. "I'm Akiko, by the way. What happened to your arm, buddy?"

"He was shot by the FBI, A—A—key—eye—o!" Macy said.

"Woah, sounds like the FBI really isn't a fan of you guys. And you can call me Aki if it's easier."

They started trudging towards the camp, Quinn groaning every few steps. They didn't speak much for a little while, despite the fact that there was a lot to say.

Eventually, Akiko spoke up in an attempt to break the silence. "So, what's everyone's name?"

"I'm Meeka. Blondey is August. Redhead is Fitz. Wounded boy is Quinn. And this little one is Macy," Meeka said as she signaled to everyone.

"Well, thanks for addressing that. Now the question I think you all know I'm going to ask: Why is the FBI all over you guys, and I kind of want a real answer this time," Akiko asked.

"We honestly have no clue. That's kind of why we're running from them. Ever since we accidentally ended up on Earth—" Meeka paused, realizing how crazy she must have sounded. She let out an exasperated groan. "I know how utterly insane this sounds, but it's the truth. They haven't stopped trying to chase us," Meeka explained.

"*What now?*" Akiko's jaw dropped. "Oh, you guys are still joking, right?"

"No. We don't belong here. We come from a planet called Esprit—"

"*ESPRIT?* You have got to be kidding me. This can't be real."

Akiko's reaction spread an unsettling feeling through the air.

"We're aware of how insane we sound. But from our perspective, it's even crazier to be on a different planet you never knew existed. Try it some time; see how easy it is,"

Meeka said.

"No, no, no. No one has ever mentioned Esprit before. I thought it was just me," Akiko said, struggling for a second to hold Quinn up.

"You're acting like—you know the place," Quinn pointed out, heaving in breaths.

"None of you are going to ever believe this."

"Try me," August retorted.

"What he said," Fitz agreed.

"I'll explain once we're all settled because here we are. Home sweet, uh... camp."

They looked around at the campsite. A huge tent was set up in the center of the clearing with a fire pit next to it. When they went inside the tent, they saw a long table covered in scrap metal and electronic parts. Gadgets, a laptop, and what looked like models of devices were strewn across another smaller table in the corner. A sleeping bag was pushed to one side of the tent as if discarded.

Akiko cleared some of the clutter off of one of the tables and had Quinn sit on top of it. He took out his first aid kit and started aiding Quinn's bullet wound.

"So, you were saying?" Meeka started.

"Right. I, too, am from Esprit. But I came here when I was little. I had this orb that I stole from my grandmother. I believe she stole it from the Esprit Empire to get revenge after being fired from her position. Anyway, I would go back and forth from Esprit to Earth, that is until the orb broke and I was stuck here. I ended up getting adopted in Italy, and ever since, I've been secretly trying to fix the orb," Akiko explained, leaving everyone astonished.

"Well, what a coincidence. The one person we meet happens to be from Esprit too," August said. "It's not just me, right? That's weird."

"Then why isn't the FBI after you too?" Fitz asked.

"No one knew. It was kind of my thing to disappear and randomly show up again. My parents just didn't care. But then, one day, I just never came home. I was eight years old. Obviously, no one ever came after me because here I am. And, honestly, the only thing I wish was different is that my brother had come with me. Being here gave me a new family, one that actually cared. I got an education and made a life for myself here. I worry about what kind of road I would have gone down if I had stayed on Esprit, but my brother was always there to help me out of a bad situation."

"What was his name?" Meeka asked.

"Ronin. We were twins," he said, fumbling with Quinn's bandages.

"Here, let me help with that." Meeka took the bandage from Akiko, and he stepped back to let her work. "This is starting to look worse. You're going to need stitches," she said to Quinn.

Quinn winced when she touched the skin around his wound. "Do whatever you have to."

Meeka searched through Akiko's first aid kit until she produced a needle and surgical thread. "I'll need to sterilize the needle first."

She looked through the first aid kit again and found a packet of wipes. She cleaned the needle and took out another

211

packet to clean the gash on Quinn's shoulder. He grimaced as she gently wiped the tender skin. Next, Meeka threaded the needle and prepared to make the first stitch.

"Uh, have you ever done this before?" Quinn asked, hesitantly.

"I've read about it before."

"That's not the same thing."

"What happened to 'just do whatever you have to,' huh?" Meeka retorted.

"Fine, just do it."

"Do you want a countdown?"

"After last time? No, thank you."

"Okay..." Meeka stuck the needle into Quinn's shoulder, and he tensed up a little. "Relax your muscles. If you keep them tense like that, this will just be more painful."

He nodded and did as she instructed.

Meeka finished stitching him up and broke off the needle and thread. "There, all better."

Quinn looked down at his shoulder. "Thanks."

"No problem."

Chapter 17

Wide Awake

"So, now what?" August asked as he sat down on the floor.

"We need to get Delphi, Asher, and Opal out of that facility," Quinn said, sliding off the table and wobbling. His face was beaded with sweat.

"Woah there," Meeka said. "I agree, but you need your strength before you're going anywhere."

"You can't leave me behind."

"You aren't strong enough," Meeka replied.

"I'll just follow you."

"I can keep him here," Akiko offered.

"I fought a room full of FBI agents. I can take you down easily," Quinn said.

"Are you sure about that?" Akiko said, walking up to Quinn and looking down at him. They would have been the same height if Quinn hadn't been slumping down out of exhaustion.

Quinn stood up to his full height with a lot of effort. "Yeah, I'm sure—"

Meeka cut him off. "Guys! Now is really not the time to see who's more manly or whatever. We have some bigger issues to discuss."

"Yeah, besides, we all know *I'm* the manly one," August

said, pointing at himself.

Fitz faked a cough. "Cough, cough peacocks, cough, cough."

"We won't leave you behind, Quinn, but you do need to rest. We also need to come up with a plan."

"Great, another plan," Fitz said sarcastically.

Everyone turned to gape at him.

Fitz turned the color of his hair to the point where you couldn't see where his forehead stopped and his hairline began. "Did I say that out loud?"

"Yup, you did, dude. And I'm glad someone said it because when have any of our plans actually worked out?" August asked.

"This time, it will," Meeka said confidently, then thought aloud, "We can't go back to the facility without knowing what's going on. That is, unless we want to get caught again. Their defenses will probably be upgraded. Escaping from a heavily secured and guarded FBI facility once is sheer luck. Twice, that's going to take a miracle."

"So, how do we get this information?" Quinn asked, collapsing down onto a bench.

"The walkie-talkies," Meeka replied. "That's it! They should still work from this distance. All we have to do is turn it to their frequency, and we can eavesdrop on everything."

Meeka took the walkie-talkie out of her pocket and changed it to channel two. A familiar voice came on over the intercom.

"Agents, bring the kids to corridor B. We have some visitors to take them back to their planet."

"Was that that screwball, Agent Smith?" August asked.

"I think it was," Meeka replied. "And they're taking the Eves back to Esprit."

"How the hell are we supposed to get there? We have a broken orb and two plastic bags full of random stuff," Quinn said.

"I have an idea," Akiko chimed in. "You guys mentioned that you had an orb. Maybe the parts of your broken orb could help fix mine."

"I mean, it's worth a shot," Fitz said.

Meeka pulled out the orb and handed it to Fitz. Fitz and Akiko walked over to Akiko's work table. They immediately started examining the orbs and fiddling around.

"Okay, while they do that, you guys should get some rest while you can," Meeka said to the others.

"What about you?" Macy asked.

Meeka bent down to be at eye level with Macy. "I'm going to stay outside and make sure you're all safe." She stood back up and addressed the rest of the group. "I'll let you guys know if I see anything."

"Shouldn't you get some rest too?" Quinn asked.

"One more all-nighter can't hurt. Besides, there's still hope for Delphi, Asher, and Opal as long as we're safe. Now sleep, or you're just going to slow us down tomorrow."

Quinn nodded his head, went over to the sleeping bag with Macy, and slowly drifted off to sleep.

Meeka left the tent while Akiko and Fitz were taking apart their orb. She breathed in the fresh, cold air and debated making a fire. She thought that, in the end, smoke would just attract unwanted attention. Meeka sat down on a log and looked around. It was colder than she had felt in a while, but the air was still sticky with the humidity from the day. The moon shone brightly over the forest, and the trees towered high above the clearing.

Meeka jumped at the sound of a twig snapping in the woods. Her breathing intensified. This was going to be a *long* night.

"Calm down," she whispered to herself. "Probably just a squirrel or something."

A few hours and many scares later, there was a rustling in the tent and an exclamation of excitement. Akiko opened the flaps and came out looking exhausted.

"I think we finally got it to work, but we won't know until we test it," Akiko said as he adjusted his glasses.

"Perfect! We can test it first thing tomorrow morning," Meeka replied.

"Yeah, that's the plan. Macy, August, and Quinn already crashed and Fitz is going to bed now too. So, I think you should go and get some rest while I take over the lookout," he suggested.

"No. I'm fine out here. I'm sure you would like to get some sleep after your hectic day."

"I doubt my day was as hectic as yours. Come on and get some shut-eye."

"Again, no. I'd rather stay up and make sure nothing happens."

Akiko took a seat next to Meeka.

"Why not? I know we all just met a few hours ago, but you

can trust me to keep an eye out," said Akiko.

"It has nothing to do with trust. I just won't let myself go to sleep until I know everyone is safe."

"You've been through a lot, huh?"

"You have no idea," she replied.

"Actually, I might. In fact, welcome to the club."

"What club?"

"The club of Esprit outcasts and their honorary Earth members. I'm the president and would like to personally welcome and congratulate you on your expertise in ticking off government officials."

Meeka gave him an odd look.

"Ok, yeah, I know I'm a little off. Lack of sleep and whatnot," Akiko said, readjusting his glasses. "The point is, at least you're not alone. You have a whole group of people rallying behind you. When I got stuck on this planet, I had no one, and being thrown into the foster system can be lonely. You have friends who care about you and will fight by your side."

"If your engineering career doesn't work out, you can always think about motivational speaking," Meeka said, smiling.

Akiko chuckled, "I'm a man of many talents. Well, since you seem insistent on staying here, I'm going to go catch some z's. Night." He nodded at her and went back inside the tent.

Meeka took a deep breath as the lights in the tent went off. A light breeze blew into the clearing, making her shiver.

✳✳✳

A loud rustle in the near distance startled Meeka awake. "*Dautor*," she grumbled to herself as she unstuck leaves from the side of her face.

She looked around the campsite to make sure everything had been left undisrupted.

"So far, so good," she whispered.

She got up and opened the flap to the tent. Walking inside, she noticed everyone was still asleep. Akiko was slumped over a table, Fitz was lying on a bench, August was curled up and drooling on the floor, and Quinn and Macy were on the sleeping bag.

Fitz slowly blinked a few times and lifted his head up. Seeing Meeka, he groggily stood up and grabbed his glasses. "Morning."

"Good morning," Meeka replied.

Akiko groaned and picked his head up off the table. "Well, that was painful. I can't believe I actually fell asleep like this."

Macy yawned in the corner, waking Quinn up. Overnight, some of the color had returned to his face, and he wasn't in as much pain. He touched his bandaged shoulder and got up.

"How are you feeling?" Meeka asked him.

"Still a lot of pain, but a little better."

"It's progress. Maybe once we get to Esprit, we can find some better medical supplies to help it heal faster."

"That would be nice," Quinn said, wincing. "I think this arm is out of commission until then."

"We should get ready," Akiko said. "The sooner we get there, the sooner your friends are saved."

August woke up and looked around. "Did I miss a meeting or something?"

"Only the super important safety precautions. You'll be fine," Akiko teased.

"Ah, no worries. I wouldn't have been listening anyway," August said as he stood up and messed with his hair. "Could I borrow your comb?"

"Uh, sure," Akiko said. "It's right in there." He pointed to a bag on one of the tables.

August combed his hair while everyone else packed up all of their supplies. Fitz brought out the orb, and everyone gathered around it.

"Okay, so Fitz tells me you guys have been dropping this thing in a sink every time you want to get it to work. The only reason that actually works is because of the water. When it comes in contact with water, the orb opens, and you can push the button to go to either Esprit or Earth. We added a safety measure to this one, so no more accidental traveling through the universe happens. Push the button three times in a row, and bam, you're on another planet. We also got rid of the noise it makes once it's opened. Got it?"

Everyone nodded. They walked out of the tent and to a stream near the campsite.

"Ready?" Fitz asked.

A chorus of "yes's" and "yups" echoed through the air as Fitz dunked the orb in the water and brought it back out. It opened to reveal the button, and he pushed it three times.

There was a pause before a burst of light shot out of the orb and enveloped the group, transporting them to Esprit.

CHAPTER 18

ESPRIT

Within moments, the world was shaken, and everything was spinning again. Lights and colors swirled around them right before they were thrown back into the real world. Meeka stumbled as she tried to regain her clear vision. August crashed to his knees; at least he wasn't sprawled on the floor like last time. Fitz also fell to the ground but quickly bounced up to his feet. Quinn and Macy both took hard hits to the sidewalk. Unlike everyone else, Akiko stood firm and unfazed. He quickly rushed to aid an extremely disoriented Macy. Meeka also attempted to help. As the majority of the group recollected themselves rather quickly, Quinn lay on the side of the street for a moment longer, dazed and taking in the new planet. Everything appeared similar to Earth but felt more lively. It wasn't anything like what he imagined. There were no odd-looking creatures, no out of the ordinary activities that stood out. It seemed so civilized. He recovered from his momentary deafness and was quickly overwhelmed with chatter from everyone around them, but he couldn't piece together any of the words.

"Why don't I understand anything anyone is saying?" Quinn called out as he sat up so quickly it looked like he'd been zapped.

"*Oblitus sum dare vobis est,*" Akiko said as he handed a small box to Meeka and then walked over to Quinn, giving him one as well.

"What? I have no clue what you just said," Quinn replied as he took the box.

Akiko gestured to his ears as Quinn opened the box.

"Oh, earpieces." He sighed as he placed one into his ear.

Meeka was off to the side with Macy, helping her place one in her ear.

Once the Russos had the earpieces in, they could understand the world around them.

"Sorry, I should have explained this to you guys earlier. I made the earpieces a while ago. They translate everything we are saying so you hear it in English. And they have built-in microphones, so whenever you speak, it comes out in Vernaculus. So we all can understand."

Quinn nodded but was clearly still a little confused. He tried pushing himself up to his feet but collapsed in pain.

"Out of commission, remember?" August said as he ran over to help him.

Quinn hissed in pain, "Yeah, count my memory jogged."

August helped him up and quickly glanced at Quinn's bandage to ensure it was still intact.

"Guys, where are we?" Meeka questioned.

"Wait, you're on your own planet and don't know where you are? Great way to start this mission," Quinn said sarcastically, still gritting his teeth from the pain.

"Hang on. I know this town," Akiko said. "I used to love

riding the trains through here."

"How far away is The Metropolis from here?" Meeka asked.

"If I remember correctly, I think it's about three or four hours by train," Akiko replied.

"Great! Lead the way to the train station," August said, mockingly bowing and gesturing down the sidewalk.

"Actually, it's this way," Akiko said, turning away from August and heading in the opposite direction.

"Oh, yeah, I definitely knew that," August mumbled as he and everyone else trailed behind Akiko.

They walked for a few minutes before stopping at a large circular building. They got in a ticket line.

"Uh, guys. I just remembered that we don't have any money. We've been using Earth currencies for the past week, but now we're on Esprit, and that stuff is worthless," Meeka said.

"Oh *faex*, you're right." Akiko adjusted the cap on his head. "Let's see, maybe we can steal a currency pecto?"

"What? No!" Meeka argued.

"It's for a good cause," Akiko countered.

"No, no, absolutely not, no."

Everyone looked at her expectantly.

"No," she repeated.

"Don't worry, you don't have to do anything. I know what I'm doing. Just give me five minutes," Akiko said.

"Are you trying to tell me you've done this before?" Meeka's voice raised an octave.

"No, well, yes, I have done this before—"

Meeka hit him with a perturbed expression.

"But what other choice do we have? Either you let me do this, or we're stuck at a train station with no way to rescue your friends," Akiko said.

"Can we find another way?" Meeka pleaded.

"Can you think of *another* way?" Akiko asked her.

She sighed in defeat. "Fine."

"Yes, great. Like I said, five minutes." Akiko turned to head off.

"Hey! I'll help you steal," August called before Akiko left the group.

Akiko quickly covered August's mouth with his hand. "Shut up! What the *infernum* are you doing? You're going to get us caught before we even do anything!" he whispered angrily and let go of August's mouth. "Just stay here. I can handle this."

"I think *someone* needs to work on his team-building skills," August grumbled.

Akiko rolled his eyes and dashed off, leaving the rest of the group behind. He walked into a big crowd of people carrying luggage and heading for the train. He made his way past the conductor and spied a woman holding an expensive handbag and yelling at the terrified staff.

"Bingo," he whispered to himself.

Akiko noticed her angrily putting her wallet back into her handbag. Part of the wallet was peeking out, and Akiko was ready to make his move. He snuck over and casually walked past her, swiftly grabbing the wallet. The woman continued to scold the staff, not noticing the sudden absence of her pocketbook.

Akiko brushed past the woman. "Excuse me," he said softly.

And just like that, his mission was accomplished with no suspicion.

He walked back towards the group and rejoined them in line.

"Told you I'd be quick," he said, smiling and holding up the pecto he had pulled out of the wallet.

"Four minutes and seven seconds, to be exact," Meeka replied, looking at her watch.

"New record." Akiko put the pecto back in the wallet.

They moved up in the line.

"So we buy six tickets, get on the train to The Metropolis where we're pretty sure but not positive they brought the Eves, break into the Empire Building, and rescue them," Meeka said.

"You know, last time we listed things like this, we were in the van heading to that facility where we left Asher, Delphi, and Opal in the first place. Doing it again doesn't really instill positivity in me," Fitz said.

"Right, sorry," Meeka apologized. "I'm just trying to get my thoughts in order."

They made it to the front of the line, where the person at the ticket booth waited.

"What can I help you with?" she asked monotonously.

"We would like to buy six tickets, please," Akiko said and swiped the screen on the pecto.

"Your transaction is complete," she replied. "Your tickets

have been transferred to your pecto." Then she yelled "Next!" to the people behind them.

They walked up to the train conductor, who was waiting to check passenger tickets before boarding.

"Can you please show me your tickets?"

Akiko held up the pecto screen, and the conductor nodded. "Alright, enjoy your trip."

Akiko nodded and led the way to the eighth small passenger car of the train. He pulled open the door and signaled for everyone to enter. They all piled into the compartment. Meeka opened the bench seat and placed their stuff inside. Across from the bench, on the opposing wall, was a map and a pull-down table. Everyone took their seats, their backs leaning against the wall labeled 'Esport,' and the train took off.

"This is so weird. So you all just get your own personal area on your trains?" asked Quinn.

"Yeah, it's for safety and privacy precautions," Fitz responded.

"Better than on Earth, right? Don't have to be crammed into one place with a ton of strangers," Akiko said.

Quinn nodded with a grin.

The train stopped at a few stations before reaching The

Metropolis center station. They got off the train and onto the platform. Maneuvering through the crowds, they managed to get out of the station and into the town.

"So, what's our plan for getting past the security keepers?" Fitz asked as they walked on the sidewalks in the direction of the Empire Building.

"We'll have to distract them or sneak past them somehow," Akiko replied.

"Gah!" Quinn hissed, holding his injured shoulder.

"What's wrong now?" August asked.

Quinn looked down at his arm and unwrapped the tight bandage. The bullet wound looked much worse compared to before. It was oozing yellow purulent, and the surrounding skin was raw and red. Meeka immediately felt his forehead. It was hot and sticky with sweat.

"He has a fever. I think it's an infection. We need to get him to a hospital," she said, looking worried.

"No, it's—I'm—fine, please, we—have to—save them," Quinn said between gasps of air.

"You're not going to be able to save anyone like this. Come on. The nearest hospital is this way," Meeka said, motioning for them to follow her and walking away.

Akiko grabbed Quinn's uninjured arm to help him keep up with her.

They walked past houses, shops, and restaurants before making it to the hospital.

"Akiko should go in with Quinn since he isn't on anyone's radar. The rest of us will wait outside. The less chance of people seeing us, the better," Meeka said.

Once inside, Quinn and Akiko went up to a stand holding a screen.

The message on it read: *Specify your injury and swipe your pecto.*

Akiko typed in *infection* and swiped the stolen pecto. The screen brought him to another page.

What symptoms does the patient show?

He typed in *Fever, Sweating, Oozing, and Raw Skin.*

A sensor beeped, and a doctor came up to them with a wheelchair. "My name is Dr. Arven. Could the patient please sit down? I will be taking you to your room."

Quinn sat down, and Akiko followed him and the doctor down the hall. They turned into another corridor but were stopped abruptly by two security keepers.

They both reflexively put their heads down to hide their faces while the doctor looked at the keepers blocking her path.

"This is a restricted wing. I'm going to have to ask you to leave," said one of the keepers.

"Oh, yes, of course. We'll take the other route to the D wing," Dr. Arven replied, turning the wheelchair around and heading in the other direction.

Akiko looked back in time to see a tall man with brown hair and brown eyes step out of the door that the keepers were guarding.

One of the guards nodded at the man. "Governor Eve."

The man nodded back and headed down the hall that led to the exit.

Akiko lost sight of the man and knitted his eyebrows together in concentration as he mapped out the path the doctor was taking to the D wing.

Finally, they stopped at the door labeled *Room 118.* The doctor rolled Quinn's wheelchair inside, and Akiko followed. Quinn sat down on the bed, and Akiko stood in the corner with his arms crossed. The doctor examined Quinn's shoulder and clucked her tongue.

"Yes, this is definitely infected." She walked over to a cabinet. "I can give you a pain reliever and clean it up right now." She took out a bottle of medicine and a few jars of ointment. "And we also have some cooling agents for the fever, but I will have to get them from another room." The doctor walked over to Quinn with her supplies and poured some medicine into a cup. "Here, take this while I clean out the wound."

Quinn took the medicine while the doctor took a small spray bottle and filled it with the ointments from the jars. She sprayed it all over his shoulder. It stung as it sunk into his gash. A prickly feeling covered his entire arm. Looking down, he saw the ooze dissipate and the swelling stop.

"Woah. How did you do that?"

The doctor shot Quinn a confused look. "Sanitation spray... haven't you ever been hurt before?"

"Of course, I've been hurt before," Quinn looked over to Akiko, who gave him a sharp look. "Just nothing this serious, I—I usually—"

"Usually just injuries requiring a *fascia* on, then it heals right away, but we have never had to deal with something this serious," Akiko interrupted.

"Oh, I see. May I ask how this happened?"

"I'd rather you not," Quinn said under his breath.

"What was that, sir? I didn't hear you."

"He got into a *cursoriam lutum* crash," Akiko spoke again.

"Were you wearing protective padding?" The doctor looked skeptical of their lie.

"Um, yes, doc," Quinn replied.

"Good, you have to be careful on those types of *cursoriams.*"

"I will," Quinn said as the doctor finished wrapping a fresh bandage around his arm.

"I will be sending the sanitary spray prescription over to the nearest pharmacy, assuming you don't have it at your home. Pick some up, apply every four to five hours, and it should heal in about a day or two." The doctor said with a smile, brushing off her skepticism. "I'm going to go get the cooling agents for your fever. I will be back in a few minutes."

Akiko and Quinn were left alone in the room.

"Quinn, wait. This might sound crazy, but I need you to dress up as a doctor. Close the door," Akiko said as he bent down and opened a few cabinets, searching for scrubs and a white coat.

"What now? I'm not sure now is the time to be playing dress-up," Quinn said as he closed the door.

"You guys mentioned that your friends' last name is Eve, correct? When we were on our way to the D wing, there were a ton of security keepers blocking off that one hall, and I saw a man come out of a room down there. One of the keepers addressed him as Governor *Eve.*"

"And you want me to impersonate a doctor to get to

them?" Quinn asked.

"Exactly, ow." Akiko hit his head on the cabinet and looked up. "Oh, here we are. Found the scrubs." He came out of the cabinet holding a pile of blue and white clothes and handed them to Quinn.

Quinn looked at the name tag on the uniform. "You've *got* to be kidding me."

"What?" Akiko asked.

"This says 'Nurse *Barbie*.'"

Akiko snickered. "Those are some sparkly pink heels to fill."

"Shut up."

"I wonder if she wanted to be a plastic surgeon."

"Very funny." Quinn pulled on the baggy scrubs and the coat over his clothes. "Okay, I'm ready."

"Just take this," Akiko said, handing him a clipboard with paper and a pen attached to it.

Quinn took the board.

"Now you're ready. You have your uniform, your clipboard; you know where you're going?"

"Yes, Mom, and I have my lunchbox and backpack too," Quinn said, rolling his eyes.

"Oh, my baby's all grown up!" Akiko mimicked.

"This is just getting weird."

"Yup," Akiko agreed, pushing Quinn out of the door. "You go, I stay. If the doctor comes back, I'll stall her."

Quinn nodded as Akiko closed the door in his face.

CHAPTER 19

DECEIVED

Delphi opened her eyes. Colored lights streaked through the fog in the distance. The sounds of an explosion caused her to whip around.

Behind her, the world was burning.

Smoke billowed from the fires below her. She was standing on a hill overlooking a city engulfed in flames.

She took in a sharp breath, her lungs filling with ash and dust. Choking, she took another look around.

After her second full turn, Delphi's eyes settled on a boy. He turned around, his messy brown hair in his blue eyes. Her memories felt muddled, but she pulled a name from the depths of her mind.

"Asher."

Five more people walked out of the fog behind him. One girl had olive-green eyes, a golden tan, and curly dark hair. A little girl with blonde hair was holding her hand. Another little girl with dark curly hair stood between two boys with green eyes. Even though six people now stood before her, someone was missing; she could feel it. She just didn't know who.

She jumped as she felt a hand on her arm.

"Delphi, wake up." A voice behind her said.

She turned around, "What?"

A tall boy with beachy, dark, disheveled hair and navy eyes was holding her arm.

"Wake. Up," he said again, this time more urgently.

His eyes darkened, looking at something behind her. The boy pushed her out of the way. She fell to the ground and looked up to see a gun aimed at the boy. The blonde man behind the trigger turned the weapon towards Delphi.

The boy who had grabbed her lunged at the gun.

"Wake up, Delphi." the man said and pulled the trigger.

***

Delphi gasped. Panting, she blinked a few times. Blaring lights burned into her retinas as she tried to sit up. The first thing she noticed was that she was wearing clean clothes. Trying not to think about it too much, she felt something cold and tight clamped against her wrist. She looked at her arm and saw a handcuff attaching her to the bedrail.

"Oh, no, no, no, no, no," she mumbled to herself as she shook her wrist, trying to free herself.

Her breathing intensified. She looked away from the handcuff and down her arm a little. She noticed a patch and followed the cord attached to it up to an IV.

"*Faex*."

Then she remembered the second part of her vision: footsteps. She heard footsteps clicking across the hard floor. Quickly, Delphi shut her eyes.

A woman who resembled Delphi sat down at the end of Delphi's bed.

"Delphi, I know you're awake," the woman whispered.

That voice, Delphi knew that voice.

She blinked open her eyes. "Mom?"

"Yes, I'm here. Let me help you sit up," Mrs. Eve said, coercing Delphi into a sitting position.

"H—how are you—why are you—where am I?" Delphi asked, using her uncuffed hand to rub a blaring headache away.

"You're on Esprit, and you're safe. Your father was just in here, but he had to attend an important meeting."

"A meeting about what?" Delphi asked, her expression dawning.

"You know you're not allowed to know about that kind of thing," her mom chastised, tucking a loose strand of her short wavy blonde hair behind her ear.

"A meeting about *what?*" Delphi repeated.

Mrs. Eve sighed. "A meeting about you and your friends. You caused numerous problems for us whilst on Earth."

"Us? You knew, didn't you? You knew about Earth this whole time, and you didn't think anyone else had a right to know?" A thought hit her. "Did *you* send the FBI after us?"

"Delphi, it's much more complicated than that. We needed to get you back home, where it was safe."

"So you *did* send the FBI? Do you have any idea what

they've put us through? They tried to *kill* us. Did you know that?"

Delphi looked into her mother's sharp, blue gaze.

"You did know. In fact, you probably issued that. And what's this?" Delphi asked, shaking her cuffed wrist. "What kind of person does this? Let me go."

"Delphi—"

"Stop saying my name."

"Delphi, I know you must be very confused right now, and you have a lot of questions. That's understandable, but you are not allowed to make demands of me."

"*I WILL DO WHATEVER THE* INFERNUM *I WANT*!" Delphi yelled.

"Don't use that tone with me."

"Stop acting like my mom. My *mom* wouldn't send assassins after me. My *mom* wouldn't chain me to a bed. My *mom* wouldn't act like nothing happened after her children were transported to another planet, thrown into a car chase, nearly escaped a building that blew up, jumped out of a plummeting plane, and ran for their lives. A *mom* wouldn't do that."

"The FBI was under strict instruction to not kill or injure you."

"*SO BLOWING US UP DOESN'T COUNT AS INJURING US?*" Delphi screamed.

"The bomb was an unfortunate accident," Mrs. Eve explained calmly. "If you had just cooperated, they would have taken you home, and there would have been no need for such monstrosities."

"Home to what? This? I'm handcuffed to a bed! That should pretty much explain how I'm feeling right now," Delphi said, a part of her wishing desperately that her mom would snap and yell back, show any emotion at all. "And what about my friends? Where are they?"

"They got away before anyone could catch them."

Delphi breathed a sigh of relief, but then panic struck her. "Are you going to be able to get them back? What about their families? Aren't Meeka's parents worried?"

There was a fast series of loud beeping noises.

"Calm down, Delphi. You're making the heart monitor spike."

"That didn't answer my question."

Mrs. Eve exhaled, clearly getting annoyed. "Your friends will be found, eventually. The ones that belong here will be returned. As for the ones that belong to Earth, I have no control over that."

A groan came from Asher as he awoke in the next bed. He opened his eyes.

"Good. You're awake," Mrs. Eve said, looking over at Asher.

"Yeah, I am." Asher started to sit up and noticed his chained wrist. "What the— What's going on? And what was that about everyone else? You're not really going to leave them, are you?"

"Of course not. Like I said before, they will be found eventually," Mrs. Eve replied.

"And what will happen to us?" Asher asked.

"My goodness, Asher! You're making it sound as if I'm a

monster planning to do horrible things to you."

"Well, I don't know, are you?" Asher retorted, his mouth set into a grim line.

"No, I am not. Subsequently, things may be different for you, but nothing horrible will happen to you. You're safe now. Everything is okay."

"Okay? *Okay?* None of this is okay. None of this will ever *be* okay. Why? Out of everyone else on this blasted planet? Why would you send killers after us?" Delphi asked.

"Do I have to keep repeating myself? The agents and troops of that planet, of that single country, were not supposed to harm you."

"They don't know," Delphi said.

"Excuse me?" Mrs. Eve asked. "Delphi, what are you talking about?"

"I said, they don't know."

Asher's face lit up with understanding. "Oh my God."

"Who else on this planet knows about Earth?" Delphi interrogated.

"Only the Director and the Board of Governance."

"So, in order to keep it a secret, you had to have people on Earth handle it. People who almost killed us," Delphi said.

"The bomb was not to go off until you got out of the building," Mrs. Eve tried explaining. "It was not going to injure you."

"Yeah, well, it did. If the bomb wasn't supposed to hurt me, I wouldn't be sitting here with a *seeping folorium* on my arm," Asher said, holding up his arm that was wrapped in a large leaf. "And you—hang on—that was an Esprit bomb.

Quinn was too confused about the shield that it couldn't have been from Earth. You gave them that weapon to use against us. If you were so adamant about not killing us, then why did you do that?"

"The plan was for you to turn yourselves in. The bomb was just a fear tactic. It was never going to hurt you."

"And if we hadn't gotten out of the building in time?" Delphi asked, already fearing the answer.

"That was a problem overlooked by our scientists and the Director."

"So this is the Director's doing?" Delphi asked.

"Yes, well, the Board of Governance also had to vote on whether or not we would send the bomb. It was the Director's proposal."

"And you voted *for* it," Asher said.

"I had to get you back. It was the simplest way."

"No, the simplest way would have been to have them just explain things to us instead of shooting at us and trying to scare us into cooperation," Delphi argued.

"And Dad? How did he vote?" Asher asked.

"He voted the same as I did, but everything turned out fine."

"Stop *saying* that!" Delphi yelled.

"Why shouldn't I say something that's true?" Mrs. Eve asked.

"You're lying, and you know it," Delphi retorted. "If it's so true, then why are things going to be different?"

"It's a complicated matter, Delphi. If we let you return to the way things once were, it won't feel normal for you. Things have changed, and you must learn to change with them."

"For example?" Asher asked, his voice filled with dread.

"Your new living quarters. You will remain here for the time being, at least until your rooms are prepared in the Empire Building."

"You mean... we're being locked up?" Asher asked.

"Oh, you make it sound so dreadful. You will each get a nice separate room."

"We're being separated?" Delphi asked.

"Why so many questions?" Mrs. Eve sighed as she stood up from the edge of Delphi's bed. "Think about it more as getting some privacy."

"You're a madwoman," Asher spat.

"Asher, it's rude to call people names," Mrs. Eve chastised. "And you and I both know that we can't let rumors start spreading about another planet. It will upset the peace and the trust that this world has in its Empire."

"The Empire can go to *infernum* for all I care!" Asher yelled. "We're your kids, and you're putting some stupid politics before us."

"This is not some 'stupid politics.' This is the fate of not only our planet but the fate of two planets on the line. Tell me, what would have happened if I let you stay on Earth? Or if we *did* have people to send in to rescue you? This peace that we have maintained between our two worlds is a fragile one that has held fast for decades but is still very fragile. The slightest crack will shatter it. You were forming a crack, and we needed to seal it before it spread. I know you will understand, even if unwillingly. This is just how things have to be. That is my final say on the subject."

And with that, Mrs. Eve walked out of the room and locked the door.

"This is—this is completely—" Asher stuttered.

"Revolting," Delphi finished for him.

"Yeah, thank you. Revolting! I mean, what the *infernum* just happened? And—ow—this cuff is really starting to irritate me."

"All of a sudden, our lives are upside down, but I guess there was always something wrong. I just can't tell if I like knowing that my mom is a lunatic or if I preferred ignorance to it all," Delphi replied.

Opal stirred in the bed on the other side of the room.

"I wish Meeka was here. She would have a plan," Asher said, then looked up sheepishly.

Delphi nodded. "Don't worry, I'm not going to say anything."

The door creaked open, and in walked a nurse, pushing a cart of food. He walked over to the space in between Delphi and Asher's beds. The nurse kept his head down as he took out two trays of food and placed them in front of each of them.

When he turned to Delphi, she recognized him. "Quinn?"

"Shhh! Yeah, it's me." He looked up at her.

"But—wha...? How did you get here?" she asked.

"No time, just be quiet and look under your tray." He looked up at their wrists. "Damnit, handcuffs." He returned to the cart, took a chain of keys off the hook, and threw them at Asher.

"Wha—"

"Shut up!" Quinn put his head back down and wheeled the cart out of the room.

They watched him leave, and Delphi opened the letter.

I left you the keycard folded in this note to open the doors. Akiko

says he has a plan, but he didn't tell me what it is. I guess we're

winging this like everything else. Everyone's safe and here on Esprit.

We're going to get you out of here.

Delphi finished reading.

"Could he have been any less vague?" Asher asked. "I mean, who the *infernum* is Akiko?"

"No clue." Delphi took out the keycard. "If this opens the doors, the keys probably open the handcuffs."

"But which ones?" Asher asked.

"Try all of them," Delphi replied, wincing as she took the IV out of her arm.

Opal stirred again but still didn't wake up.

Asher tried ten keys before he found the right one. "Got it!"

He unclamped his cuff and handed the keys to Delphi. Asher shook Opal awake while Delphi undid her own cuff.

"Hey, Opal. Come on. It's time to wake up," Asher whispered to her.

Opal opened her eyes and yawned. "Mommy?"

"No, it's just me," Asher said.

"Are we safe now?" Opal asked.

"We're going to be. We just have to get out of this room

first," Asher replied.

"I want Mommy," Opal said.

"Trust me, no, you don't," Delphi replied, coming over and undoing Opal's chained wrist.

Opal sat up and slid out of the bed, looking confused.

"So what now?" Asher asked, changing the subject.

"Quinn said that this Akiko person has a plan. I guess we just have to wait to see what that is," Delphi said.

***

Quinn quickly made his way back to Akiko, who was pacing back and forth in the patient room.

"Hey, I'm back," Quinn said as he let out a deep breath.

"Great. Are they okay?" Akiko asked

"Sure. You could say that. So, what's your plan?"

"Don't have one," Akiko said, looking around. "You know what..."

He walked over to a glass-covered fire alarm. Akiko jabbed his elbow into the glass, shattering it. He cleared out some of the shards of glass and hit the button with the palm of his hand. Alarms and sirens filled the air.

"Now, we make a scene," Akiko said with a mischievous smirk. "*FIRE!*" he screamed, running into the hall. He looked over at Quinn, who stood in utter shock. "Time to have some fun. You coming?"

Quinn joined him, and they both ran around screaming "*FIRE!*" and rushing people out of the building.

"Go get the Eves and meet me at the back of the hospital. I got this," Akiko whispered as he passed Quinn.

Quinn rushed back to where the Eves were being held. People were sporadically running around, and he had to push his way through a sea of bodies before finally reaching the hallway.

"I'll take care of the Eves, sir," Quinn said to the guard. "I was instructed by their mother. Go get to safety."

Quinn rushed to get his keycard, then remembered that he had given it to Delphi. He prayed the door was open as he turned the handle. It opened to Asher, Delphi, and Opal standing in the doorway, their expressions full of confusion and fear.

"Dude, we have to get out of here. There's a fire!" Asher called out.

"Yeah, definitely," Quinn said sarcastically.

"Oh, looks like someone upgraded their lying skills," Delphi said.

"Don't worry, all part of the plan. Let's go," Quinn said with a smile.

They ran out the door and in the opposite direction of the stampede of people trying to escape the building. They continued until they made it to the back end of the hospital, where Akiko was waiting.

"Nice to see you guys," Akiko said, leaning against a wall.

"And you are?" Delphi asked.

"Akiko, or Aki. Whatever feels right. I assume you're

Delphi?" Akiko replied.

"Yeah?" she answered with a suspicious look.

"And you two are Asher and Opal," Akiko said, turning to them.

"I think we'll have more time for introductions later. They'll eventually realize that the fire alarm was a dupe and that you guys are missing. Let's go meet up with everyone else," Quinn said, discarding his scrubs on the floor.

They ran through the empty halls, darting around corner after corner until they reached the back of the building. Akiko and Quinn opened the doors and stepped outside.

"What took you two so long? We heard sirens and people started running out of the building like maniacs. I was about ready to go in there myself!" Meeka yelled.

"Sorry, but—" Quinn started.

"But we have a surprise for you," Akiko said, stepping out of Meeka's view to reveal the Eves standing behind him.

Everyone's faces lit up. Delphi was the first out the door and ran right up to Meeka, giving her a big, relieved hug.

They all crowded around, and everyone reunited. After many hugs and tears of relief, Asher finally made his way up to Meeka.

"Asher I was—" she started.

"Now, where did we leave off?" Asher smiled as he pulled Meeka in by the waist. He briskly leaned in, pressing his lips to hers.

Her stomach dropped. The world felt as if it had been put on pause. Her surroundings slowly blurred as she embraced the moment. She forgot about all the chaos, stress, and everything else. The rest of the world just fell away.

Asher was overwhelmed with exhilaration as he finally, after years, got the courage to make his move. He couldn't have been happier. He didn't care who was around watching; he didn't care what they were thinking; he didn't even care about the mockery he was going to endure. He was on top of the world, and no one was going to bring him down.

After a few seconds, Asher reluctantly pulled away. They locked eyes.

"Excuse me?" Delphi interrupted the moment with a faint laugh.

"Shut up, Delphi," Asher said, refusing to break eye contact with Meeka.

Meeka smiled and took Asher's hand. "I was—"

"Yo, Asher! Meeka admitted to being in love with you!" August interrupted.

Asher smiled at Meeka. "Oh, really?" he teased.

"Yeah, dude! She had a whole mental breakdown and everything," he added.

"You *culus*!" Meeka hissed at August.

Asher laughed with the biggest smile on his face. He looked over at his twin sister, who shared the same expression.

"You're good with this?" he asked her.

Delphi simply nodded with excitement. "Yeah, but I think you need some work on the pickup lines. That was so unbelievably cliché."

Asher rolled his eyes and put his arm around Meeka. They walked back up to the group, and August gave Asher a pat on the back.

"Pretty bold of you, man. But we all know I could've done better," August said playfully.

"Sure, buddy," Asher replied.

August smirked, "Give me a hug, you big idiot. You finally got the girl you've been chasing for what? Ten years?" August wrapped his arms around Asher, patting him on the back. "You did good, bro."

Asher stood there awkwardly.

"Dude, I'm seriously not letting go until you hug me back."

Asher laughed and embraced August. "Don't mess with me. You've never been serious a day in your life."

"And hope to keep that record. Thank you very much." August let go of Asher, and they stepped away from one another. "Well, I guess if you get the girl, that makes me the funny best friend."

"August, you *are* the funny best friend," Delphi said.

"Hear that, guys? Delphi thinks I'm funny!"

Chapter 20

Winging It

"So, did you guys have a plan for after you rescued us, or are we still working towards that 'just wing it' reward?" Delphi asked.

They had gotten away from the supposedly 'on fire' hospital and were now sitting on a bench in the nearby park. Children ran around under the bright sun, and a light breeze blew past the group. Opal and Macy were playing on a swing set just a little out of earshot.

"The second one," Fitz replied.

"Go figure." Delphi sighed, looking around. "You know, things used to be normal, and they were kind of boring. Now, look at everything. We're running for our lives through the *universe*. How many other people can say that?"

Meeka looked concerned. "Delphi, have you snapped?"

"No, I haven't *snapped*. And I'm definitely not saying that this whole thing was enjoyable. I mean, we almost died, we did get hurt, and I found out my parents are nuts, but—"

"I think I know what you're saying." Asher cut in. "Before, in the hospital, Mom said that things have changed, and she's right, everything's changed, but maybe it's possible that change isn't always bad?"

"Well, of course, *you* would say that," Delphi remarked.

Asher shot her a confused look, and Delphi focused her gaze on Asher and Meeka's intertwined hands.

"Okay, come at me with it all now. I can take it," Asher said, straightening up.

"Nah, I think I'd rather make this slow and painful," Delphi replied, laughing.

"Delphi!" Meeka said.

"Meeka!" Delphi mocked.

"Oh, this is going to get good," August smirked, rubbing his hands together.

"Yeah, well, apparently not right now," Asher said, shooting Delphi a look.

She teasingly glared back at him, and he looked away.

"So, plan, anyone?" Asher asked.

"Why does this feel like déjà vu for my déjà vu?" August asked. "Haven't we done this whole 'planning' thing a gajillion times?"

"He's not wrong," Fitz agreed.

"Well, what do you suppose we do? We have to go somewhere," Quinn said.

"What about my house? It's in Caput-Rubrum. That's over eight hours away from here," Fitz suggested.

"I mean, we really have nowhere else that could be a potentially safe atmosphere," Meeka replied.

"Alright, I'll get us some train tickets," Akiko said as he stood up.

Everyone followed him to the train station. They utilized an alternative route that, unfortunately, took longer to get there, but they were able to avoid the hospital.

When they arrived, Akiko made his way over to a kiosk to buy the Eves hats so they could better hide their faces. Then he went to the counter and purchased their tickets.

They boarded the train and took off towards Caput-Rubrum.

"So, we get there, then what?" Quinn asked as they trundled past the rolling grasslands on the outskirts of The Metropolis.

"Ring the doorbell?" August suggested.

"Okay, then what? It's not like we can really tell Fitz's parents the truth," Quinn said.

"Why not?" August asked.

"Why not? Why *not?*" Meeka blustered. "I don't know. Maybe because, first of all, who would believe us? Second of all, we are kind of wanted right now, and third of all, and I'm not sure if I mentioned this or not, but who would *actually* believe us?"

"I think she's losing her crackers," August whispered to Asher.

"I think you might be right," Asher replied.

"I'm being realistic!" Meeka yelled.

"I was just kidding. And you're right, most people wouldn't be able to take a bunch of kids showing up and saying that they're wanted by the Empire."

"Way to cave, man," August whispered.

"Shut up, August," everyone said in unison.

"We were talking about an excuse, then?" Delphi asked.

"Yeah. Fitz, you obviously know your parents the best out

of all of us. Any good ideas?" Asher asked.

"I don't know," Fitz said.

"Uh, Fitz made friends, and we wanted to go to his house because The Metropolis was boring?" Opal suggested.

"Good try, but I don't know how well that will work. Keep thinking," Asher said.

"Ooh! Ooh! I got one!" Everyone stared at August expectantly. "What if we say we're on a trip for school? Huh? Huh?"

"August, it's *summer*," Delphi reminded him.

"Wait—oh *faex*," August slumped into his seat. "Then I've got nothing."

"Could Fitz sneak us in?" Quinn asked.

"That depends on how long you're planning on staying," Akiko cut in.

"I'm pretty sure I wouldn't be able to hide the fact that you're in my house for very long. Plus, I'd have to explain why I'm home. Plus, plus, when they find you, that would make things a *lot* harder to explain," said Fitz.

"Party!" Macy exclaimed.

"Sorry, Mace. Parties don't usually last for weeks," Quinn said.

"What if we try convincing Fitz's parents that August was supposed to come to their house this summer and not the other way around?" Delphi said.

"But what about you guys?" Fitz asked.

Delphi shrugged. "It's August. He brought friends unannounced. He shows up unannounced. It would be *weird* if his showing up was planned."

"I don't know how concrete that is," Meeka said.

"Do you have any ideas?" Delphi asked Meeka.

"Maybe there was a natural disaster in The Metropolis, and Fitz's house was the best place to go," Meeka proposed.

"Wouldn't they have heard about it, though?" Delphi asked.

"I know. It's just so difficult to come up with an excuse for this."

"What if we say we're homeless? I mean, we don't look too good, so that's a start," August said.

"If *I* were my parents, I wouldn't let a bunch of homeless people into my house just like that," Fitz replied.

"And I'm not pretending to be homeless," Meeka added.

"And a lot of people would recognize our last names," Delphi put in. "Since Meeka's and my parents work in the Empire."

"If we can't come up with a concrete reason, what then?" Meeka asked.

"Try to find somewhere else to go?" Asher replied.

"But we're already on the train, and where else would we go?" Delphi asked.

Opal looked at Delphi. "Home."

Asher opened his mouth to explain, but Delphi shook her head, concern written all over her face. Opal wasn't ready for that yet. Frankly, neither were they.

"If we go home, the bad guys can easily find us, so we have to avoid it." Delphi wasn't lying per se, just withholding the truth. Either way, she felt terrible.

"But Mommy and Daddy can protect us," Opal argued.

"It's just too risky, and we don't want to get caught, right?" Delphi replied.

"I guess."

Meeka looked at the Eve siblings with sympathy. She knew Delphi would skewer her if she started pitying them, but the situation was just so, well, pitiful.

August cleared his throat. "So... any other ideas?"

After hours and hours of bickering, brainstorming, and staring blankly at the ceiling, they finally settled on pretending to visit a carnival in town. Their plan was to say that they were just dropping by and hopefully be invited to stay. It was a weak plan, and they knew it, but it was all they had.

Eventually, the gentle motion of the train rocked Opal and Macy to sleep. They laid curled up on the floor, their heads propped up on the backpacks full of supplies. As they rested, blurred scenery flew past the compartment's window, and the group continued to talk.

"How is it that Esprit is so clean and Earth is so, well, *not*? The world feels fresher here, if that makes any sense. It's not just me, right?" Quinn asked.

"It's probably because of how natural Esprit is to Earth. Most people on Earth don't put the natural world hand in hand with technology, so they end up with pollution and acid rain and stuff like that. Esprit decided to merge the two. Keeps the planet alive and advances us at the same time. It's a win-win," Akiko explained. "That's why I became a sustainable engineer back on Earth. Someone's got to fix their *faex* before they run out of time."

"People on Earth battle with their planet while we work with ours," Meeka added.

"So now that we have sufficiently bashed your planet, what's your impression of this one so far?" Asher asked Quinn.

"Kind of overwhelming in the beginning, especially since you were all speaking in another language. Less terrifying once Akiko gave me the earpiece translator. Not super great when we found out that the people running this planet almost killed us. But all in all, it's just like anywhere else, extremely flawed, just in different ways," Quinn answered.

"How about you, Aki? How do *you* feel about being *back* on Esprit?" Meeka asked.

"I really missed it. Actually, maybe this would be a good time to mention this. Once we get off the train, I'm afraid I'll be departing from you guys. I want to go find my brother."

"That's great!" Meeka exclaimed.

"Oh, and speaking of brothers," Akiko turned to Delphi, then back to Meeka. "I didn't know you guys had the whole 'my best friend's brother' friendship dynamic going on," he eyed Asher, who perked up from resting his head on Meeka's shoulder.

"What's the problem?" Asher asked.

"Ugh! It's been like this for *years.* The worst part was that they thought they were actually good at hiding it." Delphi rolled her eyes.

"While we're being honest, it's always been obvious. No one wanted to say anything, though," August added.

"Oh, shut up," Asher said, laying his head back down on

Meeka's shoulder.

✳✳✳

The train pulled up to the station a few hours later. They woke up Opal and Macy and hopped off. The group maneuvered their way out of the crowded building and into the light of the sunrise outside.

"I guess I'm off then," Akiko said. "Thanks for helping me get back here."

"Thanks for saving us," Asher replied.

"No problem, anytime. I'm guessing you're going to stay under the radar for a while, so contacting you will prove difficult."

"I can give you my parents' house number if you want," Fitz said.

"Sure, I'll call you guys when I find my brother," Akiko said, taking the piece of paper Fitz handed him.

Meeka patted him on the arm. "I'm sure you'll find him soon."

Asher looked jealously at Meeka's hand touching Akiko's arm.

"Hormones suck," he mumbled to himself.

"Thanks. I hope you're right. Oh!" Akiko slipped his hand into his pocket and took out the pecto. "You guys will probably need this more than I do. I'll just swipe a new one off of someone else." He handed Meeka the currency card. "Catch you guys later."

They watched him walk into the distance and disappear back into the crowd.

At that moment, a gray blurriness passed over Delphi's conscience.

"I guess we're on to Fitz's house," Meeka said. "This is our last chance to turn back."

Asher shook his head. "We have to try. Let's get a ride—"

"AH!" Delphi screamed and sank to the floor, cradling her head in her hands.

Hello, dear one.

"Delphi! What's wrong? Is it another flash?" Asher knelt next to her.

"No, no—"

You're making a scene, young one.

"Who ARE you?" Delphi asked the voice.

"Delphi, it's Asher. I'm your brother. Are you okay?"

I'm you. Well, a part of you.

"I'm going crazy," Delphi mumbled, rocking back and forth.

"Why? What's wrong?" Meeka asked.

People often confuse insanity and power. You are not crazy; you are powerful.

"Can you hear that voice?" Delphi asked.

"Delphi, there aren't any voices," Quinn replied.

"Like I said, crazy. I'm crazy." A sharp pain in Delphi's head made her cry out again.

You must relax, darling. You are far from crazy.

"Go! Away!" Delphi yelled.

Meeka ran over and helped Asher lay her down.

You don't want me to leave. We could be so powerful together.

"I said, go AWAY!" Delphi forced herself to sit up.

The gray haze faded from her mind in a split second, leaving her stunned and out of breath.

"*Faex*, Delphi. You good?" Asher asked.

"*No!* No, do I look okay?" Delphi snapped.

"Honestly, I think she's right. She is crazy," August said, standing wide-eyed.

"I'm telling you all right now, and I need you to believe me. That wasn't me. That wasn't my voice in my head. It wouldn't leave," she said, heaving ragged breaths.

"Yep. Definitely crazy," August responded.

"I believe you," Meeka said firmly.

Delphi looked over at Asher. His expression was obviously unsure.

"I—I guess I have to believe you," he stuttered.

"Well, if it wasn't your voice, then who was it? Was it familiar? Did it sound like anyone you know at all?" Quinn asked.

"No, it was just some, some echo, I guess. That's the only way I can explain it," Delphi said, pressing her fingers to her temples. "It sounded like a woman's voice, coming from far away but clear at the same time."

"So what was this echo saying to you?" Meeka questioned.

"She was saying how powerful I am and practically making me aware of her existence."

"Echo sounds intense. Think she's got a boyfriend?"

August asked.

Delphi glared at August. "What is wrong with you?"

"Many, many things," August replied. "But I think you should be more worried about what's wrong with *you* right now."

"We should get her to my house fast," Fitz suggested.

They rushed Delphi to her feet and found a row of streetcars. The vehicles were hooked into their docking slips. Meeka swiped the pecto to unhook one. They clambered through the door and slipped onto the benches lining the four walls. The tinted glass dome ceiling showed rays of light streaking across the sky as the sun rose. Fitz plugged in his address on the screen in the center of the streetcar, and the vehicle whirred to life. They rode through the community, past houses, some vaguely resembling trees and others with domed ceilings and children playing in front yards.

Eventually, the car stopped in front of a house made up of three cylinders with domed glass roofs. They got out of the street transport and walked up the path to the front door. A recognition system rang and alerted the people inside that someone was there. Lights were on inside, and a woman with short, curly copper hair opened the door. Her warm brown eyes flicked from kid to kid until resting on Fitz.

"Honey? Is everything alright? I thought you were going to stay at August's house for the summer." Her eyebrows knit together in a worried expression.

Fitz opened his mouth to answer, but August made his way to the front of the group first. "Hi, Aunt Naudia."

"Can someone please explain to me what's going on?"

Fitz's mom asked.

"What's going on?" A man came up behind Naudia. He had the same green eyes as Fitz and August.

"That's what I was just wondering," Naudia said to the man.

"Do you want the truth or one of the dumb explanations we came up with on the train?" August asked.

"*August!*" Meeka, Delphi, and Asher hissed.

"The truth," Naudia said, looking at them all.

"Okay, so we kind of ended up on this whole other planet where we met these two." August gestured to Quinn and Macy. "Then these people started chasing us, so we wrecked Quinn's car trying to get away. Then they blew up his building, then we tried to go to another part of the planet. Well, long story short, that didn't work out either. We ended up back on Esprit, where we found out that the Empire was who sent those people after us. Now we're here." He took a deep breath.

"I said the *truth*, August."

"That *is* the truth, Aunt Naudia."

"I can vouch for that." Asher stepped in.

"Me too," Meeka said.

"Yeah," Delphi agreed.

Quinn, Macy, and Opal nodded in agreement as well.

"He's not lying, Mom," Fitz said.

"Kids, we aren't stupid. I would like to know the real reason why six strangers are on my stoop. August, tell me the truth before I call your parents," Fitz's dad said.

"Uncle Lock, please do *not* call my parents. It will make

this whole situation worse. The Empire will find us again, and we all will be thrown into the Empire building to be locked up forever! I promise I'm not lying. I know we have no way of proving this to you, but we need shelter. We are literally trying to hide from the rest of the world," August pleaded.

Everyone was in shock at how well August begged. He actually seemed to be handling the situation pretty well.

"Mrs. Ray, I assure you we are telling the truth," Meeka interjected.

"This still sounds ridiculous, and at this point, I really have to call your parents, August," Naudia insisted.

"Please, no! Please, no! I'm literally begging here! Anything!" August panicked.

"Okay, okay. I won't call them... for now. Why don't you come in, and we can discuss this a little more over breakfast?" She stepped out of the doorway to let them enter.

"And you won't call the Empire?" August asked.

"Promise," Naudia replied.

August looked at his uncle, who put his hands up in defense. "I promise too."

August nodded his approval and stepped inside. Everyone else followed him to the kitchen, where they sat around a round table.

Bacon and eggs were cooking on the stove, and Naudia poured a few extra glasses of some sort of fruit drink, then sat down and knitted her hands together. Lockson readjusted his glasses and did the same.

"Now, if you *are* telling the truth, and I want Fitz to answer this time," Lockson said, stopping August from replying, "then when did this happen?"

Fitz was about to answer when the sound of footsteps came down the stairs. "Wow, Mom! It smells great down here. What are you talking about, 'telling the truth?' And, woah, I just realized there are a bunch of strangers in my house, and I just came rambling down the steps in my pjs." A twenty-year-old girl walked into the kitchen, pulling her red hair up into a messy bun.

"Hi, Ivan," Fitz said.

"Fitz? I thought you were going to stay with—oh—hey, August."

"Hello, Ivanna Banana," August greeted her with a smirk.

"I thought I made it clear that you aren't allowed to call me that."

"What's wrong with 'Ivanna Banana'?" Lockson asked.

"Nothing, Dad. I just don't like it when he calls me that."

"Picky, picky, picky." August shook his head mockingly.

Ivan rolled her eyes and sat down. "So, is someone going to introduce me or...?"

"Right, yes. This is, uh, they are— I'm sorry, I don't think I caught your names yet," said Naudia.

"Oh! Sorry. I'm Meeka, that's Opal, there's Macy, next to me are Delphi and Asher, and the other one is Quinn."

A chorus of 'hi's,' 'hey's,' and 'hello's' followed the introductions.

"Nice to meet you all, but why are you here?" Ivan asked.

"Whose turn is it to explain? Because I'm done," August said.

"I'll tell her." Fitz sighed and started telling Ivan the

whole story.

When he finished, Ivan snorted with laughter. "I can't believe you took a whole five minutes telling me such an elaborate lie. Did August put you up to this or something? Did you lose a bet with him?"

Delphi yanked on her own hair in frustration. "No, he's not lying. If someone says that again, I'm going to scream."

"You do know how crazy that sounds, right?" Ivan asked.

Delphi winced at Ivan's use of the word 'crazy.' "Listen, we've been through an *infernum* of a lot. I'm tired, sore, and really on edge. If you don't believe us, that's your choice, and in your position, I probably wouldn't believe us either, but you're wrong. We really just need a place to stay and lie low for a while. By the looks of things, this isn't the place. If you'd excuse me, I'm leaving."

She got up from her seat and everyone else followed.

"Wait," Naudia said, stopping them from taking another step. "This is all true, Fitz?"

"Every word of it."

"I believe you then, and I believe I speak for all of us."

Ivan and Lockson nodded.

"This is really weird," Ivan remarked.

"You're telling us," Quinn replied.

CHAPTER 21

SHAKEN UP

Three days passed with no excitement. The boys were bunking in Fitz's room while Meeka and Delphi were with Ivan. Opal and Macy took the guest room.

They gathered around the kitchen table, which had become their meeting spot, while Macy and Opal played upstairs.

"Now that we have established that you can stay as long as you need, what do you plan on doing now?" Lockson asked.

"I don't know. Maybe we can try going back to things being as normal as possible," Fitz replied.

"Normal? Who's normal? I think I'd like to meet this fellow," August remarked.

"You know what I mean," Fitz said.

"We just need to try to create a normal routine. Start fresh," Meeka said.

"Kiddos, tonight's movie night. Anyone have any snack recommendations?" Naudia walked into the room. "Fitzy? How about strananas? I know they're your favorite."

"*Fitzy?*" August asked.

"What's a stranana?" Macy asked.

"We can get to that question later. The real question here

is, *Fitzy?*" August said.

Fitz turned red. "Mom!"

"What? Oh, did you not want me to call you that in front of your friends? Okay, I won't call you that anymore, Fitzy," Naudia smiled mockingly.

"Mom!"

"Okay, okay. I'm sorry."

"Thank you."

"Hey Fitzy, can you pass me that glass of water?" Ivan asked.

Fitz turned even brighter red.

"Be careful. He might go crazy and end up dousing you with it instead," August remarked.

"Okay, guys, settle down," Lockson cut in. "If he doesn't want to be called Fitzy, then we won't call him Fitzy."

"Why don't we just change the subject?" Meeka asked.

"Thank you." Fitz sighed.

"Stranana sounds delicious for tonight," Meeka said to Naudia.

"Great, I think I have some left over in the fridge." Naudia was about to walk back into the kitchen when a sudden rumble shook the ground.

"What was that?" Delphi asked, nervously.

There was another shudder as the ground vibrated.

"What's going on?" Asher called out.

"Kids, get down low to the ground," Lockson instructed.

They all knelt down and waited, silently holding their breaths, for another shudder.

"Well, everything seems okay to me." August started to

get up but was stopped by another, this time much stronger, tremble. The ground quivered beneath their feet, and the house began to shake.

"Oh, boy," Asher said.

The vibrations grew, getting stronger and rocking the house more and more. It seemed as if the ground would split open and swallow them at any second. They heard a crash in the living room as a vase slid off a table. A glass on the counter in the kitchen, along with a few plates and some other cooking materials, crashed to the floor. The glass shattered on impact, flying everywhere. More vibrations followed, each stronger than the last.

"Quick! Under the table!" Naudia yelled.

"Oh no," Meeka whispered, the force of realization hitting her. "Opal and Macy are still upstairs! We have to go get them!"

Delphi tried to stand up, but the ground shook violently, and she hit her head on the table as she fell back down.

August, who still hadn't gotten under the table, quickly surveyed his surroundings. He was the closest to the staircase and could hear screams coming from the second floor. Without a second thought, he darted up the stairs. When August reached the top step, he slipped as another tremor rocked the house. He just barely caught himself, narrowly avoiding bashing his skull. He managed to get back on his feet and wobble over to the guest room. Stuff littered the floor of the room: broken picture frames, vases of flowers, puddles of water, and Ivan's old toys.

Opal and Macy were huddled in a corner, trying to avoid

the falling objects. August hurried over to them.

"Man, are you girls lucky. Let's get downstairs."

The house groaned, and they each grabbed one of his outstretched hands. He pulled them out of the corner just as a shelf came crashing down. It slammed into the ground where the girls had just been sitting. They descended the stairs as fast as they could without falling and stumbled over to everybody else.

It was a tight squeeze, but they managed to get most of everyone under the table. Quinn grabbed Macy's hand and ruffled her hair.

"Why do you keep getting stuck in dangerous places?" he asked with obvious relief.

Macy shrugged. "Maybe it's payback for throwing my stuffed animals?"

Quinn chuckled and pulled Macy closer.

Opal hugged Delphi, Asher, and Meeka.

"Are you ok?" Delphi asked.

Opal nodded. "It was weird. August came and got us."

"You're welcome," August replied.

The ground shook forcefully, and a crack formed in the laminate wood floor.

"We can finish this conversation later when the ground's not trying to eat us," Asher said.

"Good idea," Fitz seconded.

More tremors shook the ground, and the crack grew until it became a maze of spider-webbed lines in the floor.

"Anyone else think that's a problem?" asked August.

An aggressive tremor shot through the house, and they all

cried out.

All of a sudden, everything was quiet. They waited. One minute passed, and everything remained still. Two minutes, nothing. Five minutes, not even a quiver.

"Is everyone okay? Anyone harmed?" Naudia asked as they all got up from their positions under the table.

Everyone was breathing heavily but nodded in reply. Everyone was ultimately left unharmed except for a few minor cuts and bruises.

Quinn walked into the living room and looked out the window. "What the?"

He dashed out the front door and down the sidewalk towards the road. The rest of the group followed him, all stopping at the edge of the sidewalk.

"Woah," Asher said.

"I agree," Delphi replied.

Their neighbors crowded along the side of the road, all staring in astonishment at the same thing.

"Why the hell is there a freakin' chasm in the middle of the road?" Quinn asked.

"And I thought the cracks in the floor were going to be a problem," August added.

Everyone stood there, gaping at the humongous cavity. It ran the length of twenty houses but only spanned the width of three feet at most.

"Maybe this time there is a perfectly logical explanation for this," Meeka said optimistically.

"Or, you know, maybe this is just more 'end of the world as we know it' *faex*," Delphi suggested.

"This thing is pretty deep," Fitz observed, looking down into the abyss.

"Woah there, buddy. Back away from the giant man-eating hole," August pulled Fitz back towards the sidewalk.

"Guys, we should head back inside before anything else happens," Meeka said.

When they got back into the house, Lockson was standing in front of the TV. The news was on, and a red alert sign was flashing on the screen. Fitz's dad didn't even notice the group come in.

"*ALERT*! Due to unwelcome invaders on Esprit, the *Lignum Vitae* is ill. The Empire is taking immediate action in hopes of fixing this crime. People of Esprit, please remain calm and stay sheltered," the news lady said.

"Unwelcome invaders?" August asked.

Their eyes darted to Quinn and Macy.

"Oh... *Faex.*"

CHAPTER 22

DARLING

Hello, my darling.

I hide behind many faces and go by many names with the hope that one day I may be able to show my true self once more. Until then, I wait and watch through others.

Oddly enough, I never thought the universe would ever become this wretched, but everyone and everything has limits. It just so happens that I've been pushed far past mine. I was vulnerable once, but everyone must be weak before they can be strong. I've paid that price already. Now I'm ready to mend the mistakes of the past and continue what I've started. Now I can stop many people from making the wrong decisions, the same decisions that landed worlds everywhere in the situations they are presently in. There are people in the cosmos that need my guidance and my power. I am the only way their full potential can be reached, but they must prove themselves first, not only to me but also to themselves.

I give out tasks to my assistants to help conduct my plans further. These plans can vary from just a conversation to taking enormous risks, but each given task betters them. Sometimes, all that is needed is a proper nudge in the right direction. And once I'm ready, I will be fighting right beside them. Maybe it's a bit of a cliché, but I know that things you want done, you have to be the one to do them. Not someone else. Trust is fragile, which is why I don't trust anyone. But many find that they are willing to trust me. Everyone has their own method of persuasion. Mine just seems to be highly effective.

Hello, my friend.

I need your help, and only you can assist me. There is a plane in danger, a person who will do more damage unless you strike first.

"What do I need to do, my liege?"

Simple, somehow find a way to crash this plane. Commandeer it. Do whatever it takes to save these innocent people.

"Are you sure this is the right approach?"

Of course, my friend. It's the only way! This will simply be an act of heroism.

"This doesn't feel right."

Oh, I promise this is what must happen. It'll be glorified!

"Yes, madam."

People are extraordinarily easy to manipulate. A reason is all they need, but too much information can lead to doubt, and too little information can lead to the same. Especially with such an important task, although if you give it too much importance, you have people lose sight of other things, more important things...

Something is wrong.

Time works differently in our minds than in the material world. I may have just given him his job to do, but hours pass in a matter of seconds and I can tell that a problem has already arisen. I feel my mind stretch over a far distance, a process that used to leave me blank for days. Now I have mastered it. I end up in a familiar space. I have chosen this part of his mind because it is the least guarded. Everyone has a special pocket in their minds, a safe place to go when pain becomes too intense or they are rendered unconscious. A place that is considered a haven is a simple spot to infiltrate.

Good work, my friend. You have saved so many lives today.
"But someone died."
Yes, that was the point.

Honestly, how thick is he?

Feel accomplished! Empowered! You've done well.
"Thank you my liege, but—"
But what?

I reach into the depths of his mind and pull out the memory.

But you killed the wrong person.

A stream of red flares through his mind as my emotions get the best of me. I feel him flinch slightly.

"Yes, my liege."

Failure is not conducive to our goals, my friend.

"Yes, my liege."

He knows better than to argue with me further.

The plane did crash?

"Yes, my liege."

Oh, these people give me headaches. If he says 'yes, my liege' one more time, I will certainly make sure he regrets it. Sadly, I cannot say that to him, and killing him will do me no good. At least not until I can gain access to more... 'friends.'

My friend, I thank you for your loyalty. Although the boy did not die, you fulfilled your task.

"Thank you, my—"

I cut him off before he can say 'my liege' again.

I must leave you now. Your negligence has caused much planning to be done, and, although I can be very patient, a woman can only wait so long.

I leave before he can do anymore groveling.

So they all escaped the plane crash, alive. I didn't lie about being a patient woman. I have spent years developing this plan and I can spend a bit longer adjusting it. The ones she loves most must die for her to be strong. My darling must experience her moment of weakness before her time of strength.

I search through my areas of control, looking for the correct people for my following tasks. I spread my mind through the universe.

"Not going to work, wrong planet, busy, busy, busy, dead, wrong planet again, also dead, and, good, you seem adequate, as well as—interesting. Isn't it lovely when things fall perfectly into place? I'll have you perform my other task."

I have much more planning to do for my 'special' task, so I close my eyes and leave the minds of my other assistants. They can be notified about their jobs when I have them completely arranged.

Now back in my own mind, I can think a little clearer.

From the start, I've always known I needed a powerful mind to work through. One that might be just as powerful as my own. Time after time, I've been let down by others who were not capable of handling such tasks. Now, I've found the one. The one who could easily have the potential to be as powerful as me someday. My darling's beloved mind holds the source that is my missing piece. With her, I can take matters through her eyes. That is, once I bypass her stubbornness, everything will be a breeze. My only problem is that she's very attached to her little group.

But no matter. Teenagers, of course, are the easiest to twist. Throw them into a situation they can't get out of, and they will start tearing each other apart. Problem after problem and the in-fighting will erupt, and a schism unfolds. Petty, really.

I go over my plan in my head as I have done a million times

before. Well, it's more actually *plans.* I have more than one goal in life. I'm not pathetic. I think through the role each person plays, and the choices people will have to make, but I win no matter what.

And behind these walls...

I am only a voice.

A whisper in your ear.

They call me Echo.

Vernaculus Dictionary

Bovis stercus: Bull Sh*t

Cane: B*tch

Culus: Assh*le

Cursor: Cell phone

Cursorium Lutum: Hydro-powered dirt bike

Dautor: Damnit

Ede faecam: Eat sh*t

Faex: Sh*t

Fascia: Bandage

Infernum: Hell

Irrumator: B*st*rd

Ita et nos sumus damnatorum: We are so damned

Lignum Vitae: Tree of Life

Oblitus sum dare vobis est: I forgot to give it to you

Prima Stella: First of Star

Quartus de Terra: Fourth of Land

Seeping Folorium: Healing plant/flower

Stercore: Sh*t

Si in cumulum stercore: In a pile of sh*t

Tertia Aquae: Third of Water

Vescere bracis meis: Eat my shorts

*These words are inspired by Latin and/or created by H.A. Stories.

*Please note some vocabulary consists of vulgar profanities. Viewer discretion is advised. We apologize for any offense taken from our word choices. :)

ACKNOWLEDGMENTS

This has been such an amazing and life-changing journey. I couldn't have done it without all of the support I've had from friends and family. As a little girl, I walked through life as though I was in a movie or a storybook. As I matured, a part of me was always connected to that creative imagination. And here I am, writing my acknowledgments for the novel I wrote with my best friend. First things first, I need to thank the one who gave me life, my momma! Without her, I mentally, and physically, wouldn't be able to be where I am today. Growing up, she let my imagination run free and even contributed to my innovative mind. She taught me to just do what I love, even if that means I change my mind a million times. I don't know what the "by the book" definition of a "fun mom" is, but in my book, she's the most fun parent on the face of this Earth. She worked with what she could provide us and made the best out of it. Giving me the best memories imaginable. But all around, there are no words that could really hit the points of how thankful I am to have her. So, thank you, Mom, for everything. I love you to the moon and back and beyond that. Other family members I'd like to recognize are my sister, Lundyn, and my brother, Mason. Thank you for all the memories and for unknowingly being part of my inspiration. Y'all are great... well, for the most part. I'd also like to thank my grandparents for being so involved in my life and for all of the encouragement. Sending a special thanks to my English teachers throughout the years. Specifically, Mrs. Kratz, my 7th and 8th grade teacher, she's truly such an inspirational woman. I got to thank Hallie's grammy, love that lady. But most importantly, I would like to thank Ms. Hallie Balogh. Thank you for putting up with my snarky comments, being late sometimes, life issues, and needing a leave of absence. This girl has been by my side through thick and thin. No matter what, I can always rely on her, without judgment, well, maybe a little judging. I'd like to upgrade her from just the "World's best friend" to "World's best friend AND co-author." I can't wait to see where our career takes us and how this journey will unfold. Thank you, Hallie, for sharing your patience, creativity, knowledge, and humor with me. Little us would be so proud of how far we've come. And finally, thank you, our readers, for being a part of this trainwreck. Welcome to our nonsense. This wouldn't be possible without y'all, obviously.

- Auttie

Being a published author has been my dream for a long time. When I was little, I would play dress-up constantly. I loved creating characters and building worlds for them to belong in. In my living room, I would act out their stories. Imagine telling that little girl that her stories are now being shared with the world, and she gets to do it with her best friend. My dream is finally a reality. But none of this would have happened without the love and support of so many people. Thank you to the incredible Gene McNamara for all of the advice with publishing on KDP, marketing, and editing. I'd also like to thank my little sister, Avarie, for always wanting to be a part of the worlds I created when we were younger and for convincing me to take breaks between long work hours (I probably would have gone off the rails a looong time ago if it weren't for her). Thank you, Aunt Rayne, for all of the Barnes and Noble birthday trips (all of those books really inspired me to write my own.) Thanks to my other Aunt, Jenn Haught, for jumping on the crazy Empire train and using her journalism degree to help me edit and her promotional career to get this novel into the hands of amazing readers. I also want to thank my grandma, Emily Cole, for the constant supply of sweets, love, and encouragement. Thanks for putting up with me and my book rants, character art, and for loving these characters as much as I do. Last and most importantly, I want to thank my parents, Julie and Blair. I don't even know where to begin because they've done so much for me. Thank you for driving me to author meetings, helping with the expensive process of publishing a novel, and giving me the confidence to accomplish my goals. (Not to mention the book rants that they also sat through:) I love you both soooo much. Okay, so I lied about my parents being the last thank you because there is one girl who really deserves all of my appreciation. Even though she got on my nerves A LOT, she can't spell for *faex*, and she is ALWAYS late for everything; she's still my best friend, and a co-authored novel wouldn't be a co-authored novel without two authors. Thank you so much, Auttie, for sharing a crazy dream with me and turning it into something real. This novel wouldn't have been half as amazing if it weren't for your hyperactive imagination, romance writing skills (that I currently lack), and humor. So, thank you to everyone (including you crazy awesome readers) who helped me on my journey to this point. I couldn't have done this without you.

~ *Hallie*

As we wrap up our first novel, Hallie and I (Auttie) would like to deliver some formal "thank you's" to the people who have worked alongside us. Thank you to all of our beta readers: Hailey Kelly, Mathew Marotta, Andrew Marotta, Brett Lefberg, Caite Panzer, Jenn Haught, Lindsay Baker, Carmel Kratz, and Crystal Wummer. We would also like to add another personal thank you to Donna Beasley for being our beta reader/editor, thanks for being so critical MOM. We want to thank our cover artist germancreative at Fiverr. A big thanks to our high school for working with us and displaying our achievements. And we can't forget about all of the boring parts of the writing process like legalities and banking which would have been impossible without the best "manager" ever, Julie Balogh (also thank you for the last-minute beta read of the first few chapters). But before closing out, a big thanks goes to you, our readers. This wouldn't have been possible without any of you, who, for some crazy reason, decided to pick up our book and read. Thank you everyone for the love and support. We appreciate you all! <3

~ Auttie & Hallie

Authors' Note

WE CAN'T BELIEVE THIS IS REAL! Neither of us ever thought that we would be published authors at the age of sixteen! Little fifth-grade Auttie and Hallie would be so proud. All of those late nights, long days, 8+ hour facetime calls, camping on a deck during COVID-19, stupid arguments, debating on who dies, learning how to spell the word piece (p-i-e-c-e, piece of pie, p-i-e), and dumb insults towards each other were ALL worth it. This is a huge accomplishment for the two of us. It started as a joke, turned to an idea, then evolved into a brainstorm, all the way to a published book, I'm sorry, not just a book, but a novel. Now, not to wail on our own horn, because we both made *sure* to humble each other along the way *cue Auttie's signature eye roll*, but we absolutely nailed this whole author thing. *cue Hallie yelling at Auttie to "take that out!"* (SPOILER ALERT: Auttie didn't take it out.)

Made in the USA
Middletown, DE
30 May 2023

31104314R00172